Love is
a time of enchantment:
in it all days are fair and all fields
green. Youth is blest by it,
old age made benign: the eyes of love see
roses blooming in December,
and sunshine through rain. Verily
is the time of true-love
a time of enchantment—and
Oh! how eager is woman
to be bewitched!

First published in Great Britain in 1957 by
Mills & Boon Ltd.,
London

First Large Print Edition
published May 1989
by arrangement with
Aidan Ellis Publishing Ltd.,
Henley-on-Thames

British Library CIP Data

Stuart, Alex, *1914–*
Last of the logans.—Large print ed.—
Ulverscroft large print series: romance
Rn: Violet Vivian Mann   I. Title
823'.914[F]

ISBN 0-7089-1999-5

Published by
F. A. Thorpe (Publishing) Ltd.
Anstey, Leicestershire
Set by Rowland Phototypesetting Ltd.
Bury St. Edmunds, Suffolk
Printed and bound in Great Britain by
T. J. Press (Padstow) Ltd., Padstow, Cornwall

ALEX STUART

THE LAST OF THE LOGANS

Complete and Unabridged

ULVERSCROFT
Leicester

LAST OF THE LOGANS

Johnny Chisholm, an Australian, was a boundary rider in Queensland, quite happy with his life until he met and fell in love with Elizabeth Anson who was on holiday nearby. She refused his offer of marriage saying she intended marrying money. Unexpectedly, Johnny inherits an estate in the Scottish Highlands and travels to meet his hitherto unknown cousin Catherine, and her daughter Fiona who resents his inheritance. Also there, waiting for him, is Elizabeth, now claiming to be his fiancée.

For my sister and brother-in-law Esmée and Johnny Ward . . . and the Australian garage mechanic who gave me the idea for this novel.

1

A HEAT haze shimmered over the paddocks, hiding all but the corrugated iron roofs of the distant station buildings and casting a tenuous, deceptive pall across the olive green of the sheep pastures. Even the low, jagged line of the Macgill Range appeared less harsh and arid than it usually did at this time of day, for the haze softened its rocky contours, so that they merged into the backcloth of blue, cloudless sky.

Johnny Chisholm, returning from his ten-day inspection of the boundary fence, reined in his leggy bay horse under the shade of a clump of gumtrees and, eyes narrowed against the strong Australian sunlight, studied the line of wire in his immediate vicinity. There was a small break in the netting and he dismounted, reaching up into his saddle-pack for pliers and the roll of wire he carried, his movements leisurely.

He was a tall, slim young man, with a

1

mop of unruly fair hair, dressed in denims and a patched and faded blue shirt which, rolled up to the elbows, displayed to full advantage his tanned, muscular arms. As he worked with the deft skill of long practice, he reflected cynically that Elizabeth Anson had told him, only a fortnight ago, that he was the best-looking man she had ever met in her life. His lips tightened. She had said this when he had proposed to her. She had let him take her into his eager, hungry arms, let him rain his clumsy, passionate, adoring kisses on her soft mouth, and then she had laughed at him.

"Marry you, Johnny?" The derisive note in her voice, heard again in memory, still rankled. "*Marry* you? Oh, don't be absurd, darling! You know as well as I do that it wouldn't be possible."

He had known, of course, he had always known in his heart that a girl like Elizabeth Anson, who was rich and lovely and a visitor, was not for him. Yet he had dreamed and she had encouraged his dreams, made him forget that they were the kind that could never be realized. She had flirted with him outrageously, and he

2

—Johnny shrugged angrily—he had made a fool of himself. He had asked her to be his wife. His big hands clenched as the pliers fell from them. He let them lie where they had fallen, took a tin of tobacco from the pocket of his jeans and rolled himself a cigarette, his fingers not quite steady. The cigarette going, he pushed back his shabby bush hat and went to lean against the fence post, staring moodily down at the tips of his dusty working boots. He didn't see them, it was Elizabeth's face he saw—her small, exquisite face with its pink and white English complexion, her lips parted in a smile in which there was both challenge and mockery . . . Elizabeth's face, as he had seen it when he bade her goodbye the morning after his foolish proposal.

She would be gone when he returned to the station: her visit over, she would be on her way back to the Old Country where she belonged and he didn't, and the chances were that he would never set eyes on her again. In a way it would be a relief not to have to see her again, but . . . he would miss her, as, achingly, he had

3

missed her every waking minute of the past ten days.

His was a lonely job, Johnny reflected. It was odd that he had never considered it so until he had met Elizabeth. He'd always liked and taken a pride in it before. But now it gave him too much time to think, and he realized that it was monotonous and largely uneventful: the long days in the saddle as he made his solitary round of the property, the interminable nights when he camped by himself, with only his horse and his small camp-fire for company. The hours which once had been filled by his dreams and had never seemed too long until Elizabeth had laughed at him and made him see himself for what he was. What had she said to him, in that brittle, mocking voice in which a hint of laughter still lingered?

"You're all right *here*, Johnny. This is your country and you're in your element. I don't pretend that you don't attract me —you do, more than anyone I've ever met. For one thing you're the best-looking man I ever met in my life—you're strong and virile and absolutely natural and unspoilt. You're honest and you don't pretend and

I adore your arrogance and the gentle kindness that lies behind it. I've enjoyed knowing you—we've had fun together, haven't we? You can't deny that and I won't attempt to. But—" She had spread her hands, Johnny remembered, in a gesture which hurt almost as much as her words had done, because of its finality and because of the look in her eyes that went with it. "Try to understand, Johnny. It's utterly impossible. I don't want to settle out here in the back of beyond. And if I did, I'd marry a man who could afford to give me the sort of life I'm used to—not a station hand, who'd expect me to live in a beastly little tin-roofed shack and cook his meals for him. As you would, wouldn't you, Johnny? Why, darling, don't you see —we'd run out of conversation before we'd been married a month! You'd bore me and I should hate you for it . . ."

Savagely, Johnny flung his half-smoked cigarette from him, ground it out with his heel as, ever since he had started smoking, he had been taught to do. Bush fires were a nightmare to all Australians, and however bitter and angry he might be, he couldn't risk a spark among these dry, close-growing gums. Elizabeth had been careless with her cigarettes, he thought, torturing himself: he'd told her till he was tired of telling her that it was dangerous to throw away the lighted butts as she did, but she had taken no notice.

"I'm English," she had said, every time he reproached her. "I simply can't remember, that's all."

So he had stopped telling her and, instead, had made a habit of taking her cigarette from her when it was smoked, himself putting it out. This had been only one of the hundred unobtrusive little services he had performed for her. He hadn't much small talk, for he was so often alone that he had virtually lost the habit of making conversation with strangers, but he had taken pleasure in serving her. Perhaps he had been a fool in that too. Elizabeth had probably despised him for being her slave—he'd have got further if he'd made violent love to her, displayed more of the arrogance she had told him she adored.

Well, it was too late now. She had gone. Back to the City, to a flash hotel, he imagined, to wait until her plane left, if it hadn't left already. Within a few days—he wasn't sure how many but knew it was under a week—she would be back in London. Johnny pushed his old bush hat still further on to the back of his head and sighed. He wondered what London was like and tried to recollect what Elizabeth had told him about it. And what he had read. Elizabeth's London had been different from the London he had read about in books—she had spoken of parties, theatres, celebrities, had grumbled about the traffic and the expense of living there, but she had told him little else.

He bent and picked up the pliers. Better finish the job, it would have to be done sometime if he was going to get back to the station house before dark. But he wasn't in a hurry to get back, to face the banter of the men. They'd known, of course, how he felt about Elizabeth, although he had tried to hide his feelings from everyone but Elizabeth herself.

Oh, stone the crows, why did he have to keep thinking about Elizabeth? London, now. He forced himself to think about London. It would be vast, a great, teeming anthill of a city: grey, he thought, on account of the climate, the rain and the fog, a city steeped in history and tradition, full of majesty and dignified buildings, rich in pageantry. The Queen riding in an open landau, surrounded by her escort of Household Cavalry with their burnished breastplates and waving plumes: the Foot Guards, brave in scarlet and gold: the famous Beefeaters at the Tower of London: the Lord Mayor in his robes: the Bank of England, the River Thames, London Bridge and the Houses of Parliament, Trafalgar Square and Nelson's Column . . .

His fingers busy with the torn wire, Johnny tried to picture what it would be like. He would never see it, of course. This, as Elizabeth had told him, was his place—a Queensland sheep station in the back of beyond.

And yet—he laughed shortly to himself —his father had been born in the Old Country, in Scotland, and had come out to Australia as a child of three, with his grandfather, who had somehow disgraced his family and had been some sort of remittance man. Until he was killed at

Gallipoli, in the First World War, at the age of fifty-two . . .

Johnny had never seen his grandfather but had been told many tales about him. He had been quite a character, by all accounts, a gambler, renowned for his wit and his good looks, who had made a fortune at Kiandra and lost it again, finally marrying, as his second wife, the daughter of a wealthy station owner whose property he had inherited. John Alastair Roderick Chisholm, with a handle, because he had been the younger son of an Earl. Johnny himself had been named after him, though he had always been careful to suppress the fact that he had three Christian names. Just as careful as he had been to hide the Christmas card which came for him every year from the Old Country because it came from the Earl and Countess of Logan and was addressed affectionately to "John from his cousins Roderick and Catherine" and would almost certainly have been misunderstood by his fellow station hands.

On the only occasion when he mentioned it—years ago, when he had been a kid at school—it had earned him the mocking nickname of "Dook" which had taken months and a dozen fights to live down and, eventually, to refute. Here he was just plain Johnny Chisholm, as his father had been before him, and, until Elizabeth Anson had come into his life, he had been content.

At the thought of his father, Johnny's jaw jutted. The repair was finished and he straightened his back, called his horse to him and replaced his tools in the saddle-pack. But although he remounted, he did not immediately move on. He was aware of a growing reluctance to return to the station house, to the questions, the sly grins and the good-natured gibes that would inevitably greet him. Even the Gilliats' unvoiced sympathy would hurt, and he wondered, sitting motionless in his saddle, whether perhaps he ought to pack in his job, move on somewhere else. But of course he couldn't, not really, not when he came to think about it—the Gilliats had been too good to him, treating him more like a son than an employee, and Harry Gilliat, his boss, had taught him all he knew. Harry was a relation of his mother's by marriage and since her death, four years ago, he'd had no one else he could call his family, for his father—following the family tradition—had volunteered for the AIF a week after war had been declared and had been killed in North Africa.

His father had been a pretty fine man, Johnny reflected, with fierce and stubborn pride. Perhaps he hadn't made the success of his life that he might have done, struggling with a small sheep property at a time when wool prices were at rock bottom, but he had been a fine man for all that and it was no use regretting the fact that he had let the property go for a song on his enlistment and that, on his death, there had been neither land nor money for his son to inherit. He had known that his duty was to his country and he had done it, without hesitation.

Johnny remembered him—not very clearly, for he had been only seven when his father had gone away—but he retained a mental picture of a big, fair-haired man with laughing blue eyes and a strangely wistful smile, who had clapped him on the head and played exciting games with him which they had both taken very seriously. His mother, he had known instinctively,

11

had been deeply in love with his father and had never fully recovered from her loss. She had been a quiet-voiced, gentle person, delicate and pretty, and she had done her best for her only son, bringing him back to Queensland, where her own childhood had been spent, and working —despite persistent ill-health—in her brother-in-law's house in order to send Johnny to boarding school in Brisbane. At sixteen, he had come back to the station as a jackaroo and now, skilled and experienced, he was a boundary rider, with the prospect—still a trifle vague—of taking over as manager when Harry Gilliat retired. Apart from two years' Army service in Korea and Japan, which he had unexpectedly enjoyed, Johnny had been in Queensland all his life.

And here, he thought belligerently, he would remain. But Elizabeth's parting words still stung him.

"You'll never do anything with your life, Johnny," she had said. "You'll never get anywhere because you've no ambition and you can't see beyond this place and won't try. There's a whole world outside, you know—a world I'm going back to. If you ever find the courage to enter it, let me know . . ."

As if he would, Johnny told himself angrily. Go running after her like a little dog, just because she'd left him! But she had destroyed his peace, taken his heart with her, made a fool of him in front of his mates and the Gilliats. He had believed himself a man, but Elizabeth had questioned his manhood and even caused him to doubt it, to wonder and to question, to feel ashamed of the little he had achieved. Because he had loved her and they had been so happy together, it simply hadn't occurred to him, in his blind stupidity and conceit, that it hadn't meant to her what it had meant to him. It hadn't entered his head, when he made it, that she would reject his proposal or laugh at the idea of marrying him.

His head came up. It was no use just standing here, wallowing in bitterness and self-pity. Sooner or later he would have to go back to the station—they would be expecting him and he had his job to do. Within the next day or so, shearing would start and they would all be too busy with that to remember about him. Elizabeth

13

had gone: the thing was over and it was best forgotten.

Johnny touched his heels to his horse and the bay moved obediently into a lope. He rode in the easy, loose-limbed style all Australian riders adopt, not moving in the saddle, his gaze on the fence and his body relaxed. Once more he encountered a break in the wire and stopped to repair it: a little further on, plaintive bleating led him to where a young Merino ram had become entangled by its horns and was held fast. He released and looked it over, sent it running with a slap across its thickly covered rump, remembering, as he did so, that Elizabeth had once told him distastefully that she could not bear the smell of sheep.

The sun sank in a blaze of scarlet glory behind the far-away Macgills. He was only a mile or so from the first of the paddock gates now, his inspection all but completed, and it was cooler, if still completely airless. Wrinkling his nostrils, he inhaled the smell of smoke and wheeled sharply in order to investigate its source. Someone, he saw, had built a tiny cooking fire just clear of the trees to his right, and, as he approached it, a thin, boyish figure in jeans rose to its feet and hailed him excitedly.

"Hey, Johnny—Johnny, I've been waiting for you! Come on, the billy's boiling and I've got some *terrific* news for you. Only it's rather sad, in a way, and I'm afraid it'll be a bit of a shock to you."

Johnny smiled, recognizing the voice of his employer's youngest daughter.

"Why, Pip," he said, sliding out of the saddle beside her, "this is quite like old times, isn't it—you waiting for me and the billy boiling? And I can do with a cupper —I'm as dry as Cooper's Creek. But what's the news, anyway?"

Philippa Gilliat shook her head at him. She was seventeen, a slim, long-limbed slip of a girl, recently released from boarding school and ecstatically pleased to be at home for good at last. She was a nice kid, Johnny thought, and it had been decent of her to come and meet him, as she had been wont to do as a child— almost as if she had sensed his reluctance to return and was seeking to make it easier for him. Unless—he stiffened. Could she have come to tell him that Elizabeth hadn't gone, that she was still with the Gilliats? Because if she had . . . he felt the hot, embarrassed colour creeping up into his cheeks.

"Pip," he said urgently, "tell me! What is it, for Pete's sake? Elizabeth's not still there, is she?"

"Oh, no," Pip returned, "*she's* gone." Her voice was cold and Johnny realized, with astonishment, that Pip, who usually got on well with everyone, was glad that Elizabeth had gone.

"Didn't you like her?" he asked, puzzled.

Again Pip shook her dark curls at him. "No," she answered emphatically, "I didn't. So there! But"—she dismissed Elizabeth with a curt gesture—"I *have* got some terrific news for you. It's so terrific that I think you'd better sit down and drink your tea before I tell you—you'll need it to prepare you for the shock."

"I doubt that," Johnny objected good-humouredly, but he tethered his horse beside hers and, returning to the fire, sat down and accepted a mug of strong, scalding tea from Pip's blackened old billy. "Well?" he prompted indulgently, because

16

he knew Pip's innocent love of the dramatic. "What is this terrific news of yours, anyway?"

Pip faced him, knees drawn up and her arms clasped about her long, slim legs. Her eyes were dark and wide-set and they met Johnny's gravely. "I did warn you," she began, "that it'd be a shock—"

"Yes, you warned me. Shall I try and guess what it is?"

"You'll never guess. It's too—too incredible."

"Well, let me try. For a start, how did it come?"

"On the phone. From Brisbane. There was a call for you."

"For *me*?" Johnny stared at her openmouthed. Had Elizabeth relented after all? Had she tried to call him up, to tell him . . . he licked at dry lips, took a gulp of his tea and then asked cautiously: "Who was it rang me?"

"A solicitor." Pip was enjoying the interest she had aroused. "A Mr. Henry of Henry, Barton and Henry."

"For crying out loud, Pip, you've made this up!"

"No." She denied it vigorously, her

17

dark eyes dancing in the firelight. Then her gravity returned and the light in her eyes flickered and died, like a candle flame extinguished in a sudden breeze. "It's a tragedy, really—well, part of it is. I didn't know any of them, of course, but all the same it was a pretty ghastly thing to happen."

"Now, look, Pip," Johnny said patiently, "I don't understand a word of this. None of it makes sense. Begin at the beginning, like a good kid, will you? A cove called Henry, who's a solicitor, called me up from Brisbane. What did he say? And who took the call?"

"Dad took it, since you weren't there. But—"

"Did *he* send you to fetch me?"

"No. He doesn't know I've come. But he'll guess, I expect." She hesitated.

"Go on," Johnny bade her. He started to roll a cigarette, no longer believing her. She was playing a trick on him, he decided, and added, grinning at her: "I suppose my rich uncle died and left me a fortune?"

Pip looked startled. "Well, yes, he did, as a matter of fact. A fortune and a title.

You're—you're an Earl, Johnny. The Earl of Logan. You—"

"*What*?" exploded Johnny. He leapt to his feet, reddening furiously, and the grazing horses raised their heads, alarmed by the sudden, unexpected movement. "Look, Pip, if this is your idea of a joke it isn't mine. I haven't got a rich uncle—"

"No. But you've got a cousin and he was the Earl of Logan. The solicitor said so. And anyway I knew—your mother told Dad years ago."

"I see." Johnny's mouth set grimly. "And suppose I have? Suppose he has died, that doesn't make me his heir—he's got two sons."

Pip nodded and now he saw the glint of tears in her eyes. "He had, yes. But the younger one was a soldier and he was killed in Cyprus a fortnight ago. His name was Hamish Chisholm. Your cousin and the other son, Alastair, flew to Cyprus for his funeral. On their way back to England the plane crashed and they were both killed. So that only leaves you. You're the only male heir."

Johnny was silent, shocked to the depths of his being. He hadn't known his

Scottish cousins, but, as Pip had said, it was a ghastly thing to happen—stark and terrible tragedy for the house of Logan. He knew now that Pip was telling him the truth, her sincerity was obvious from her tear-filled eyes. Besides, she knew the names of his dead cousins and there was no way that she could have found these out, except the way she had described, from the Brisbane solicitor. Pip, admittedly, liked to play tricks on him, but this wasn't the sort of trick she would ever have played, she was too kind-hearted and had too much sense. But if it was true, then . . . he took a deep, painful breath and dropped to his knees beside her.

"Pip," he said in a low, shaken voice, "what did he want—Henry, I mean, the solicitor? Does he want to see me?"

She inclined her head. "Yes. He said you'd have to go to Scotland. There's a castle, an estate, a lot of money. They—they belong to you now."

"Do they?" All the colour drained from Johnny's face. "Yes, I suppose they do. But what would I do with them? I wouldn't want to live over there. This is my home, this is where I belong. I'd be—

I'd be out of place in a Scottish castle. I can't be an Earl. Look at me, Pip—how could I?"

Pip looked at him, gravely at first, and then a little smile curved her lips. "You're all right, Johnny," she told him with shy pride. "Of course you are. You're a fine person, the best there is. We all think the world of you, Dad and Mum and me and the others. Whatever anyone else says."

He knew she meant Elizabeth and two bright spots of colour burned in his cheeks again. Elizabeth hadn't wanted to marry him because he was only a station hand in the back of beyond, but now, without warning, everything had changed. He wasn't just a station hand now, he was— Johnny swallowed hard—he was the Earl of Logan, heir to a great Highland estate and an old and honoured name. If he went to the Old Country now, Elizabeth wouldn't scorn him. He could meet her on equal terms.

He stood up, suddenly impatient. "Let's go, Pip."

She rose with him and together they doused the still smouldering ashes of the fire. It was quite dark now and stars

21

gleamed in the night sky. Familiar stars, stars which had looked down on him many times as he lay rolled in his blanket at the end of his lonely patrol. Johnny's gaze went to the Southern Cross. He wouldn't see the Southern Cross in the Old Country, but he knew, in that moment, that he had to go. Not only because of Elizabeth but for his own sake and because it was his duty. There was his cousin Catherine who was now so tragically bereaved and who might need him. And her daughter, who was a year or so younger than himself—Fiona. He knew nothing about them save their names, but they were his family, he must go to them because he was the last of the Logans and his place wasn't here any longer, it was with them.

Pip was unusually quiet as they jogged through the paddocks side by side. Johnny glanced at her once, but in the dim light it was impossible to make out more than the outline of her face.

She broke the silence at last. "Johnny—" Her voice was tremulous and Johnny turned in surprise, realizing suddenly that she was crying.

He reached out a hand to take hers. She was a sweet kid, he thought, as precious to him as a sister, and he wondered why she was crying. "Look," he admonished gently, "you mustn't grieve for my cousins."

"I . . . wasn't. I'm awfully sorry for them, of course, but that wasn't why I was crying." She freed her hand, drew it, childishly, across her eyes. "Johnny, you'll go, won't you?"

"To Logan? Yes, Pip. I must. But I'll be back. I won't go for ever."

"Won't you?" She sounded incredulous.

"No," he said firmly, "of course I won't. You'll see."

"I'll miss you," Pip whispered miserably. "I've only just started to realize how —how much. At first I was pleased for your sake—that you'd be rich, I mean, and—oh, and everything. But now—" She broke off and he felt her eyes on his face, searching it. "Well?" he asked. "Now?"

"I wish you hadn't to go."

"I told you—it won't be for ever. Anyway, you can come to Scotland and visit me. Your dad promised he'd stand you a trip over, didn't he? Long before this happened."

"Yes," she agreed but without conviction. They reached the last of the paddock gates and Johnny went forward to open it. The lights from the station buildings blazed at them out of the darkness, bright and welcoming.

"Will you—will you marry Elizabeth now?" Pip questioned suddenly. Johnny spun round in his saddle, letting the gate go. He didn't answer her at once but sat motionless, his brows coming together in a pensive frown.

"If she'll have me, Pip," he said at last. "But she refused me once, you know."

"She won't now," Pip returned flatly. She thrust past him, bent forward to grasp the catch on the gate and her voice was muffled as she added: "She's not right for you, you know. She's hurt you once and she won't hesitate to do it again."

"Now look, Pip—" Johnny began, on his dignity, but Pip interrupted him. "You don't know her, Johnny. She's different with men. She put on an act with you but she didn't bother with me. And she's hard. As—as hard as nails."

"You oughtn't to talk like that, Pip."
Johnny was angry but he controlled his
temper with an almost visible effort. "You
don't know anything about it, you're only
a kid."

"Am I?" Pip had got the gate open. She
slipped through it, held it against her knee
so that it was between them. "I'm seventeen. And"—she caught her breath on a
sob—"if this hadn't happened and you'd
stayed here, you'd probably have married
me in the end. So there!" The last two
words were uttered with childish defiance,
and when she had said them she put heels
to her horse and was off at a canter, recklessly ignoring the station wagon which
rounded one of the buildings and had to
skid to avoid her.

Johnny stared after her helplessly,
recognizing the truth of her assertion in
spite of himself. Because it *was* true—if
he'd stayed here, he might easily have
married Pip Gilliat . . . in the end. He
didn't meet many girls and Pip was nearest
to him in age, he had known her for most
of her life and he was fond of her. In a
year or so, when she had filled out and
matured, she would be an attractive girl,

a wife any man could be proud of, but . . . he wouldn't be here for a year or so. He was going away. His heart sank and then lifted again. He had the world at his feet, a whole vast new world . . . Elizabeth's world. And she had doubted that he had the courage to enter it.

Johnny squared his shoulders. Well, he would show her, he would show them all, even Pip.

He bent and jerked open the gate. Harry Gilliat got out of the station wagon and came towards him, a big, broad-shouldered, smiling man, his hand out-held.

"Well, Johnny, congratulations, boy! I reckon Pip forestalled me with the news, didn't she?"

Johnny dismounted. He took the out-stretched hand and wrung it hard. "Yes," he said, "she told me."

"Come on in, then," Harry Gilliat bade him. "I expect you'll want to be on your way to Brisbane in the morning. I'll run you in to the railhead first thing." He put an arm about the younger man's shoulders. "Mother and the girls have seen to your packing, everything's ready and the solicitor promised he'd see about an air passage for you on the first available plane, so you haven't a thing to worry about."

"No," Johnny conceded uncertainly, "I suppose not."

"You haven't." There was pride in Harry Gilliat's voice, pride and a deep affection. "You'll do all right, don't worry. This couldn't have happened to a better man, you know—I'd stake my oath on it. And on you."

Johnny took comfort from his words. They walked together to the station wagon and then a crowd of men came tumbling out of the bunkhouse, to fling themselves upon him and wring his hand. They hoisted him on to their shoulders and carried him in triumph back to the house . . .

2

FIONA CHISHOLM was sitting in the drawing-room at Logan Castle, with the television switched on, when Dr. Cameron was shown in. She looked up with a brief smile of welcome and motioned the visitor to a seat beside her.

"Am I disturbing you?" The young doctor hesitated.

"No, of course you're not." Her smile widened. "I'm waiting for *In Town Tonight* to come on. The new head of the family is being interviewed, I believe." Her smile abruptly faded and David Cameron thought: She's taking it hard, poor girl. But who can blame her? Her father and both her brothers killed within a week and now a complete stranger—an uncouth Australian cousin—arriving out of the blue to take everything she and her mother ought to have had. She must be going through hell. He wished, quite desperately, that he could help her, but couldn't find anything to say.

Fiona faced him. She was a beautiful girl, with her long dark hair and candid, smoke-grey eyes—the image of her mother, who had been a famous beauty. They were both typical of the Chisholm women, tall and proud and dignified. Involuntarily, Dr. Cameron glanced up at the portrait-lined walls and sighed. He wondered what the new Earl would be like, and Fiona said, uncannily, as if she had read his thoughts: "Stay and see him, won't you? It shouldn't be long now, the News is nearly finished."

He sat down. "Your mother seems a little better this evening," he volunteered diffidently, and was rewarded by the return of her smile.

"Yes, I thought she was, David. You've been awfully good to her—to both of us."

A tinge of colour crept up beneath the smooth tan of David Cameron's cheeks. "I wish there was more I could do."

"You've done what you could. There isn't a cure for a broken heart, is there? I don't suppose there ever will be."

"No." His eyes searched her face anxiously. He knew that, beneath her apparent calm, she was unbearably tense and strung up, near to the limit of her endurance. Everything had fallen on to her shoulders—the funeral arrangements, the memorial service, the cables to Australia and the protracted legal wrangling—for her mother had collapsed when the news had been brought to her and still lay in that strange limbo to which the heart-broken escape and from which he had so far failed to bring her back. Perhaps, for Lady Logan's sake, it was better so, but the strain on Fiona was appalling.

The News was followed by the weather forecast: the bright screen flickered in front of David Cameron's eyes but he wasn't consciously aware of it. When the Sports Round-up began, Fiona leaned forward and turned down the sound.

"You don't mind?" she asked politely.

He shook his head. "Is there anything I can do for you, Fiona? Anything at all? You know I'd give my right hand to help you if I could."

"Yes, I know." Her voice was gentle. "But you've given me sleeping pills, haven't you? And your shoulder to weep on. You've been a wonderful friend to me, David."

"I wish I could be more than a friend."

"You can't, my dear." Her expression hardened. "I shall have to marry money now. We haven't a penny, you know, Mummy and I. I don't mind for myself a bit. It's different for her, she's always been used to living here, having everything she wanted—and Daddy's adoration. It's going to be a terrible blow to her, on top of everything else, when we have to leave Logan."

"Leave Logan?" David stared at her in shocked astonishment. "But surely you don't have to leave? This Australian won't turn you out—"

"No, I don't suppose he will. But we shall have to go, all the same. It doesn't belong to us any more—everything is entailed, you see, in the good, old-fashioned Scottish way. The heir gets it all. He'll want his own people here, not us."

"But he's young. And he's not married."

"I know." Fiona's lovely mouth tightened in distaste. "But already one of his girl friends has tracked him down. A Miss Elizabeth Anson. She has installed

31

herself in the village, at the Logan Arms, and keeps ringing up to find out if he's arrived. I've had to disappoint her—he was due here this evening, but"—she gestured to the television set—"*that* held him up. The Press have splashed his name and his romantic story all over their front pages and now the BBC are having their whack. He telephoned to say that he would be coming on the night train. Oh, David!" Suddenly her voice broke and her eyes were bright with tears. "Hamish was killed by Cypriot terrorists—they shot him in the back and the papers printed pictures of him lying there. And then Daddy and Alastair died in a burning aeroplane and I couldn't open a single newspaper without seeing ghastly pictures of the wreckage— the pitiful, horrible wreckage that I see in nightmares when I try to sleep. And now . . . all this. I should think everyone in the country knows the name of Logan now. It's—it's like trying to go on living a normal life under a huge, glaring spotlight that's never turned off. I thought they'd stopped, that they'd lost interest in us, but now it's all been resurrected again because *he* has arrived at last. We had photographers here yesterday, taking pictures of the Castle . . . *his* inheritance. I hate him, David, without even knowing him. I know I oughtn't to, that it's not reasonable to hate a person you've never set eyes on, but I can't *be* reasonable. He's got what Alastair should have had and I hate him for that."

"You couldn't really hate anyone," David insisted. He took her hand, fondled it gently. It was ice-cold and it trembled in his. Fiona looked up at him. Her eyes, behind the film of tears, were as cold as the hand he held.

"I can. I'm a Chisholm and a Highlander. They both know how to hate."

David lowered his gaze. He saw the picture of the sports commentator fade from the television screen, to be succeeded by the medley that served as introduction to *In Town Tonight*. "Shall I turn this off?" he asked. "If you feel like that about your Australian cousin, seeing him might upset you." He didn't take her passionate outburst seriously, aware of the strain under which, for weeks, she had been labouring, but his trained physician's instinct warned him that she was near

33

breaking point. He wished that she would let herself go and find some relief in tears: she was so young, so tragically young and lovely that his heart went out to her. "Fiona," he pleaded, "darling, you mustn't be bitter. Honestly you mustn't, it won't do any good."

He drew her to him and, for a moment, felt her relax against him, tasting the salty bitterness of her tears as his lips touched her cheek.

"Sweet, you aren't alone, you know. You've got me. I love you, I—"

With swift revulsion of feeling, Fiona jerked herself free of his encircling arms. "Don't, David"—her voice was harsh with pain—"please don't. I can't love you, I won't—" She leaned in front of him, her fingers fumbling unsteadily with the controls of the television set. "I *want* to see him," she said. "And it won't upset me—heavens, why should it? I've got to meet him in the flesh tomorrow, he's coming here, don't you understand? This place is his now, not ours. He has a right here and I shall have to make him welcome."

The announcer's voice cut her short.

The sound of it was so loud that it wakened echoes in the quiet room. David adjusted the control. They waited, in silence, whilst a young Spanish guitarist was interviewed. He played and sang, but, although they didn't speak, neither of them consciously heard him. He bowed himself off, to be followed by a middle-aged couple who had been medical missionaries in New Guinea.

David found his attention wandering from the screen to Fiona, and the blank, dead look on her face filled him with anxious disquiet. She sat very still, gazing fixedly at the screen, and from the walls of the lofty-ceilinged room her ancestors looked down on her. It was as if the whole turbulent history of the Chisholms of Logan was written in their proud, bleak faces, the young physician thought.

He knew their history well enough: it was impossible to live and work in this district without hearing it in song and legend. The great Castle which towered over the glen had been a Chisholm stronghold since the twelfth century, when Red Roderick had come with his fierce, marauding clansmen and laid its first crude foundations, which later Chisholms had added to as the years went by. And which, David thought grimly, they had defended to their last breath, against King and commoner alike. Chisholms had fought in the Fifteen and the Forty-five, had beggared themselves for the sake of their Bonnie Prince Charles and followed him into exile: they had carried on a bitter and relentless feud against the Campbells and the red-coats of King George and had not been subdued until granted a pardon and an earldom, together with a promise of independence which amounted, virtually, to victory.

Afterwards, they had served King and country with valour and distinction throughout succeeding generations. They had all been soldiers, many of them well known. A Chisholm of Logan had fought at Waterloo, another at Sebastopol, a third under Gordon of Khartoum: their names occupied much of the space on the village memorial which commemorated the last two world wars.

David glanced over his shoulder, into the eyes of a pictured Chisholm colonel who had followed Havelock into beleaguered Lucknow during the Indian Mutiny, a tall, fair-haired giant of magnificent physique, whom Fiona's elder brother Alastair had closely resembled. They all resembled each other, he reflected, the men tall and fair, the women—like Fiona herself—slim and dark-haired.

Not all the family portraits were in this room, of course—there were others in the great hall, still more in the dining-room and long gallery—but there were enough here to make him understand and sympathize with Fiona's bitterness. For the first time in its long history, headship of the family was to pass out of the direct line, the proud Logan title to belong to a young man who had been born and had lived all his life in Australia. A sheep farmer, not a soldier. A Chisholm in name but not in upbringing, an obscure, un-known cousin whose grandfather had disgraced the name and been cast off . . . whose father had served in the ranks of the Australian Army and earned no distinction in peace or war. David found himself wondering again, as he studied the portraits, what this new Chisholm would be like.

Beside him, Fiona tensed suddenly. She said, her voice quite flat and devoid of emotion: "He's coming on now, David."

"Yes," David said, forcing himself to concentrate again on the television screen. The interviewer briefly and tactfully traced the events which had led to his next subject's appearance on the programme. In spite of his tact, David could feel Fiona's pain when her father's name was mentioned. He felt for and found her hand, clasped it in his own and heard her give a little, smothered gasp as the camera panned slowly down to the young man who was seated in an armchair beneath a strong cluster of lights.

He looked ill at ease and acutely embarrassed, David saw, but as he rose to his feet there was a strange, moving dignity about him that, somehow, he had not expected. He was tall and well built, this young Australian, with a frank, open countenance and a pleasantly diffident smile. David realized, studying him, that, in spite of not belonging to the direct line, he was a typical Chisholm. On the black and white screen it wasn't possible accurately to judge his colouring, but his hair was obviously fair, his skin so much darker than that of the interviewer that, David decided, he must be deeply tanned.

A strikingly good-looking young man who reminded him of the Indian Mutiny colonel and—yes, definitely of Alastair.

The interviewer motioned to him to resume his seat and took his own place opposite as the camera came closer.

"Well, Lord Logan, it is extremely good of you to put off your journey north in order to give us this interview. I imagine that you must be anxious for your first sight of your inheritance?"

Under the betraying eye of the camera, David saw a flicker of some emotion he didn't attempt to analyse cross the young man's face. He inclined his head.

"Oh, yes, I—I am." His voice was deep, faintly accented.

"You've never been in this country before, have you?"

"No. I was born in Queensland. This is my—that is"—he corrected himself—"this is the first time I've been Home." He sounded the capital letter and the interviewer pursued: "You call it 'Home', Lord Logan?"

"We all do out there. That or 'the Old Country'."

"I see. I think that's rather nice. Will you tell us about your life in Queensland? You worked on a sheep station, didn't you?"

"Yes, sir. I was a boundary rider. That's to say . . ." he explained, gaining confidence now that he was on his own ground. He made it sound interesting, David thought, but beside him he felt Fiona shiver. "Does he have to—to parade it like this?" she whispered fiercely.

"He's not doing badly," David defended. A film sequence was shown; the new Lord Logan was faded out but his voice, steady and even, continued to describe the shots of an Australian boundary rider at work. When it ended and he was once more on the screen, he seemed more at ease, the pleasant diffident smile again in evidence as the interview progressed towards its conclusion.

Fiona and David, as if by common consent, leaned closer to the screen. They were so absorbed that neither of them heard the door open and slow, hesitant footsteps cross the parquet. It wasn't until

40

she spoke that Fiona realized that her mother was with them.

"Fiona," she said and there was joy in the question, mingled with an odd, compelling urgency. "Is that him, is that the boy?"

Fiona turned, startled, to look up into her mother's lovely, tragic eyes. "Yes," she admitted, "it is. But—"

"He's like Alastair," Lady Logan said softly. "I'm so glad. I shall like him if he's like Alastair."

Fiona leaned forward and switched off the television set. David, glimpsing her expression, put out a hand to her but she ignored it. She went to her mother's side and said gently: "Darling, you shouldn't have got up. Let me help you back to bed."

They went out together, the old woman and the young, walking slowly past the Chisholm portraits. David paused uncertainly and then followed them. He was a doctor, he reminded himself, and they both needed him.

3

IT was raining when Johnny Chisholm left the BBC's Riverside Television Studio. A car had been put at his disposal to take him to Euston for his journey north and he shared it with the medical missionary from New Guinea who, with his wife, had been on the *In Town Tonight* programme with him.

They were a pleasant, unassuming middle-aged couple who set themselves out to be friendly, and, as the big limousine sped swiftly through the rain-wet streets, Johnny found himself talking to them both as if he had known them all his life.

Whilst not fellow-Australians, they knew Sydney and Brisbane as well as he did, if not better, and—because it was many years since either of them had been home—they shared his awed interest in London and he felt completely at ease with them. He confessed, without shame, that he had found his television interview a terrifying ordeal, and was absurdly pleased and relieved when they agreed with him.

"Not that they didn't do everything they possibly could to make us feel at home," Dr. Naseby remarked thoughtfully. "But" —he took a worn and blackened old pipe from his pocket and sucked at it noisily— "it's the thought of all the millions of unseen people watching one that is so alarming. Especially if one comes from a part of the world where the sight of another white face is an event of major importance! Still, we got through it, didn't we? And from now on we shall probably find people we've never set eyes on before staring at us in a puzzled way and wondering why our faces are familiar to them. I believe the television announcers and, of course, the stars suffer from that sort of thing to a quite extraordinary degree—people recognize and hail them as friends and, in fact, *regard* them as friends, because they've seen them so frequently on their screens that they really imagine they know them."

"I think they must rather enjoy it," his wife returned, smiling across at Johnny. "It's wonderful to have friends, don't you agree, Lord Logan? I know *I* can't have too many and I always talk to people on trains and buses when I get the chance. Not that I do very often," she added wistfully, "but we've got six months in England and I shall certainly make the most of it while I'm here. If the fact that we've appeared on TV breaks the ice and makes it easier for me to talk to the people I meet—well, then, I'm glad we were on the programme and it'll be worth all the nervous strain we endured, waiting to go on!"

Her husband laughed at her affectionately. "You're quite incorrigible, Jess— why, I honestly believe you'd walk into a cage full of performing lions if you thought the lion tamer looked an interesting person to talk to! For myself, one experience of television is going to be ample, I think, to last me a lifetime. I'm a solitary man and I infinitely prefer the wide-open spaces where I do my job in decent obscurity and no one cares who I am, so long as I do it."

Johnny smiled sympathetically, sharing his feelings. His own reaction had been very similar, he had been nervous, dreading the moment when the cameras would turn in his direction and project his face and his voice and his hesitance on to millions of tiny screens in millions of homes whose owners were strangers to him.

He did not enjoy being in the limelight, but he had been unable to escape from it ever since his arrival at the Brisbane solicitor's office—now nearly a month ago —when he had been besieged by eager newspaper reporters and had woken next morning to see, to his horror, his story splashed over the front pages of both the *Telegraph* and the *Courier Mail*.

Mr. Henry, the senior partner of the firm which was handling his affairs, had been understanding and helpful, but he could not save Johnny from his unwelcome publicity; neither, it transpired, had he been given any funds with which to finance his client's journey to England. He had, acting on the instructions he had received from the Logan lawyers in Glasgow, got in touch with the new earl, summoned him to Brisbane and gone carefully into such proofs of his identity as he could produce, and he had tentatively reserved him an air passage from Sydney to London.

But there, it seemed, his responsibilities ended. It had occurred to no one that the new Earl of Logan, heir to a vast estate and to undreamed-of wealth in the land of his forebears, might experience any difficulty in raising the price of his fare home. The estate, Mr. Henry had told him weightily, would be subject to probate and there would be heavy death duties to be paid when the total had been assessed— settlement would take time. Johnny, doing a swift mental calculation of his savings, decided against cabling for funds, and he rejected both Mr. Henry's offer to lend him money and his suggestion that he should borrow some from Harry Gilliat.

"I'll manage," he had told the solicitor briefly. "But you'll have to postpone my air booking."

In the darkness of the luxurious car, Johnny grinned to himself. He *had* managed. First there had been the astute Sydney newspaperman who had offered him fifty guineas for an exclusive story— which Johnny hadn't even had to write— and then there had been a fortnight's shearing. He had returned to the Gilliats' station and, by dint of working overtime, had added considerably to his slender resources, grimly silent under the banter of his fellow workers and obstinately refusing to answer even Pip's questions. Harry had, of course, offered to lend him as much money as he wanted, but that, Johnny reflected, wasn't the way he liked to do things. It never had been. He had always stood on his own two feet and he didn't intend to stop now. Besides—whilst wild horses would not have wrung the admission from him—he still regarded his sudden acquisition of a mythical fortune with a certain mistrust. There might have been a mistake—didn't the fact that the Logan solicitors had sent him no money point to something of the sort? And even if Mr. Henry appeared to be satisfied with the proofs of his identity—his birth certificate, his mother's marriage lines and the rest—it was surely still possible that someone else, some relative of whom he had never heard, might produce a better claim to the title than his own?

There were moments when, back in the safe familiarity of the place he knew,

Johnny almost wished that someone else would turn up to dispute his claim. The fortnight before he finally left Australia had been both happy and painful: there had been nostalgia in everything he did, even in the heat and bustle of the shearing sheds. He had sought out Pip in his few moments of leisure—had even, he recalled with a faint twinge of anxiety, kissed her in a far from brotherly way on his last evening, because he was fond of her and kept remembering what she had said to him in the paddock, the day she had brought him the news of his cousin's death. If he had stayed, he might have married her. He knew it and so did she but, in spite of the kiss, neither of them had mentioned it again.

But it was curious, Johnny recalled, looking back, how, during those last days, he'd scarcely thought of Elizabeth . . .

He sighed as the car halted at a set of traffic lights and Mrs. Naseby drew his attention to the windows of a famous department store, ablaze with lights and containing more fur coats than he had ever seen in one place in his life. He made an effort to listen to what she was telling him, but his thoughts were with Elizabeth now. He had her London address, but he hadn't attempted to get in touch with her during his short stay. He would, of course, in a day or so, once he was settled at Logan. But his lack of money, embarrassing and absurd, still worried him. It was no use ringing up Elizabeth if he couldn't afford to take her out to lunch at one of the expensive restaurants to which she had so often told him she was accustomed. And it had been out of the question to entertain her at his small, shabby hotel—she wouldn't have understood why he was staying there. But he had had to buy himself a suit, in order to face the *In Town Tonight* cameras, and even a ready-made suit, in London, cost far more than he had imagined it would, so that the cheap hotel had been a necessity.

He wondered, replying abstractedly to Mrs. Naseby's excited comments on the fur coats, whether Elizabeth had been watching television this evening and whether she had been surprised to see him on her screen. He would write to her, he decided, the moment he arrived, and, perhaps, suggest a meeting in London. It wouldn't do, of course, to invite her to Logan until he had found out what his cousins Catherine and Fiona felt about his entertaining a visitor at the Castle. They would be in mourning, neither would welcome the intrusion of a stranger—his own arrival would be intrusion enough, in all conscience—and probably, once he had paid his respects to them, both would be relieved if he took himself back to London for a time.

Besides, he wanted to see more of London. He had dreamed so often of what it would be like that he longed to explore it and find out for himself. And all he had been able to see of it, so far, he had seen on a coach tour this morning. They had visited the Tower, he had seen the Thames and the Houses of Parliament and they had driven past Buckingham Palace and through Hyde Park. But they had missed the Changing of the Guard and he hadn't yet seen the Queen in her landau. True, he had glimpsed the Horse Guards sentries in Whitehall, but it had been raining and they had been under the cover of their boxes, so that he really hadn't seen more of them than the noses of their splendid black chargers and the plumed tops of their helmets. He could hardly send Pip the postcards of these sights that he had promised her when he himself could not, in all honesty, claim to have witnessed them in ideal conditions.

"Well," said Dr. Naseby, peering out of the rain-obscured window as the big car glided to a halt beneath a gloomy archway crowded with taxis, "here we are—this is Euston Station and this is where, alas, our ways must part, Lord Logan." He held out his hand. "It has been a great pleasure to meet you like this—for both of us, hasn't it, Jess? I hope one day it may be our good fortune to see you again, but in the meantime"—his handshake was warm —"the very best of luck to you. And success in your new life!"

Johnny took regretful leave of them and, shaking his head to an approaching porter, he stood uncertainly amongst the milling throng of arriving and departing passengers to watch them drive away. When the big black saloon had vanished from his sight, he glanced at his watch. There was nearly an hour before his train left: his luggage was in the station cloakroom where he had deposited it earlier and he had only to collect it and buy his ticket, which should not take him long.

He decided to buy the ticket first and then have coffee and a sandwich in the refreshment room. Or a pie. He wondered if they served hot pies on British railway stations, as they did in Queensland. Pies were just the job, on a train journey. He thrust his way through the crush, joined a queue at the first ticket window he saw and patiently waited his turn until, nearing the head of the queue, he saw to his dismay that it was for First Class tickets only. The Second Class window was further down and this, too, had a queue in front of it. Cursing his own stupidity, Johnny went to the tail of the small procession and again settled down to wait.

His ticket secured at last, he made his way to the nearest refreshment room. It was full of people—soldiers, sailors and airmen in uniform, soberly clad civilians and a few children, muffled up against the bleak chill of the evening and blinking sleepily at the food in front of them. There wasn't a free table and Johnny went to lean resignedly against the counter, once more to wait his turn.

"Well?" There was a girl in front of him, her apron crumpled, her eyes tired and without interest as they met his. "What's yours?"

"I'd like some coffee, please. And—do you have pies?"

"Yes," she answered indifferently, "pies a shilling and two and three." Her hands were busy, drawing his coffee from a steaming urn. "Coffee with or without sugar?"

"With," Johnny supplied. "Er—are the pies hot?"

"Hot?" The girl stared at him, displaying a faint flicker of interest with her surprise at his question. "No, they're pork pies. We don't serve those hot. If you want something hot there are sausage rolls. One and three, they are, for two, and you can have HP or tomato sauce with them, if you like."

"Thanks," said Johnny, unaccountably disappointed that this enormous, important railway station should have so little to offer him. He was suddenly hungry for a Queensland pie and homesick for the casual, friendly service of his own Wahrangi Junction, where every traveller was known by name to the station staff, and the refreshment room, with its homely deal tables, a meeting place for the exchange of news and local gossip, whilst people waited, without impatience, for the coming of the thrice-weekly mail-train.

"Well?" prompted the counter girl, as he hesitated. "You going to have the sausage rolls or not?" She thrust his coffee cup across the counter, slopping the pale liquid it contained into the saucer. Johnny nodded. Sausage rolls, he supposed, would be better than nothing. The girl pushed a bowl of sugar in his direction, warned him severely to "put the spoon back" when he had done, gave him two anaemic-looking rolls of pastry and snapped brusquely: "Sauce is up the other end. That'll be one and ten . . . ta . . . two bob, here's your change. Who's next, please?"

A tall, great-coated Air Force sergeant, with rain dripping from his cap, pushed past him with scant ceremony, and Johnny retreated, losing more of his coffee as he searched for a place at one of the crowded tables. He was glad when it was time to join his train, although this—like the refreshment room he had just left—was filling rapidly and most of the Second Class seats were reserved.

Eventually, however, he found an unoccupied corner in one of the forward coaches, hoisted his two shabby suitcases on to the rack and settled down. His fellow passengers greeted him with smiles but made no attempt to converse either with him or with each other, and as the long train started to draw away from the platform they all, thankfully, made preparations for sleep. Johnny followed their example. He was tired, he realized. It had been a long, eventful day, culminating in the strain of his first appearance in front of the television cameras, and tomorrow would come the even greater strain of his arrival at Logan and his first meeting with his cousins.

He wondered, as he composed himself for slumber, what they would be like and in what spirit they would receive him. Would they resent him, as a stranger and an interloper? Or would they be pleased, in spite of everything, that he had come—would he be able to make them understand that he had come because he wanted, if he could, to help them and to offer comfort to them both in their bereavement? He hoped his cousin Catherine wouldn't imagine that he had any intention of turning her out of her home: that was the last thing—the very last thing—he wanted to do. The prospect of living in the great, forbidding castle he had seen in the newspaper photographs filled him with misgivings, but at least, if his two cousins shared it with him, it might not be so lonely. He couldn't, of course, possibly occupy it by himself, that was out of the question.

Perhaps though . . . Johnny sat up . . . perhaps, if he saw the family solicitors in Glasgow, he might be able to waive his claim to possession of Castle Logan—even make it over, legally, to the late Earl's widow during her lifetime. It was her home, after all, she had lived there for nearly thirty years, and, he felt sure, wouldn't want to leave it. And, even if both castle and estate were entailed, as Mr. Henry had explained to him they were, it ought to be possible for him to grant her —what was the legal term for it? Security —security of tenure. And he could make her a substantial allowance for its upkeep, make sure that she did not lack for anything. Fiona, too, could be given an allowance. He knew that, because the capital was entailed, he would be unable to touch it, but he could, surely, manage both allowances out of income—he himself wouldn't want much in the way of money. He had never had expensive tastes nor the slightest desire to live in luxury. And even if he married Elizabeth, that didn't mean that he was likely, suddenly, to change his whole mode of life. If possible, once he had got everything settled and his cousins provided for, he would return to Queensland, buy himself a small property there and divide his time between the Old Country and Australia.

Elizabeth hadn't said that she disliked Australia—certainly she had enjoyed her visit to the Gilliats, on her own admission. The reason she had refused to marry him wasn't because it would have meant living in Queensland on a sheep station, but rather because, when he had proposed to her, he had been only a station hand, without any money. She had said that she wanted to marry a man who could afford to give her the sort of life she was used to —well, he'd be able to do that now, if he took her back and bought a property of his own. She would *not* have to live in a tin-roofed shack and cook his meals for him . . .

Johnny glanced cautiously round the carriage to see that he was unobserved and then took out his wallet, shuffling through the photographs it contained. He hadn't a proper photograph of Elizabeth, but he had several snapshots of her, taken when she was staying with the Gilliats. One on horseback, with Pip beside her, he particularly liked, for in it she was smiling and so obviously enjoying herself that it gave him reassurance.

They made quite a contrast, she and Pip, he reflected, studying the snapshots —Pip dark and thin and boyish in her faded jeans, Elizabeth fair and lovely and extremely feminine, her long blonde hair blowing out behind her. She wore the conventional English riding kit, too, which somehow added to her femininity: a tailored silk shirt, perfectly cut breeches and an elegant pair of hand-made boots. Both girls were expert horsewomen—Pip, of course, had ridden from the time she could walk and, as a child, had attended her first school on horseback. But Elizabeth brought a grace and elegance to her riding that Pip couldn't match: she had hunted in the Shires and was a successful point-to-point rider—she had *style*. Admittedly she couldn't tackle the wild, half-broken brumbies Pip handled so well, but—she had style and it showed in the snapshot, just as the difference in their ages showed. Pip was a child, Elizabeth an adult, sophisticated young woman who knew how to charm a man's heart out of him and set his pulses racing . . .

Looking down at their two pictured faces, Johnny sighed, his conscience pricking him afresh. He oughtn't to have kissed Pip as he had, that last night, oughtn't to have reiterated his invitation to her to come and visit him at Logan. He had been a bit carried away that night, had scarcely known what he was saying, and Pip was a funny kid, who got funny ideas at times. He hoped that he hadn't given her any and that she hadn't taken him too seriously. He didn't want to hurt Pip or do anything which might upset her parents, from whom he had received so much kindness that he would be forever in their debt. But . . . Johnny sighed again and replaced the snapshots in his wallet. Gradually the swaying train lulled him into a broken and uneasy sleep and he slept fitfully until the grey light of early morning, seeping in through the carriage windows, roused him to wakefulness.

They would reach Ardloch at a little after nine, he knew, and from there it would be a drive of about ten miles to Logan. Johnny unpacked his shaving gear and went along the corridor to wash and shave. He had a clean shirt in his suitcase and he changed into this when he had completed his toilet. It was important that he should make a good impression on his cousins, the first impressions, he reminded himself, were often the ones that counted. He eyed his reflection in the mirror anxiously. His new suit which, when he had bought it yesterday, had seemed so correct and well cut, now bore unmistakable signs of having been slept in. And was a blue pinstripe suit the correct wear in the Scottish Highlands? He had seen plenty of such suits in London, where they seemed to be almost a uniform, but perhaps, in the Highlands, those who didn't wear the kilt sported tweeds? Obviously no one would expect him to wear a kilt, since he was Australian, but—he frowned. He was entering a house of mourning, he should have bought himself a black suit, not a blue one, as a mark of sympathy and respect.

Wretchedly, Johnny tugged at his blue tie. He had a black one somewhere, if he could only find it. And a clothes-brush . . . he hunted frantically in his suitcase, finally running the clothes-brush to earth. But the black tie eluded his search, and in the end, when impatient rattling on the door of the washroom warned him that others beside himself wanted to use it, he was forced to make do with a fairly sober brown one. It didn't go with his suit, but at least it wasn't as gaudy as the blue tie that had been his initial choice, and his suit, now that he had brushed it, didn't look too bad.

He emerged into the corridor to be greeted by the concerted disapproval of some half-dozen of his fellow-passengers. Returning to his own compartment, he found everyone awake and rain beating relentlessly on the windows, blotting out everything save a few stunted bushes growing beside the track. A thick, swirling mist covered the surrounding country like a pall and, strain his eyes as he might, he could make out very little, except once, when the mist cleared for a moment and he glimpsed the ruffled waters of a loch. And then the mist closed in again and the loch vanished.

Johnny shivered and turned his back on the window, to find the eyes of the elderly woman opposite riveted on his face.

"Excuse me"—she spoke with a strong Glasgow accent—"but have I not seen you before? Your face is unco' familiar."

He shook his head, reddening under her scrutiny.

"I don't think so. I don't see how you could have done."

"What makes ye so sure?" She was still unconvinced. "I'm no' one to forget a face. And I would swear that I know yours. Do you travel this way often?"

"I've never travelled this way before," Johnny assured her. The other passengers were looking at him curiously now, their interest caught and held. One of them, a bright-eyed lad in a school blazer, put in eagerly: "The telly, Gran, do you not remember? We were watching it last night before we left to catch the train. Was this gentleman not on it?"

"Oh, aye, of course!" The elderly woman was delighted. She beamed at Johnny, the mystery solved. "The laddie's right, is he not—'twas you we saw on *In Town Tonight* surely? I don't mind your name—'tis your face I remember. Well, guidsakes but this is a coincidence—seeing you last night on the telly and travelling with you in the same railway carriage! I'd not have believed it possible. But 'tis true, is it not—it *was* you we saw?"

Redder than ever, Johnny admitted that it was. But before he could change the subject from himself, the boy said triumphantly: "I mind your name, sir. You're from Australia and you're the new Earl of Logan."

They all gazed at him, their astonishment mingled with awe as they realized who he was. Recalling his conversation with the Nasebys, Johnny knew that denial was useless: these people had seen

63

him whilst sitting at their own firesides, it was as if he had entered their homes as a friend, and, even if he had wanted to, he could not behave towards them as if they were strangers. And, suddenly, he didn't want to. They were decent, kindly people, impressed more because he had appeared on television than because a strange fate had made him a Scottish peer.

The elderly woman shook hands with him, introducing herself as Kirsty Mac-Bride: her grandson followed suit and soon they were all talking, asking him eager questions, plying him with the sandwiches and the thermos tea they had brought for the journey. He felt happier than he had felt since leaving Australia, and when the train began to slow down and he realized that he had reached his destination, he gathered his things together despondently, reluctant, now that the time had come, to part with his new acquaintances. He descended to the platform with their good wishes ringing in his ears and looked about him for some sign of his cousin Fiona, who, he thought, would be the most likely person to come to the station to meet him.

But the platform had a sleepy, Sunday morning air and was deserted, save for a solitary porter waiting to collect tickets at the barrier and the small handful of passengers who, like himself, had just left the train.

Puzzled, Johnny looked at his watch. The train was a few minutes early, he saw, which might account for his cousin's absence.

He picked up his suitcases and made for the station exit, seeing that there were only two vehicles parked in the yard outside—a red Post Office mail van, whose driver was busy loading a sack of mail into its rear, and a dark blue Rolls-Royce coupé which was unattended.

He approached the postman and then halted in astonishment as the man raised his head. He was a young man, with red hair and a round, cherubic face which—although almost all the time Johnny had seen it previously, it had been covered with Korean mud—was quite unmistakable. They stared at each other for a long moment in silence. Then the postman said, his tone incredulous:

"It's you. It's *Snow!* Why, man alive, I

never expected to set eyes on you again! How did you get here, for heaven's sake?"

"I came in the train, Jock." Johnny seized the outstretched hand and the young postman wrung it enthusiastically.

"Do you mind that last patrol we did, in front of the Hook?"

"Do you remember the night we met at the Moto Club, on Tokyo leave?" They both spoke together, both laughed and both began again, their words tumbling over each other as the memories came flooding back. There were so many memories—memories of the fighting they had shared, the lonely patrols, the fear and the tension, the occasional excitement and the cold. Always the cold: Johnny could never think of Korea without remembering how cold it had been. He shivered involuntarily, recalling the long weeks of inaction which he and Jock had shared, huddled in their cheerless bunker, talking their heads off to each other, because there was little else they could do.

Jock had been with the Argylls, a corporal Bren-gunner from Glasgow, who had volunteered to act as guide to the Australians when they first came into the

66

line, and for some reason he had been forgotten when his unit pulled out and so he had stayed until belatedly reclaimed, several weeks later. By that time, he and Johnny had become firm friends and they had met again, by chance, in Tokyo just before Jock's demob. Johnny's eyes gleamed as he remembered that leave when they had drunk vast quantities of beer together and laughed and enjoyed themselves, as fighting soldiers will in a foreign capital, their pockets full of money and time their only enemy.

For a few minutes, oblivious of everything else around them, they indulged in excited reminiscences, reliving it all, absurdly and unrestrainedly pleased to see each other again. Johnny forgot his mission, Jock the sack of mail that was half in, half out of his van and neither of them noticed that a tall, dark-haired girl in a tweed suit had come to stand beside the parked Rolls, regarding them with silent disapproval.

It was Jock who saw her first. He coloured furiously and pointed. "You're him, aren't you—the new Earl? You're on your way to Logan?"

"Yes," Johnny admitted. He had his back to the Rolls and saw neither the girl nor Jock's pointing finger. "But look, Jock, we—"

Jock swallowed hard. "I never dreamed it was you. Mind, I kenned your name was Chisholm, but the Diggers called you Snow, didn't they? 'Twas just I didn't connect you, somehow, with Logan. And you a corporal like me." He sounded a trifle reproachful. "You never said, you never told me, with all the talking we did, that you were related to *them*. And the newspapers didn't make it sound like you, did they?"

"No, I don't suppose they did."

"Well," said Jock helplessly, "her ladyship's come for you—Lady Fiona. You'd best not keep her waiting." Recalled to his own duties, he sighed and gestured to the sack of mail at the back of his van. "And I've to deliver that to the sorting office before I can get away for my Sunday dinner. Goodbye, Snow—your lordship. 'Twas grand seeing you. Maybe we'll meet again and maybe we won't. There's the Terriers and the Legion and"—he grinned good-humouredly—"I deliver the mail to Logan, week about."

Before Johnny could say another word, he slammed the doors of his van, slipped quickly into the driving seat and was off out of the station yard in a flurry of churned-up gravel.

Johnny turned, aware now that he had been standing bareheaded and coatless in the rain and that his suit looked worse than ever. He walked stiffly over to the waiting girl, clutching his suitcases, and came to a halt in front of her, smiling uncertainly.

She was beautiful and extremely well dressed, he saw, which added to his confusion: a girl of about twenty-two or three, with a lovely pale oval face and startlingly intelligent grey eyes, which met his appraisingly for an instant and were then swiftly lowered. Her tweed suit was dark but she was not in deep mourning, and she had drawn a waterproof over her shoulders.

Johnny held out his hand. "Good morning," he said nervously. "Er—I'm Johnny Chisholm, I—that is, you're my cousin Fiona, aren't you?"

She acknowledged his awkward greeting with a grave little inclination of her head, her smile perfunctory and without warmth. She accepted his hand, but the gesture was purely formal, and Johnny, who had been wondering if she would expect him to kiss her, withdrew his hand quickly and bent to pick up his suitcases again.

"Shall I put these into the car?" he asked.

"Mackay will do it," his cousin returned. The coldness of her tone struck him with the force of a physical blow. There was a chauffeur, he now realized, as the man came to relieve him of his bags, a white-haired chauffeur in impeccable uniform who murmured something about "his lordship" and took the shabby cases from him as if their touch offended his finer feelings.

Johnny felt the hot, resentful colour rising in waves to the roots of his hair.

"If loading my bags is too much trouble for you," he said bitterly, "I can do it myself, you know. I managed to take them off the train."

The chauffeur looked shocked. "My

lord, I assure you, it is no trouble at all."
He put both cases into the boot of the
luxurious coupé, even his well-tailored
back expressing reproach and injured
dignity.

"I'm sorry," Fiona put in, her tone
more icy than it had been before, "that
Mackay missed you on the platform, John.
He was waiting by the entrance to the
sleeping car and I was at the bookstall,
otherwise I might have seen you get off.
Didn't you travel by sleeper?"

"No," said Johnny, "I didn't." He experienced a strong desire to shock his
cousin from her complacency, as he had
shocked the chauffeur a moment ago, by
telling her that he could not afford to
travel in a first-class sleeper because his
journey from Australia had been expensive
and had taken every penny he had. But he
restrained himself. She was a woman and
had recently suffered a tragic bereavement:
it would be uncouth and uncharitable to
be rude to her or to reproach her for his
lack of funds. It obviously didn't occur to
people who were used to having money
and driving around in Rolls-Royces that
ordinary people like himself might have

difficulty in paying their rail and air fares. But he was glad now that he hadn't cabled to the Logan lawyers for money: it gave Fiona one less reason to despise him. He had got here under his own steam, maintained his independence, asked them for nothing.

"Shall we get in out of the rain?" Fiona Chisholm suggested. She motioned to the car, and the chauffeur, his face impassive, opened the rear door for her. Johnny got in after her, Mackay closed the heavy door soundlessly, went round to the front of the car and took his place behind the wheel. They glided majestically out of the station yard.

Fiona was silent, her gaze on the chauffeur's back, but her hands, Johnny noticed, were restless, pleating and re-pleating a fold of her skirt, moving to touch her handbag and returning once more to her lap, to clasp each other tightly.

"This," he said, when the silence had become uncomfortable, "is a bonzer car." He was conscious, as soon as he had made it, of the inanity of his remark. Normally he didn't use much Australian slang, but the "bonzer" came out before he could prevent it, and out of the tail of his eye he saw his cousin wince.

"I'm glad you like it," she rejoined curtly. "I hope you'll decide to keep it. My father bought it for my mother last year."

"But if it's your mother's car—" Johnny began, and broke off at the sight of her expression. In all his life he had never seen hate in a woman's eyes before, but he saw it now in Fiona's and instinctively recoiled. "*I* don't want your mother's car," he said desperately, "don't you understand—I don't want anything, anything at all that belongs to either of you! That's not why I've come—why, for crying out loud, Fiona, surely you must know that?"

"I know nothing whatever about you," Fiona answered flatly. "And what you want and what you don't want scarcely comes into it—under the entail everything belongs to you. The car, of course, was a gift to my mother, it's registered in her name and is her private property, but, since she won't be running a car in future, it occurred to me that you might want to keep it for your own use. It could be arranged—the estate could buy it from her —if you wanted to take it over."

Johnny opened his mouth to protest but closed it again, the words unspoken. Instead he suggested weakly: "We—we shall have to have a talk about things like this, about everything. Perhaps your mother—"

She interrupted him fiercely. "My mother isn't in a fit state to be worried, I'm afraid. She's been ill, she still is, much too ill to concern herself with business matters. I shall deal with these on her behalf, with the assistance of our solicitors. The head of the firm will be coming to see you tomorrow—I thought it would be best to get things settled with as little delay as possible, for all our sakes. Once that's done, my mother and I can leave Logan. We are both anxious to go."

"Anxious to leave your home, Fiona?" Johnny echoed, appalled. "But you can't be. *I* don't want you to go."

"Don't you? Well, I am sorry, but neither of us has any desire to stay." Her tone was repressive and it brooked no argument. Johnny stared at her, the wind taken completely from his sails. He felt frighteningly at a loss, and, though he racked his brain for words, could think of nothing to say to this strange, beautiful girl who made no secret of the contemptuous dislike with which she regarded him. She was his cousin, Johnny thought despairingly, but she hated him, without his having done anything to incur her hatred. Unless she had misunderstood his meeting with Jock or resented the way he had spoken to the chauffeur . . . a glance at her face told him that it went much deeper than that. But, lest he should be mistaken, he decided to explain Jock.

Fiona heard him in silence, not looking at him.

"I see," she said when he had done, but he sensed that she neither saw nor understood, and he wondered even if she had listened to what he was saying. Anger rose in his throat, transcending pity. There was no need for her to adopt this attitude, he thought. She hadn't given him a chance, she had judged and condemned him long before his arrival. Good heavens, did she really believe that he had come here in order to dispossess her mother and herself, to turn them from their home, rob them of all that had been theirs?

They drove swiftly through the grey, wind-swept streets of Ardloch, the rain beating a savage tattoo on the roof of the car and finding its echo in Johnny's heart. Had he travelled thirteen thousand miles for this? He was a stranger in a strange land who had thought to find a welcome from his kinsfolk, but instead he had been met with bitterness . . .

He glanced again at Fiona's lovely, shuttered face.

"Look, Fiona," he pleaded humbly. "Couldn't we try to understand each other? I think you've got me wrong, honestly I do. I'm every bit as sorry as you are for the—the reasons that have brought me here."

"Are you?" Her voice cut like a whiplash. "I scarcely imagine you could be. But go on. What—apart from understanding —do you want of me?"

"Well—" Johnny hesitated, eyeing her unhappily. "Couldn't we be friends? I don't know a soul here, except Jock MacPhail. I'm completely on my own and—"

"On your own, John?" Fiona's tone expressed courteous disbelief. "But you're not. Your fiancée is waiting to welcome you. She wouldn't come to the station, although I did suggest it, but she's coming to lunch. I invited her because I thought that would be what you wanted."

"My . . . fiancée? But—"

"Elizabeth Anson," Fiona supplied coldly. Her eyes met Johnny's then, with a question in them. "Isn't she your fiancée? She told me that she was expecting to marry you when I spoke to her on the telephone this morning. Didn't you know that she was staying in Logan?"

4

JOHNNY was so taken aback by Fiona's completely unexpected announcement that, for a moment, he couldn't speak.

Elizabeth here . . . in Logan? Staying in Logan . . . apparently coming to lunch at the Castle . . . he could hardly believe his ears. And—she had told Fiona that she was expecting to marry him, that they were engaged . . .

He swallowed hard. That, of course, was wonderful news, it was what he had always wanted, but—it was a shock, all the same, and the very last thing he had imagined would happen. He had visualized a cautious and tactful approach on his part to a still slightly reluctant Elizabeth, a slow and carefully planned renewal of his courtship—lunches to begin with at the Savoy or the Berkeley perhaps: an occasional theatre or a drive into the country, when the weather improved. Even dinner, if she seemed to be enjoying his company, and when he had acquired the right clothes and a rudimentary grasp of the duties of escort to a girl like Elizabeth on her home ground.

He was in love with Elizabeth, of course, Johnny reminded himself. She was the girl he had dreamed of making his wife, but—she had refused him once and hurt him deeply. And Pip had warned him that she wouldn't hesitate to hurt him again, which—although he hadn't really taken Pip's warning seriously—had been the reason for his decision not to propose to Elizabeth a second time until he could be fairly certain of the outcome. But now she was here, waiting for him, calmly informing his cousin that they were engaged before he knew it himself! It *was* a shock, and, coming on top of all the other shocks he had received, it was a little hard to take in.

"Well?" prompted Fiona unsmilingly. "Didn't you know that Miss Anson was staying in Logan, John?"

"I—no." Johnny was conscious once again of her hostility and he added quickly, defensively: "But I'm awfully pleased that she is. It's—it's wonderful news."

"Then I did the right thing in asking her to lunch?" his cousin pursued. "I wasn't sure if I had."

"Oh, yes. Yes, indeed." Realizing that she expected some sort of explanation, Johnny hesitated. He didn't have to explain himself, really, but obviously it must seem a trifle odd that he hadn't known of Elizabeth's arrival, and he didn't want his cousin Fiona to misjudge Elizabeth as she had already misjudged himself. He said, choosing his words with care: "Miss Anson was staying out in Queensland—she was a guest of the people I worked for and we saw a lot of each other during her visit. But I left in a bit of a rush and I've been rushing ever since—I hadn't time to get in touch with her, let her know what was happening. I was going to, naturally, as soon as I'd introduced myself to you—you and your mother."

"Naturally," Fiona agreed. Johnny glanced at her suspiciously but her face was blank and withdrawn, her expression inscrutable.

"I didn't want to—well, to intrude on

80

your grief," he told her diffidently. "That was why I didn't invite Elizabeth to come here myself. I thought it would be better if I saw her in London a bit later on. But she wouldn't know that, she wouldn't realize that you and your mother—" He broke off helplessly, unable to put his feelings into words.

"That my mother and I would not feel like entertaining strangers just now?" Fiona finished for him. "Is that what you mean?"

"Well, yes."

"It is kind of you to worry on our account. But I assure you, it isn't necessary. My mother is keeping to her room, on our doctor's advice—I told you that she was ill, I think?" Johnny nodded and Fiona went on, still in the same flat, unemotional voice: "We'll leave the Castle as soon as my mother is well enough, but until then, of course, you must feel perfectly free to entertain anyone you wish. I will supervise the domestic arrangements for you until I go—unless you would like Miss Anson to do so. There is not a great deal to do—we have a fairly large staff and a competent housekeeper."

"I see." Johnny licked at dry lips. He felt chilled by his cousin's brusque, matter-of-fact dismissal of his attempts to spare her. "Shall I be able to—that is, does your mother wish to see me?"

At that, Fiona turned to look at him and he saw a flicker of something suggesting uncertainty in her grey eyes. But then they hardened and she said: "I imagine she would like to meet you and—bid you welcome. But I hope you won't try to talk to her of anything remotely connected with business or legal matters. She isn't fit to discuss anything like that—I've kept everything from her. You understand that she has suffered a terrible shock, she—she isn't herself."

"I'm very sorry," Johnny said with such sincerity that her expression relaxed a little.

"I'm sure you are, John. But things like this happen, don't they? One just has to accept them, put on the bravest front that one can and . . . go on living. At my mother's age it isn't easy to go on living when you have lost everything you love and hold dear." For the first time, there was emotion in her voice and Johnny was conscious of her pain, so bravely hidden until this moment. He wanted to put out a hand and take hers, to tell her again how sorry he was, but the instinctive conviction that she would resent it prevented him. She didn't want his pity. He respected her courage and her proud, independent determination to ask for no quarter and yield none: in her place he would have felt as she did, he thought, and deliberately avoided her gaze.

A little silence fell between them, but now it wasn't a hostile silence, as it had been before. The car gathered speed, climbing a steep, curving hill with effortless ease. Because of the rain Johnny could see little more of the country through which they were passing than that it was mountainous and rather bleak. Here and there a grey stone cottage stood by the roadside, and once they passed through a small village, but both it and the wayside cottages appeared to be devoid of life, the windows of the houses blank and inhospitable, with only the smoke rising from an occasional chimney to suggest that they might be occupied.

He found it depressing. To cover his

uneasiness, he took out his tin of tobacco, with the intention of rolling himself a cigarette, only to realize that he had no made cigarettes to offer his companion. He could hardly offer her one of his rolled ones, still less smoke himself, without offering her one—and he knew Elizabeth's opinion of his "bush cigarettes". His failure to carry "tailormades" had always annoyed her and she had often reproached him for it.

"Please smoke, John," Fiona said, breaking the silence, "if you want to—I don't."

Relieved, he started to tease the tobacco into shape. His cousin watched him without comment. When the cigarette was made she said briefly: "You do it very neatly," and then, leaning across him, pointed to a clump of fir trees on the skyline and announced: "Logan stands behind those—the Castle, I mean, the village lies in the glen below it."

"Is it a big village?"

"Yes, fairly big. It serves all the estate farms and crofts. There's a post office, a general store and, of course, the church and the manse and the school. The Logan Arms, where your—where Miss Anson is staying, is very comfortable and has about twenty guest rooms. It caters for summer visitors, and we get quite a number, for fishing and shooting. The Arms owns a stretch of the river below the Castle and Colonel Macreay lets them his grouse moor every year." She went on telling him about the village, but Johnny listened with half an ear. He wondered whether, when they left the Castle, Fiona and her mother would settle down in the village or whether they intended to go right away. The thought of their leaving on his account worried him, and after a while, when Fiona finished her description of the village and started to talk about the estate, he interrupted her.

"Fiona—"

"Yes?" She turned her head sharply.

"Where do you and Cousin Catherine intend to go, when you leave the Castle?"

His question obviously took her by surprise. He saw the guarded, hostile look in her eyes again and regretted his impulsiveness. "I'm sorry," he said, "if you think I'm prying into your private affairs but—"

"I *do* think you are. And I should prefer it if you didn't. We should *both* prefer it."

"Was it"—he had to know, Johnny thought obstinately—"was it your mother's decision or yours that you should leave?"

Angry colour burned fiercely in Fiona's pale cheeks.

"It was—and is—the only possible decision we could make," she returned at last.

"But did your mother make it? Does she know of it?"

"She doesn't know of it yet—I told you, I have tried to keep such matters from her. But when she does know, she will agree, of course." Fiona made a small, impatient gesture with her hands. "I shall look after my mother, you need not concern yourself about either of us. I am perfectly capable of taking care of her, I promise you. And now"—her tone held finality—"if you don't mind, I'd rather not discuss it with you. We shall have to go into the position with our solicitor tomorrow in any case. That's why he's coming."

"Very well," Johnny conceded, "if you say so." But if she imagined that this was the end of the matter, then she was mistaken, he thought grimly. He might buy her mother's car, if that was what she wanted, but he would not—no matter what Fiona said—turn either of them out of their home. That was unthinkable.

The car rounded the last bend and began the descent into Logan village. It looked as grey and unwelcoming as the other villages had looked, but it was larger and there were some signs of life—a milk lorry, halted outside the gateway to a farm: a policeman, muffled in his raincape, pedalling slowly down the hill: a handful of raincoated women gathered about the doors of the Kirk and, further on, a little procession of children hurrying in the same direction. All turned their heads to look at the passing car and Johnny felt their eyes on him as the chauffeur slowed down in order to make a sharp, left-hand turn opposite the general store.

He didn't see the Logan Arms and Fiona made no attempt to point it out to him. Nor did she suggest that they should call there, but as if she had sensed what he was thinking, she said briefly: "I've arranged for a car to pick up Miss

Anson at half-past twelve. We lunch at one."

"Thank you," Johnny acknowledged, with equal brevity.

The car turned into a drive entrance, flanked by a stone-built lodge and an imposing pair of heavy, wrought-iron gates, and began to climb. He peered through the streaming windscreen, conscious of the quickened beat of his heart as, out of the mist, the vast grey bulk of Logan Castle came suddenly into sight.

It was a massive, formidable structure, a fortress as unyielding as the rock from which it had been hewn, a castle in the truest sense, with towering battlements and a central keep, its windows—except for those on ground level which had been enlarged—the arrow-slits of mediaeval days. It was surrounded on two sides by a deer park: to the east, behind a belt of screening trees, Johnny could just make out the silvery gleam of water—a river, he decided, or perhaps a loch—over which the mist hung sluggishly, writhing about the trees.

He sensed rather than saw the mountains at its back and knew a sudden thrill of pride as he gazed for the first time upon his inheritance. This was the castle of the Chisholms of Logan, this the home they had known, the fortress they had defended throughout the long, turbulent centuries that it had been in their possession. The history of Scotland and of the Highlands was written in its weather-worn stone: from here, long-dead Chisholms had gone out—clansmen in rough, homespun tartan, soldiers in scarlet and khaki—to do battle for their country's honour, to crown a king or defy one, to join in fierce carnage with their neighbours, in prosecution of some long-standing feud.

And—Johnny drew a deep, awe-struck breath—it was *his*. He was Chisholm of Logan now. His grandfather had been born in this place and his father too. He was the only one who had not, but he had returned here . . . returned to claim it for his own. Here, God willing, his son would be born.

Beside him, Fiona stirred. "John"—her clear, cold voice broke into his thoughts, bringing him abruptly back to earth—"is it as you imagined it would be?"

He shook his head. "No. No, it's not."

89

"In what way?"

"It's bigger," Johnny answered lamely. "I never imagined it would be so—so enormous. It's so big that I don't see why you and your mother couldn't go on living here with me. I can't see any reason why you have to leave, honestly, Fiona."

He knew, from the contempt in his cousin's eyes, that this was not the reply she had expected or wanted from him. Her low-voiced, bitter: "*Can't* you?" told him plainly that their brief moment of intimacy was over. He had let his chance of winning her respect and tolerance slip through his fingers and he might not be given it again. Fiona resented him, hated him for the interloper he was, and she despised him so much that she would not even permit him to be generous to her.

As the Rolls-Royce glided smoothly to a halt outside the impressive front door, Johnny felt a stranger, unwanted and unwelcome. His bright hopes faded, the vision he had seen disappeared. He might be the last of the Chisholms of Logan, but he didn't belong here as his forebears had belonged: he would never belong here: the ghosts he had seen were allied with Fiona against him.

The chauffeur came round to open the car door. At the same moment the front door swung back on its massive iron hinges and a butler in a neat black jacket stood waiting, his smooth, well-shaven face blank and expressionless. Fiona got out of the car and Johnny followed her miserably.

"This is Jamieson," Fiona said. "Jamieson, his lordship's bags are in the car. Will you see that they are taken up, please?" The butler bowed and stood aside politely to allow Johnny to pass him. He took the two shabby, rain-wet suitcases from the chauffeur and came to Johnny's side.

"If your lordship will follow me . . ." He led the way across a long, stone-flagged hall, its walls hung with stags' heads and other trophies of the chase. A log fire burned cheerfully in a great stone fireplace at its far end, and a graceful, turkey-carpeted staircase led upwards to what appeared to be an open-fronted gallery, protected by a railing in the same dark, highly-polished wood as the banisters.

As they gained the second floor, Johnny saw that the gallery extended for almost the whole length of the house, the parquet surface partly carpeted and the walls lined with portraits. Several corridors opened off it, panelled in dark oak, from which rose other, smaller staircases.

"Lady Fiona," Jamieson said, "has put you in the Red Suite, your lordship." He opened a door and again stood aside so that Johnny might precede him. Johnny went in, to find himself in a large, high-ceilinged room, furnished with a huge four-poster bed, with dark red hangings. Carpet and curtains, as well as the chintz-covered chairs, continued the dark red colour scheme: an electric fire, set in the wall, emitted a pleasant warmth, and the windows overlooked the park. Beyond the bedroom, through a communicating door, there was a dressing-room, lined with heavy mahogany cupboards and a chest of drawers.

The butler carried Johnny's suitcases into the dressing-room, set them down neatly side by side and turned to look at him inquiringly.

"Well?" challenged Johnny, somewhat at a loss.

"Your keys, my lord. If I might have them, I will unpack for your lordship."

"They aren't locked." Johnny braced himself. His cases were a mess and he wasn't going to have this supercilious flunkey laughing his head off at his scanty wardrobe. "I'll unpack for myself, thanks."

"Very good, my lord. Er"—Jamieson coughed delicately—"your bathroom opens off the dressing-room." He displayed it. "Is there anything I can bring your lordship? Some coffee, perhaps? Or a tray of tea? Unless your lordship would prefer whisky—"

"Thanks," said Johnny. "I could do with some tea, I reckon."

"Certainly, my lord." The butler moved towards the door, his feet making no sound on the thick carpet. "I will bring it up at once—if there is nothing else I can do for your lordship?"

"No," said Johnny, "nothing, thanks." He wished that the man would go and leave him alone, was relieved when at last he did so.

Left to himself, he went into the dressing-room, opened the first of his suitcases and surveyed its contents ruefully. Shirts, ties, his hairbrushes, the framed photograph of herself that Pip had given him, his crumpled flannels and his old suit were hopelessly jumbled together, disturbed in his hunt for the black tie in the train this morning. Well—he sighed—better get them out of sight, before that infernal butler returned and renewed his offer to do it for him . . .

Johnny was just completing this task when a soft tap on the bedroom door brought him to his feet.

"Come in," he called, expecting it to be Jamieson with his tea, but as he hurriedly shut the last drawer, he heard a woman's voice and turned, startled, to see his cousin Catherine coming towards him, both hands outheld.

She was a tall, slim, grey-haired woman, in whose shadowed eyes tragedy lurked. Her resemblance to Fiona was so striking that it told him instantly who she was, but her smile, unlike Fiona's, was warm and friendly, her handclasp affectionate. She had once been very beautiful, Johnny realized as he looked down at her, and her face, despite its pallor and the lines which pain had etched across it, still retained more than a hint of its former comeliness. He bent, without a second thought, to kiss her cheek and felt her tremble as she went into his arms. She was very thin and alarmingly frail, and he held her with gentle reverence, conscious suddenly of an overwhelming desire to protect her.

"So you're John—" She stood back, gazing up at him with smiling approval.

"And you're Cousin Catherine." Johnny's voice wasn't steady.

"You're like my eldest son—you're like Alastair. I thought you would be when I saw you on television last night."

"You saw me?" Johnny questioned and she inclined her shapely head. "Oh, yes. You were very good. I was proud of you, very proud. It couldn't have been easy for you. I don't suppose any of it has been easy for you, has it?"

"No," he confirmed, "it hasn't. I don't know how I'm expected to behave, you see. And there's been no one I could ask."

"There's someone now," she told him softly. "You can ask me, John—about anything that worries you. I shall be glad to help."

"Will you?" He stared at her, filled with compassion because, like himself, she was lost and alone and yet anxious to help him: she, who had lost everything, was yet ready still to give, if there was anything he wanted from her. "Oh, will you, Cousin Catherine? I should be so grateful." His throat was stiff. "I can't take your son's place, I can't begin to, but if you would help me, I—I'd try not to fail you. I'd do the best I could."

"I know you would, John. But—" she touched his sleeve—"you've been out in the rain, your jacket's wet through—goodness, you'll catch a chill, you aren't used to this climate. You must change at once, my dear boy, and have a hot bath—don't linger here, getting colder and colder. Off you go at once. I will tell Jamieson to bring a suit of Alastair's for you to change into and a hot drink . . ." She bustled him off, ignoring his protests, and Johnny, feeling like a little boy again, permitted her to have her way.

When he emerged from his bath, he found a tweed suit laid out for him in his dressing-room. It fitted him perfectly. Returning to the bedroom, he saw his cousin Catherine waiting, a tea-tray on the table beside her. She had Pip's photograph in her hand and, as he joined her, she looked up from it inquiringly.

"Fiona told me that your fiancée was coming to lunch. This is her photograph, I suppose?"

Reddening, he shook his head. "No, Cousin Catherine. That's Pip Gilliat. Her father owned the property I worked on. My—er—that is, it's Elizabeth Anson I'm going to marry."

Lady Logan's delicate dark brows came together.

"Oh, I see." She replaced Pip's photograph on the mantelpiece. "Then it is Elizabeth Anson who is coming to lunch?"

"Yes. She's staying at the Logan Arms."

"Is she Australian?"

"Oh, no, Cousin Catherine—she's English, she lives in London. She was only staying with the Gilliats."

"Come and sit down, John," his cousin invited, indicating the armchair beside her, "and tell me about your Elizabeth while we drink our tea." She gave him her slow, charming, oddly youthful smile and added quietly: "This was my Alastair's room, you know. He and I often used to have tea in here together like this when he was at home. We were—very close to each other, Alastair and I."

"Were you?" echoed Johnny huskily. He took the chair beside her and reached out his hand to take hers.

"I'm glad you look like him, John," Lady Logan said. She let her hand lie in his for a moment and then drew a long sighing breath and released it, reaching for the teapot. "Tell me about Elizabeth, dear," she prompted gently. "Are you very much in love with her?"

"Yes," Johnny answered. He met her gaze. "Yes, I'm very much in love with Elizabeth, Cousin Catherine. She's . . ." He hesitated, searching for words and his eyes went to Pip's photograph, perched on the shelf above his head. He smiled at it. "Elizabeth is a wonderful girl," he said firmly and realized, as he said it, that he had addressed his assertion to Pip.

Lady Logan watched him in silence, sipping her tea.

5

IN her bedroom at the Logan Arms, Elizabeth Anson was making a careful toilet. She stood in front of her mirror, regarding her reflection critically. The grey worsted dress, she thought, was, perhaps, a pity, but it was right for today's luncheon—one couldn't wear bright colours when one's hostess was in mourning. And the touches of blue she had added, in scarf and belt, brought out the colour of her eyes, whilst still not detracting from the subdued effect she had set out to create.

She donned her coat, which was a dark grey tweed, and wondered about wearing a hat. Obviously she ought to wear one, but all her hats were gay, new season's jewel colours and much too bright. People in the country—especially in Scotland— were much less formal than they were in London: privately Elizabeth considered them rather dowdy, but . . . she hesitated, doing a swift mental review of the hats she had brought with her. There *was* the off-white fur felt: it would tone with her coat, which had a white fleck in it, and, however informal the Chisholms might be, she would feel happier in a hat.

She got it out, perched it neatly and expertly on her head and smiled. Yes, it was right—or would be, if she gave it a touch of blue, to relate it to her scarf. She had some chiffon somewhere that would be just perfect, and it wouldn't take more than a minute or two to stitch into place. She hunted in the drawer of her dressing-table, found the chiffon square and set to work with her needle. She wanted Johnny to be impressed—not that it was difficult to impress Johnny, but . . . Elizabeth drew a quick, uneven breath. She had very nearly lost Johnny, might still lose him, if she didn't play her cards extremely care-fully. Because she knew that she had hurt his pride when she had rejected his proposal all those weeks ago, knew too that she had wounded him deeply by laughing at the idea of marrying him.

And yet it was ironic in a way that her laughter had been as much for herself as for him. Johnny had attracted her more than any man she had ever met, and she had found it hard, against all reason, to refuse him. So that she had had to laugh at him to save herself: she had had to make him appear ridiculous in order to escape from him and break the spell he had cast over her. Because, of course, as things had been she really couldn't have married him. It wouldn't have worked and she had had the good sense to realize it. She could not and did not blame herself. Her decision had been the right one at the time, the only possible decision, for who—short of a fortune-teller—could conceivably have imagined that events would take the fantastic turn they had? Who in their right senses could have foreseen that Johnny Chisholm, an obscure young station hand from the Australian outback, without a penny to his name, would become almost overnight a Scottish peer and the heir to a fortune?

Such things didn't happen as a rule, except in fairy stories: nothing like it had ever happened in Elizabeth's experience, and even now she found it a little hard to believe, in spite of seeing it in black and white in every newspaper she had picked up during the last few days. She was thankful, though, that she *had* seen it in the newspapers, because this had given her time to make plans and act on them, to come up here, so that when Johnny arrived she would be waiting for him.

That he would be pleased to see her she had no serious doubt. The attraction between them had been very strong, and every instinct she possessed had told her that Johnny Chisholm was in love with her. He was too honest and too innocently naïve to be able to hide his feelings from her, and, at the Gilliats', he hadn't tried. They had all known how he felt about her, from Harry Gilliat himself to his precocious younger daughter, Pip. Elizabeth flushed, remembering how Pip had reproached her on Johnny's account. Pip's accusations had been quite unforgivable —prompted by childish jealousy, of course, but nevertheless hurtful because, in a way, they had been true. She *had* treated Johnny badly, but—that was over now. She had made reparation. She had come here the instant she had heard that Johnny was on his way and she had made it clear to his cousin that she intended, after all, to marry him.

Elizabeth finished stitching the trimming in place and studied the hat, head on one side. It looked very nice, she decided, suitable and in good taste. Johnny would be proud of her, proud to present her to his aristocratic Scottish relatives as his future countess. He would need a wife who had some social standing, in order to make up for his own lack of it. Whilst she could not actually boast of any titled relations, her father had been a rich and successful businessman who had left his only daughter well provided for and had sent her to a good school. She knew the "right people", Elizabeth reflected complacently, and her mother, who lived in an expensive Eaton Square flat, served on numerous charitable committees and was quite an asset.

There was a brisk knock on the door. "Yes?" queried Elizabeth, putting on her hat. "What is it?"

"If you please, Miss Anson"—it was the chambermaid's voice—"there's Dr. Cameron waiting on you downstairs. He said to tell you that he had called to drive you up to the Castle."

"Very well," responded Elizabeth, wondering who Dr. Cameron might be and why he—instead of the car Lady Fiona Chisholm had promised—should have called to pick her up. "Tell him I won't be long."

She had half expected Johnny to call for her himself, and knew a moment's uneasiness because he had not. But, she thought, perhaps it was as well that their reunion should take place in public. There could be no recriminations then, and if Johnny acknowledged her as his fiancée in front of his cousins, the next step would be the official announcement of their engagement in the *Telegraph*. She had deliberately refused Lady Fiona's invitation to accompany her to the station this morning, when she met Johnny's train, in order that he might hear of her decision to marry him from his cousin, rather than from herself. In a way her decision had been an impulsive one: she had never intended to claim Johnny as more than a very good friend, but Lady Fiona had sounded so brusque and off-hand, when Elizabeth had first telephoned her to ask when Johnny was expected that, in sheer self-defence and a certain pique, she had said: "After all, I *am* going to marry him, you know," and that had been that. She had known she couldn't retreat and hadn't wanted to, when—as the result of her impulsive words—Lady Fiona's attitude had undergone a subtle change. Instead of offhanded evasions, she had received an invitation to lunch, and Lady Fiona, Elizabeth felt sure, would have mentioned the presence of his fiancée at the Logan Arms to Johnny as soon as he arrived.

Or, if not then, at least reasonably soon after it. She would have to, if Elizabeth was coming to lunch . . .

Picking up her bag and gloves, Elizabeth permitted herself one more critical glance into the mirror and made her way downstairs.

A broad-shouldered, stockily built man in a raincoat was standing warming his hands in front of the fire in the lounge. He turned at the sound of Elizabeth's approach, and she saw that he was about thirty-two or three, with a cheerful, friendly smile and dark hair which was greying prematurely at the temples. There was something about his air of quiet, unassuming competence that suggested the physician, and Elizabeth went over to him unhesitatingly.

"Dr. Cameron?"

"Yes, indeed, Miss Anson. How do you do?" They shook hands solemnly but there was a twinkle in the doctor's dark eyes as he added: "I understand that you are also bidden to the Castle in order to welcome the new Earl? Fiona asked me if I'd pick you up—I hope you don't mind a rather mud-spattered car, but, contrary to the usual practice on a Sunday morning, a great many of my patients have required my services today and in this weather the roads are in a pretty bad state. So"—he spread his big, blunt-fingered hands ruefully—"I'm a trifle late, I'm afraid, and the car isn't fit to be seen." He led the way out to where an old, pre-war, Lancia sports saloon was parked close to the kerb and courteously handed her into it.

Getting in beside her, he pressed the starter and the engine sprang noisily to life. He said, as they roared down the village street: "Have you seen the Castle before?"

"No," said Elizabeth shortly, piqued by his casualness. *Bidden to welcome the new Earl* indeed—didn't this uncouth young doctor realize that she was engaged to Johnny and the Castle's future mistress? Apparently he didn't, for he went on talking about it as if she were a tourist and he a local resident, condescending to a mere Sassenach.

But she was forced to concede, when a bend in the drive gave her her first glimpse of Logan Castle, that it was an impressive and even a breathtaking sight. The newspaper photographs hadn't given her any conception of its size or of its grim, majestic dignity. And . . . it was Johnny's. She wondered, her lips curving into a delighted smile, what Johnny thought of it. He would be overwhelmed, of course, and, she imagined, rather lost: she knew, from servants' gossip at the hotel, that the place was kept up as few stately homes were kept up nowadays—the Chisholms were wealthy and maintained a large staff. Johnny couldn't possibly live in a place this size on his own and he would not have the first idea of how to run it. Obviously, when his cousins went—as, of course, they would have to—Johnny would turn to her, would suggest that they should marry at once. There was no reason on earth why they should delay, Elizabeth told herself. They would have to be married in London. That went without saying: she was the bride and she lived there. The wedding would be at St. Margaret's or, perhaps, in view of Johnny's Scottish ancestry, at St. Columba's, Pont Street. Not that it would really matter which, because their wedding would, in any case, stand a very good chance of being the wedding of the year, and she could trust her mother, she knew, to play her part in seeing that it was.

She wondered, as Dr. Cameron made a racing gear-change with considerable skill, whether Lady Logan would attend the wedding. Its interest would be greatly enhanced if she did, and if Fiona Chisholm could be persuaded to act as bridesmaid, with Jennifer Edwardes, Lallie Hilton and, perhaps, Rosemary Lucien-ffrench, that would undoubtedly set the seal on its success.

Although, of course, Fiona and her mother were in mourning: she had forgotten that, and it might, after all, be necessary to postpone the wedding until spring. Elizabeth stifled a sigh. She didn't want to postpone her marriage to Johnny, but it was important, for his sake even more than hers, that his cousins should come to his wedding. It was vitally important, since both his parents were dead.

She stole a glance at the doctor's profile. Rumour had it among the hotel staff that Lady Logan was very ill—prostrate from grief and shock, poor lady, the chambermaid had said—but rumours were so often exaggerated. Dr. Cameron appeared to be the local GP and, if not actually treating Lady Logan, he probably knew who was and would be aware of what was wrong with her. She wondered if she dared ask him and decided that a tactfully phrased inquiry could not possibly do any harm.

She made it, in a lowered, solicitous voice, but, owing to the noise his car made, was forced to repeat it in a louder tone.

Dr. Cameron shrugged. "If," he told

her noncommittally, "you're wondering whether you'll meet her at lunch, then I can tell you that you won't. She's keeping to her own rooms, on my advice. It would be too much of a strain on her to be asked to meet strangers just now."

"But surely Johnny—Lord Logan—will see her?" Elizabeth insisted. "I mean to say . . ." She left the sentence unfinished.

Again he shrugged. "Oh, yes, I expect she'll want to see him. But I shan't force it on her and I shouldn't think he will, if he's the chap I think he is."

"What sort of *chap*"—her faint emphasis on the word was deliberate—"do you think he is? Have you met him?"

"No." He answered her last question first. "I saw—and heard—him on TV last night. He struck me as a rather decent lad, considering."

"Considering what?" demanded Elizabeth, nettled by this guarded praise.

Dr. Cameron laughed. "Considering he's not a Scot," he returned with irritating smugness. "Well,"—he swung the car in a tight circle, drew up with an unnecessary flourish a few yards from the front door and turned in his seat to look down at her—"here we are. I hope it hasn't been too uncomfortable for you, Miss Anson. This isn't what I should term a lady's car, but it's an old friend of mine and I've become rather attached to it." He got out and came round to help her to alight. "Come on in," he invited carelessly and, to Elizabeth's shocked astonishment, opened the front door and led the way into the hall.

"Do you always walk in here unannounced?" she asked, intending her surprise as a mild reproof. "Surely Lady Logan—"

He interrupted her, with a hint of impatience. "Good lord, my dear girl— I'm a doctor and a busy one. If I waited to ring bells, I'd never get any work done. Lady Logan doesn't mind and neither does Fiona. Jamieson, the butler, is the only person who does, but that's because he regards it as a reflection on his efficiency —he usually hears me coming and—ah, he has. Here he is. 'Morning, Jamieson. I beat you to it, didn't I? We'll be supplying you with that hearing aid yet, you know. Er—" he gestured vaguely in Elizabeth's direction—"this is Miss Anson. Perhaps

111

you'd look after her. I'll just run up and have a word with her ladyship before she has her lunch."

He left her, to Elizabeth's relief, and she turned to the butler and said, with icy dignity: "Will you tell his lordship that" —it would be as well, she decided, to make her status clear at the outset—"that his fiancée is here? I understand that he is expecting me."

"Certainly, madam. I believe his lordship is changing, but if you will come this way, I will inform him of your arrival. Lady Fiona will also be down in a moment."

He showed her into a huge, gloomy drawing-room, furnished in heavy Victorian style, its walls hung with what were obviously family portraits, and left her.

Elizabeth looked about her disapprovingly. The Castle might be enormous and impressive from the outside, but inside, she thought, it was quite hideous. Well, she would change all that. When she married Johnny, she would refurnish this room, anyway. It was simply ghastly and . . .

The door opened and Johnny came in.

They stared at each other for a long moment in silence and then Johnny said:

"Oh, Elizabeth, it's good to see you! I can't begin to tell you how good it is because I—because I never thought I should see you again, you know."

"Didn't you?" answered Elizabeth softly. "Surely you knew that I was in love with you, Johnny?" She went into his arms and Johnny held her close.

As he kissed her, she knew suddenly that he had changed . . .

6

FOR Johnny, holding Elizabeth in his arms, many things had changed and he was becoming aware, gradually, of a change in himself. But it had been a subtle change, as yet too nebulous to find open expression in his actions. He had always worshipped Elizabeth and, as he sought for her lips with his own, he felt as if, by some miracle, the clock had been put back and they were still in Queensland, returned once more to the point from which they had started.

He strained her to him hungrily, living again those precious, never-to-be-forgotten days when he had first known the ecstasy of being in love with her and had seen, in her fresh English beauty, the fulfilment of all his dreams.

Elizabeth had been gentle and gracious to him at first. She had sought his company so consistently that he had believed her to be as much in love as he was himself, and had begun to dream of the future they would have together when, at last, he summoned the courage to ask her to be his wife. His happiness in those first days had been a lovely, fragile, secret thing, built from his dreams, and, because he was a solitary man, unused to the company of girls of his own age, he had shrunk from putting it into words, even to her.

He had imagined that she knew and understood without the need for words, which, from him, must inevitably be clumsy. So he had waited, living in his fool's paradise, biding his time until the opportunity to tell her that he loved and wanted to marry her should present itself. He hadn't imagined that she would refuse him, because she had welcomed his courtship and permitted his lovemaking, diffident and untutored though it was.

Love, he had always believed, brooked no refusal and took scant heed of differences in rank and race and outlook, sweeping them aside as if they didn't matter. To find that such differences did matter to Elizabeth had been a bitter blow, both to his pride and his illusions, a blow from which, even now, he hadn't fully recovered.

And yet . . . she had come back to him. A moment ago she had told him that she loved him. He had seen in her eyes that she spoke the truth and, if he still doubted, there were her eager lips under his to give his fears the lie. She belonged to him, he could feel it in the trembling of the soft, pliant body he held so close against him and in the strong, swift beat of her heart under his hand. She was his girl, the girl he was going to marry, sweet and familiar, unbearably dear, and he wanted to believe her, wanted with all his heart to believe in their love.

He had told his cousin Catherine that he was still in love with Elizabeth—not an hour ago—and had been conscious, as he said it, that he wasn't sure, that he was afraid to say too much because once she had hurt and scorned him. He had experienced a similar uncertainty this morning, when Fiona had said that Elizabeth had come to Logan. But uncertainty was ended now—she had come back and everything was as it had been between them at the beginning. She would—she *must* have some explanation of what had happened and why she had gone away.

Johnny sighed, held her at arm's length and stood looking down at her. "Oh, Elizabeth!" His voice shook. "I don't know what to say. I don't know how to start."

"Couldn't you just say that you love me?" Elizabeth pleaded.

"But you know that. You've always known how I felt about you."

"Oh, darling, yes, I suppose I do. But I couldn't be sure that you'd forgive me for my—my stupidity in trying to pretend that I could do without you."

He stared at her. "*Can't* you do without me?"

She shook her head, in the absurd, charming little white hat she wore, and Johnny caught the glint of tears in her eyes. "No. I tried—heaven forgive me, I tried. But I couldn't. I missed you so terribly, Johnny. I must have been mad to imagine that I could ever do without you —or that our marriage wouldn't work because we were so different. I'd have gone back, you know, to Queensland, if you hadn't come here. Oh, Johnny, you do forgive me, don't you? You do understand?"

Gently, he took off the absurd little hat whose trimming matched her eyes, touching her hair with reverent fingers. He had always loved to touch Elizabeth's hair. It was so soft, so incredibly fair, like ripe corn in the sun.

"Of course I forgive you," he said, "but"—his brows came together—"I can't pretend that I understand. If you loved me, why did you go away?"

"Because I was a fool. I thought I could stay away. I was wrong, Johnny, so dreadfully, crazily wrong. I had to come back."

"You told Fiona that we—that we were engaged—"

She hung her shining head, laid it for a moment against his chest and drew a little sobbing breath. "I know. I was impatient, I wanted to see you—to explain, to put things right, to *prove* that I still loved you. It was the only way I could think of to —to make you understand. Johnny"—her head came up and she faced him, lips parted and sudden fear in her eyes— "Johnny, you do still want to marry me, don't you?"

"If it's what *you* want, Elizabeth. If you think I'm good enough for you. I'm just the same, you know. They can call me Lord Logan, but I still haven't any manners or any big ambitions. And I still can't smoke tailormade cigarettes!"

He had thought to make her smile, but she regarded him gravely. "Oh, darling, as if that mattered! You'll learn, and"—her tone was earnest, persuasive—"I'll help you. You won't have to worry about anything like that, truly you won't. Because you're the Earl of Logan, people will accept you. And already you've realized the sort of clothes you ought to wear up here. That suit is absolutely right."

Johnny stiffened. "It belonged to my cousin Alastair. I was lent it because my own got wet. *I* didn't choose it."

Elizabeth's brows rose. "You were *lent* it?"

"Yes. By Cousin Catherine."

"Well, you look marvellous in it, anyway. And you can buy plenty of your own. I'll help you to choose them, take you to a good tailor in London who will be able to advise you."

"But I don't need a lot of clothes," Johnny objected. "I shouldn't know what to do with them, Elizabeth. And—"

"Don't be silly, darling," Elizabeth chided firmly. "Of course you do." She drew away from his embrace, crossed to a tall, Victorian mirror framed in gilt which hung above the fireplace and began to set her hair to rights. "Goodness, you have made me look a mess! Have you got my hat, because I ought to put it on for lunch —oh, thank you, darling. Talking of lunch"—she turned to face him—"when do you suppose we are going to have it? Isn't your cousin Fiona having it with us?"

Johnny reddened. "She said she was. And there's a doctor coming too, I believe —the one who's looking after Cousin Catherine."

"Yes," agreed Elizabeth. "Dr. Cameron." Her mouth tightened. "He drove me up here and then disappeared. He said he wanted to see Lady Logan before lunch. I imagine that *he's* holding us up. But"—she glanced round the room—"at least they ought to have put out some sherry for us, if we're to be kept waiting like this."

"Ought they?" Johnny followed the direction of her glance. "Why? Do you drink sherry?"

"Yes. It's the correct thing to drink before a meal. Ring for some, Johnny."

"*Ring?* But—"

"Darling, of course. There's the bell over there. Ring it. And when your butler comes, tell him to bring us some sherry. He ought to have seen to it without being asked."

Obediently, Johnny rang the bell. He supposed that Elizabeth knew what she was talking about, but he didn't much relish giving orders in this house to a butler whom, by no stretch of the imagination, could he seriously consider "his". But at that moment, to his heartfelt relief, the door opened and Fiona came in. She had a young man in a shabby dark suit with her and, when she had introduced him as Dr. Cameron, she crossed over to Elizabeth's side and said apologetically:

"Miss Anson, I'm Fiona Chisholm. I do apologize for not having been here to greet you when you arrived, but one of the maids scalded herself—really quite badly, poor girl—and I've been helping Dr. Cameron to administer first aid." She smiled. "But you haven't helped yourself to sherry—do let me get you some. Lunch

121

won't be long, but we've just time for a drink before we go in." She lifted the lid of a walnut cabinet set against the wall to the left of the fireplace, revealing a display of decanters and glasses that took Johnny's breath away. "There's Tio Pepe and Manzanilla or a brown Jerez. Which would you prefer?"

"Tio Pepe," answered Elizabeth. She coloured faintly but her tone was assured. "John?" questioned Fiona.

Johnny hesitated. He said, avoiding Elizabeth's gaze: "I'm afraid I only drink beer. But if that's not in order, it doesn't matter."

Dr. Cameron grinned at him. "You're a man after my own heart, Lord Logan— beer's my tipple too. And here's Jamieson, who has evidently read our thoughts. His lordship, Jamieson, is another Philistine. He, too, will drink beer. Thank you."

"Thank you, sir—my lord." Jamieson poured beer into the silver tankards he carried, offered them on a salver, his face expressionless. When he had gone, Johnny joined the young doctor in his corner, leaving Fiona and Elizabeth together. The doctor eyed him appraisingly for a moment

122

and then raised his tankard in friendly salute.

"Your health, Lord Logan. And welcome!"

"Thanks." They talked together, lightly and inconsequentially but with ready ease. Johnny found himself liking Dr. Cameron and sensed, from his smile, that his liking was returned. This, he thought, was a man he could understand, down to earth and without pretensions, good at his job, probably, and completely honest. The sort of doctor *he* would want, if he were ever ill.

When Jamieson announced lunch, Fiona led the way with Elizabeth, the two young men bringing up the rear. Fiona and Elizabeth were talking to each other with every appearance of enjoyment, Johnny noticed, and was again conscious of relief. For some reason he didn't then attempt to analyse, he had wondered if they would get on, had even feared that they might not. But perhaps, he thought, his own reception from Fiona had led him to imagine her unfriendly to everyone, which —judging from the way in which she was now behaving to Elizabeth—was not the case. And it was possible that he had imagined her hostility towards himself or, at any rate, exaggerated it.

Certainly his Cousin Catherine's welcome had more than made up for Fiona's lack of warmth. Cousin Catherine had been kindness itself to him, and this, strangely, had had the effect of making him feel more tolerant of Fiona. The position wasn't an easy one for her, heaven knew: it wasn't easy for any of them, but Cousin Catherine's gentle, dignified acceptance of it had done much to dispel his own feeling of strain. He felt confident that, when the time came, he would be able to persuade Cousin Catherine not to leave Logan, using as a lever his need of her, which was very real and of which, he thought, she was already aware. Had he not given her ample proof of it this morning? Cousin Catherine was another person he understood. Their talk this morning, when they had drunk tea together in the room that had once been Alastair's and was now his, had, Johnny felt, forged a strong bond of sympathy between them.

And now he had Elizabeth to help him, to stand at his side and guide him through the bewildering complexities of his new role. He glanced at her proudly, thinking how beautiful she was and how effortlessly assured she looked as she took her place in the chair Jamieson drew out for her, half-way down the long table. The dining-room was immense, like all the rooms in this great house: the table, set with silver and cut glass, could have seated twenty guests, instead of the four who were now preparing to lunch at it. He looked about him with a hint of panic for his own place and Elizabeth said smoothly:

"You're at the head of the table, darling. I'm on your right. Isn't that so, Lady Fiona?"

Fiona agreed, briefly, that it was, and Johnny sat down. Dr. Cameron, taking the chair at his left, remarked pleasantly that he had always been interested in sheep farming in Australia and had been looking forward to hearing about it at first hand from someone who had actually worked on a station property. This topic—intro-duced, Johnny suspected, in order to put him at his ease—absorbed them for the first few awkward minutes whilst they were settling down. Jamieson and a black-frocked maid in impeccably starched cap and apron served their first course with silent deftness, and, from her place opposite the doctor, Elizabeth smilingly enlarged on his halting description of the Gilliats' farm.

It surprised Johnny a little that she could talk so fluently and knowledgeably on the strength of her few weeks' experience, but he was well content to relinquish control of the conversation to her, himself relapsing into silence. Both Fiona and Dr. Cameron listened politely, Fiona interposing an occasional question, and the meal progressed in an atmosphere of apparently unforced geniality.

Over coffee, which they took together in the drawing-room, Elizabeth started to ask about the Castle. When Dr. Cameron, looking at his watch, reluctantly announced that it was time he returned to his sick-visiting, Fiona said, her tone suddenly formal again: "Perhaps you and John would like me to show you round, Miss Anson? It's too wet to do much out of doors, and in any case, it would be better if the Factor took you round the farms and the estate. But I could show you the Castle, if you would care for me to do so."

"I should like that," Elizabeth assented, with restrained eagerness. She went to Johnny, linking her arm in his. "And you would, too, wouldn't you, John darling? And then we can start to plan. So many of the rooms seem to me to be asking for modernization. It will be such fun doing them, and I know just the man to advise us on it—he's an Italian interior decorator called Guido Vincente. My mother discovered him and she's recommended him to dozens of our friends, who have been delighted with his work. He has wonderful taste and a flair for colour. I'm sure if we got him up here, he would know just what was required. Not," she added hastily, when Johnny was silent, "that I mean I want to furnish this house in contemporary style or anything startling like that. But I do so *hate* Victorian plush and mahogany, don't you?"

"I don't know," Johnny returned helplessly, aware that Fiona had stiffened. "I thought the furniture was very good. It looks good to me, anyway. Sort of right and in keeping with the size of the rooms.

I wouldn't want to alter anything, Elizabeth."

He looked about him, honestly puzzled. The big, brocade-covered sofa and the wing chairs on either side of the fireplace seemed to him appropriate to this setting: he liked the rugs on the floor, with their mellowed reds and blues, and the heavy dark blue velvet curtains, drawn back from the wide windows. It was a solid, comfortable room, a room one could live in. He liked the warmth and luxury of the huge log fire, the gleaming expanse of parquet by the door, the bookcases with their leather-bound, gold-tooled, matching volumes and the great chandeliers which hung from the ceiling. Most of all he liked the portraits of his ancestors, looking down at him from their gilt frames. But, when he had first entered it, he had found the house a trifle awe-inspiring, and perhaps, he thought, it was still having this effect on Elizabeth. She would like it, as he did, when she became accustomed to it . . .

He heard Fiona say something about Chippendale in an icy voice and then she was leading them out into the hall. Elizabeth continued to walk at his side, her fingers resting lightly on his arm, but he sensed that he had displeased her, and knew, without either Fiona or Elizabeth having spoken another word, that each resented the other's presence now. And he had imagined that they liked each other and had made friends! He found himself wishing that Dr. Cameron had stayed, to ease the tension with his brisk, dry humour and hearty uninhibited laughter. But his cousin Fiona led them on, coldly impersonal as a professional guide conducting a party of tourists.

"This is the billiard-room . . . the gun-room . . . the cellars are down those steps, the kitchen and larders at the end of that passage . . . the servants' hall is at this end and the butler's pantry is beyond it. If you'll come up by the back staircase, it will save time. This is the Long Gallery, it was used as a ballroom when my father was alive . . . the library opens off it . . ."

When at last their tour came to an end, Fiona politely excused herself, with the plea that her mother would be alone. "I'll read to her for a little," she said. "She likes being read to and finds the day very long, so I'll have my tea with her, if you'll forgive me. Perhaps you'd ring for yours when you're ready, John." She left them at the door of the drawing-room.

Jamieson, in response to Elizabeth's ring, brought in tea, setting it on a table which he drew up to the fire. Elizabeth, seating herself in front of the crested silver tea-pot, smiled across at Johnny, patting the chair beside her.

"Well, darling," she invited, "aren't you going to sit down?"

He sat down, inexplicably restless and ill at ease. The size and magnificence of the Castle had come as a revelation to him: it was a small world of its own and he felt weighted down, crushed by the burden of responsibility that was his. But Elizabeth seemed to have no qualms: she chatted gaily and excitedly about her plans for its redecoration and, apparently unaware of his brooding disquiet, went on to talk of the entertaining they would do, the dinner parties and the balls they would give, the people they would invite to visit them. Johnny didn't attempt to interrupt her— these, he thought, were *her* dreams and he would have, somehow, to share them.

Obviously they would have to live here for a time: it would be expected of him, Elizabeth would expect it, it was his duty. But he knew, as he sat there listening to her, an almost unbearable longing to return to Queensland, to the places and the people and the sights that were home to him, to the work he loved and could do with his hands, as a skilled craftsman, to the land where he had his roots.

He wanted to tell her so, but, looking into her eager, shining eyes, hearing the glad note in her voice, had not the heart. Instead, rising to his feet, he suggested:

"Look, Elizabeth, let's dine out somewhere, shall we?"

"Dine *out?* But, Johnny, why, for goodness' sake?"

"I'd like to get away from here for a bit. It's—well, it's a bit overpowering, for a start. I'm not used to it." He reached for her hand. "Come on, what do you say?"

Elizabeth got up reluctantly. "Where can we go? You surely don't want to have dinner at the Logan Arms, do you? It's excruciatingly dull and the food isn't up to much. Quite apart from that the service is appalling."

"Well . . ." He did not mind where they went, so long as he could escape from the Castle. "We could go to Ardloch. It's quite a big place, there ought to be somewhere where we could get a meal. Come on, we'll find somewhere."

"All right, darling. But you'll have to order a car, won't you? We can't walk to Ardloch."

A car, Johnny thought—the Rolls, with the supercilious Mackay to drive them? His jaw set obstinately. It wasn't his car, yet: it belonged to his cousin Catherine and he couldn't take it. What was more, he wasn't going to. He glanced out of the window and saw, with relief, that it had stopped raining. He helped Elizabeth into her coat and led her into the hall. "We'll walk up to the Logan Arms," he said firmly. "It'll be nice to get some fresh air, after being cooped up indoors all day. I can't take being a hot-house flower, Elizabeth. I'm sorry."

She opened her mouth to argue but closed it again, warned by his expression that this was an occasion when she would be wiser to let him have his way. They walked together down the long, curving drive, the twilight closing about them. Johnny's spirits rose. It was a clear night, a trifle damp still but fresh after the rain, and, as a bend in the drive hid Logan Castle from his sight, he saw the first star come out and quickened his pace as if, by the mere act of hurrying, he could reach up and touch it. He smiled down at Elizabeth.

"This is better, isn't it?"

"It would be if you'd walk a bit slower," Elizabeth answered crossly. "It's dark and cold and beastly and I can't keep up with you. Why you couldn't have ordered a car, I don't begin to understand. Honestly, Johnny, this is a bit much, you know. I'm not dressed for cross-country rambles."

Johnny slackened his pace and tried to explain.

"You see, it's Cousin Catherine's car. I can't just demand it—not until things are settled with the solicitors tomorrow. But don't worry, we'll get a taxi from the village and go to Ardloch."

"A taxi?" Elizabeth wailed. "When you've got a garage full of cars and at least two chauffeurs? Really, Johnny, I think you must have taken leave of your senses!"

"I haven't, Elizabeth. It's just that—"

"It's just that you let that high-handed cousin Fiona of yours twist you round her little finger," Elizabeth retorted bitterly. "Why, you even stood up for her against me. Saying you liked that hideous furniture! How could you like it—it's simply ghastly. *And* unfashionable. And in bad taste . . ."

She lectured him severely all the way to the Logan Arms, which they reached, damp and chilled, half an hour later. Johnny had no reply to her arguments. He supposed them justified and the knowledge added to his depression. But he continued obstinately with his plans for the evening. A taxi was ordered, whilst Elizabeth had a drink in the lounge: after it, she retired indignantly to her room to change whilst the taxi, with its meter ticking, waited outside in the yard.

Half-way to Ardloch, the rain started again and was falling in a steady stream by the time they pulled up outside the Station Hotel. But inside it was warm and cheerful, with a blazing fire in the lounge and another, even larger one in the dining-room and, to his relief, Johnny saw Elizabeth smiling at him again.

They enjoyed their meal, Elizabeth delighted by the reception the hotel staff accorded Johnny as soon as they realized who he was. She was tender and charming to him throughout the rest of the evening, and, driving back at last, over the hills, she laid her head companionably on his shoulder and let him kiss her gently into drowsiness, held close in his arms.

They bade each other goodnight at the door of Elizabeth's hotel. She said, lifting her face to his:

"It will be all right, Johnny darling—everything will be all right, you'll see. Once we're married—and when your cousins go. The sooner they leave, the better. You haven't a chance while they're still living in the Castle, undermining your authority and putting the servants against you. Believe me, I know what I'm talking about."

"But"—Johnny stared at her incredulously—"I can't turn them out of their home, Elizabeth. I want them to stay, both of them, for as long as they want to—

Cousin Catherine especially. Don't you see—"

"No," said Elizabeth, "I don't see. But *you* will, in time. I'm too tired to argue about it now, I'm exhausted. So I'll say goodnight and we'll have a long talk about it tomorrow."

She kissed him lightly on the cheek, smiled at him briefly and vanished into the darkened hotel, leaving him staring after her, shocked and appalled.

The taxi drove him back to the Castle and he sat in it miserably, the bright magic of the evening shattered by Elizabeth's parting words, his thoughts chaotic. The great front door was unlocked and he let himself in, careful to make no sound that might bring Jamieson hurrying to meet him. All the lights were on, the fire still burning in the hall. He found his way to the drawing-room, which was in darkness, save for a faint glow from the fire, and he had crossed to it and was already holding out his hands to the glowing embers when the sound of a swiftly stifled sob, coming from behind, warned him that he was not alone.

He spun round, startled, and saw that

his cousin Fiona was sitting hunched up in one corner of the vast sofa, watching him in wide-eyed alarm. In the dimness of the firelight, he could see only that her face was pale and shadowed, but he knew, as soon as she spoke his name in a small, choked voice, that she had been weeping and, remembering Elizabeth's words, his heart went out to her in pity. He hurried to her, dropping on his knees beside her and taking her two small, ice-cold hands in his own.

"Fiona, please, Fiona, you mustn't cry, you mustn't worry. I haven't come here to drive you away . . . you or your mother, I give you my word, I swear it! I want you both to stay here, this is your home, it belongs to you, not to me. I'm going to arrange it tomorrow when your solicitor comes. It's the first thing I'm going to do, the one thing I *want* to do—don't you understand?"

Fiona freed her hands and got to her feet. She stood looking down at him, not saying a word. Johnny rose awkwardly, puzzled by her silence. He faced her. "Fiona, I—"

"You don't understand, do you?" The

interruption was swift, her tone bitter. "You and that girl. You'll never understand, either of you. But I'll make it plain, shall I? You seem to have won round my mother—my poor mother, who thinks that because you look like Alastair she should love you, that it's her duty to accept you. *I* won't accept you and I won't stay with you—I'd rather never see this place again than stay here with you and Elizabeth Anson."

"But, Fiona"—in his anxiety and his eagerness to make her understand how he felt, Johnny sought to recapture her hands —"we . . . *I* want you to stay. Whatever Eliz—whatever anyone says. Won't you believe me? I mean it with all my heart, I never meant anything more sincerely in my life. Your mother—"

"You have put my mother against me," Fiona accused. A sob tore at her, binding her throat.

Johnny drew her towards him, holding her gently by the shoulders, forcing her to look at him. "I haven't. Please, Fiona, at least listen to me. Give me a chance to explain."

She shook her head. "There is no explanation. Let me go. I want nothing from you, neither your pity nor your charity—nothing you can give me. If my mother wishes to stay, that is her affair, but I do not think, when she realizes what it is going to be like here when you marry Miss Anson, that she will stay for long." She looked down at his hands, where they rested on her shoulders. "I would rather you didn't touch me. Please let me go."

"No." He held her tightly now, his heart pounding, caught up in some strong, surging emotion he was powerless to resist, drawn to her in spite of himself, aware that it was madness and that he was behaving like the boor she thought him. "Not until you promise to stay at least long enough to give me a chance. You haven't given me a chance yet, not the ghost of one. You judged me long before I ever got here, didn't you?"

"And if I did?" Her eyes were scornful. "You've done nothing so far to cause me to revise my judgment of you, John. And keeping me here against my will isn't likely to make things any better."

"All the same, I'm going to keep you here," Johnny said obstinately.

"You're not, you have no right to, why—" Fiercely she struggled free of him. Her eyes were blazing in her white face and she was breathing hard. "Perhaps," she told him bitingly, "Elizabeth Anson enjoys this sort of thing from you—I don't. You are engaged to her, you are going to marry her. But try to get it into your head that I hate you, not only for what you've done since you came here but also for what you are. You can't deceive me as you've deceived my mother. I shall not remain here for one day longer than I have to—and I mean *that* sincerely and with all my heart. Goodnight."

"Wait," Johnny pleaded, "wait, Fiona! You haven't heard what I intend to do."

"It's of no interest to me," Fiona said coldly, from the door. "I hope I shan't be here to see it."

Johnny's arms fell to his sides as the door closed behind her. Why, he wondered helplessly, did she dislike him so? What had he done? He had tried, tried as hard as he knew how, to be fair to her, and to make it clear that he wanted to give her back all that had been hers. But she wouldn't listen. She hated him, hated and despised Elizabeth, who, as she had just reminded him, was the girl he was going to marry. His lips compressed. Very slowly, he moved after her to the door, mounted the stairs to his own room. But, when he had undressed and got into bed, sleep eluded him. After half an hour, he got out of bed and seated himself at the table. He would write to Pip, he decided: he owed her a letter and perhaps, if he wrote down all that had happened to him since his arrival, it might become a little clearer to him.

He picked up his fountain-pen and began to write . . .

7

PIP GILLIAT had just finished breakfast when the mail arrived, fetched in a sack by one of the aboriginal truck drivers who had been to the railhead.

Johnny's letter was on the top of a little pile addressed to her father, and she seized it, thrust it into the pocket of her jeans and, thankful that she had escaped observation, went out, whistling with assumed nonchalance, to get her horse.

She rode out for some distance from the station buildings and then, dismounting, tethered the horse and settled down in the dubious shade offered by a thin clump of eucalyptus saplings in order to examine her prize. It was a long letter, consisting of eight pages in Johnny's neat, boyish script, and Pip read it through three times with great concentration before she was able fully to take it in. Then, her brow anxiously furrowed, she replaced it in its envelope and sat back on her heels to consider what Johnny had said.

Beside her, her horse Barney—the bay which had once been Johnny's—whinnied softly, impatient to be on. He was a boundary rider's horse and the mild exercise Pip gave him wasn't enough for him. Normally, Pip would have talked to him, for she was fond of all animals and horses were her life, but this morning she ignored Barney's plaintive whinnies and, in fact, scarcely heard them.

Johnny, she sensed, reading between the lines of his letter, wasn't happy. He hadn't said so in so many words, but she knew, could almost feel his bewilderment as she recalled the incidents in his new life which he had described to her.

He was engaged to Elizabeth. That was, perhaps, the worst news of all, Pip thought glumly, although she had more than half expected it. Elizabeth would want him now, though she hadn't wanted him before, and she hadn't wasted any time in getting him back. She had been waiting at Logan when he arrived, so that Johnny, who was absurdly chivalrous, had had little chance of escaping from her. Even if

—Pip sighed—even if he had wanted to escape . . . but—what else had he told her?

He had appeared on television. He had met a Scottish soldier called Jock MacPhail who had served with him in Korea and Jock had been delighted to see him. He had done a coach tour of London but it had been raining, so that he hadn't been able to see as much of it as he had wanted to. He liked London and he thought Logan and what he had seen of the surrounding countryside very beautiful, in spite of almost continuous rain. He had described the Castle so vividly that, sitting there, the letter in her hand, Pip could imagine she had actually seen it herself. It sounded very big and grand and a little frightening. And so—although Johnny hadn't said a great deal about her—did his cousin Fiona. Well, she wasn't big, of course, but grand and a little frightening, anyway. Johnny's description of his cousin Fiona puzzled Pip rather. It was oddly contradictory. At one moment he seemed to admire her, the next he wrote of her as if she had hurt him.

But of Lady Logan—to whom he

144

referred as "Cousin Catherine", with a capital letter—he wrote with warm affection and approval. She had evidently received him kindly, made him feel welcome and wanted and at home.

Pip took out the letter again, re-read the bits about Cousin Catherine and then, frowning more deeply than ever, she re-read all he had told her about Lady Fiona, still at a loss to understand what Johnny really thought of her.

I'm going to make over the Castle, if I can [he wrote], to Fiona and her mother. It's large enough to house us all and an army besides, so that even when Elizabeth and I are married, we can each have our own separate establishments.

In any case, I shall make over a portion of the income from the estate to Cousin Catherine and Fiona, whatever either of them says. They have more right to it, heaven knows, than I have and more need of it, too. It's perhaps a bit soon to decide these things but, honestly, Pip, I wish I were back home on the station, doing the job I know how to do. I'm no use here, always doing and saying the wrong thing and managing to offend someone without meaning to at all. The long and short of it is that I'm simply not cut out to be an earl . . .

"Poor Johnny!" Pip said aloud. "Oh, *poor* Johnny!"

Her hands clenched fiercely and she felt tears sting her eyes. She wished she could go to the Old Country, to be with Johnny and help him. He was such a dear but too good-hearted, too chivalrous and kind. He let people take advantage of him. Like many physically strong men, he was gentle and easy-going by nature, reluctant to use his strength in order to triumph over his weaker opponents, with the result, of course, that in the end they triumphed over him. As Elizabeth had triumphed . . .

Pip sat up. Elizabeth Anson didn't *deserve* Johnny. She was mean and small-minded and selfish, a gold-digger, out for all that she could get. She hadn't wanted Johnny when she was here, except as a temporary escort, someone to amuse and flatter her—why, she'd scarcely noticed him until the day of the Wahrangi Picnic Races, when he had won the Barber Cup and carried off all the prizes in the rodeo which had followed the meeting. She had wanted him *then* all right, when his rivals had carried him shoulder-high round the arena and he had been everybody's hero: she had set her cap at him quite shamelessly from that moment on, Pip recalled indignantly, but—Johnny being Johnny—he hadn't seen through her, hadn't suspected.

Someone ought to tell him the truth about Elizabeth—now, before it was too late. But how to tell him? It was no use writing it in a letter, he simply wouldn't believe it. Whoever told him would have to go to England, would have to *prove* to him that Elizabeth was what she was and . . .

Pip got to her feet, reaching for her horse's rein, jerking it free. "Come on, Barney," she urged, slipping on to his back. The bay needed no second bidding. At the touch of her heels, he was off at breakneck speed in the direction of the distant station buildings. Pip considered ways and means as she rode. She would have to show her father Johnny's letter: that would be the first step. And then if she could persuade her mother to phone the Awkwrights, to persuade them to let her travel with them to London . . . or, better still, suppose she were to ring Betty Awkwright first and ask her to get her mother to approach Pip's mother, as if the idea had originated from them and not from herself?

Pulling up by the first of the paddock gates, Pip smiled to herself. It would be best to get the Awkwrights on her side first, and she didn't think it would be too difficult, she and Betty had always been good friends and they'd been at school together. Anyway, it would have to be done: the Awkwrights were the only people Pip knew who were going to England. The fact that they were leaving the week after next did not unduly perturb her: she had the best part of a fortnight in which to make her arrangements, she told herself comfortably—you could do a lot in twelve days, if you set your mind to it. Admittedly it would mean putting up with Bob Awkwright, who had recently conceived a youthful passion for her, but she could handle Bob, with the help of Betty, who was his twin . . .

She swung open the paddock gate, thrust Barney through it and let it click shut behind her, pleased with her spur of the moment plan. It wasn't ideal: her mother would oppose it, but she thought she might find an ally in her father. And Johnny *had* invited her to visit him at Logan, her father *had* promised—albeit vaguely—that she could go.

Pip dug her small heels into Barney's flanks again and began to rehearse what she would say to her father.

"After all, Dad, I'm eighteen next month, you know. And you promised I could go to England, honestly you did. I'd be perfectly all right with the Awkwrights and they want me to go with them. They'll be there for three months and I could come back with them too . . ." She was taking the Awkwrights' co-operation a bit for granted, of course, but if she explained to Betty . . . Betty had a soft spot for Johnny and she hadn't liked Elizabeth Anson any more than Pip had, so that she knew she could count on Betty at any rate. And, probably, on Bob.

Pip made a face at the thought of young

Bob Awkwright but resolutely continued with her rehearsal.

"And you see, Dad, there's Johnny, isn't there? Johnny needs one of us to keep him out of trouble or he'll be in it, up to his neck. I shouldn't be surprised if he's already in it, getting himself engaged to that Elizabeth Anson . . ." But—no, it would be wiser not to mention Johnny's engagement as one of the reasons why she wanted to go to England—her father might misunderstand. Parents were apt to, where their eighteen-year-old daughters were concerned. It would be enough, Pip decided, just to read out judicious extracts from Johnny's letter and trust to the Awkwrights to do the rest.

Her tension lifted. Reaching the last of the paddock gates, she glimpsed her father's tall figure rounding the corner of one of the woolsheds and hung back until it vanished from sight. She must get to the telephone before she talked to her father.

Pip dismounted, humming a tune to herself under her breath. She whispered to Barney, as she took off his saddle:

"I wonder what Johnny will say when I

tell him I'm coming to England the week after next?"

Barney eyed her indifferently, tossing his head.

8

DURING the week that followed his arrival at Logan, Johnny spent most of his time in a complex discussion of his financial affairs with Mr. Angus Menzies, senior partner in the firm of Glasgow solicitors entrusted with the administration of the Logan Estate.

There was much to be discussed, and Mr. Menzies, a quiet-voiced, middle-aged man, obligingly set aside all his other business and took up temporary residence at the Castle, where—with Johnny and the Manager of the Ardloch branch of the Bank of Scotland, who was his co-executor —he went carefully into the new Earl's legal position under the entail.

Elizabeth, despairing, after the first day, of ever getting Johnny to herself during the solicitor's visit, cut short her own and returned to London, ostensibly in order to acquaint her mother with the news of her engagement. This—subject to her mother's consent—was to be made public on her return to Logan.

Johnny saw little of Fiona. She was present at meals, a coldly dignified, courteous but unenthusiastic hostess, who addressed him when good manners demanded that she should and avoided him whenever possible. By contrast, her attitude to Mr. Menzies was extremely cordial, and Johnny became increasingly irritated when, at some pause in their intricate conferences, both the solicitor and the bank manager vied with each other to sing her praises.

"A charming young lady," was Mr. Menzies' invariable comment when Fiona's name was mentioned. "You are indeed fortunate, Lord Logan—indeed fortunate!"

He approved wholeheartedly of Johnny's wish to make financial provision for his cousins, but—presumably instructed by Fiona herself—was at some pains to point out that neither desired to accept anything in the nature of an allowance from him.

At their final interview, which took place in the library, and at which the bank manager was not present, Mr. Menzies summed up. "The Castle, together with its contents and the estate proper, comes under the entail, and is the property, during his lifetime, of the legal heir and holder of the title—yourself, Lord Logan, neither of the late Earl's sons having survived him. The entail cannot be broken . . ." He went into a long list of legal technicalities which Johnny attempted vainly to interpret and added, seeing his bewilderment: "You cannot sell nor deed it away without an alteration in our present law, which would require an Act of Parliament to revoke. Judgments have been given in the recent past . . ." he listed a number of them, his gaunt, bespectacled face suitably grave . . . "where death duties had to be paid and a sufficient sum could not be raised other than by a sale of some part of the entailed estate. But *you* need have no anxiety on this score."

"Needn't I?" Johnny's tone was doubtful.

"No indeed. The Logan Estate is a very wealthy one for these hard times—both the late Earl and his father administered their trust wisely and, as you will have realized, most of the developments in Ardloch over the past thirty years, and almost all the building, have been on land which is owned by the Estate. Ardloch is a growing and prosperous town, Lord Logan, and the land has trebled in value. In order to meet the charges, I would advise you to dispose of the properties I have marked for you on this plan in red, all of which—having been the personal estate of the late Earl—are excluded, of course, from the entail."

Johnny had not seen the plan before, but he found himself looking at it with interest, suddenly appreciating its significance. "Do you mean that the Earl bought these properties himself at some time?"

The lawyer shook his head. "They came to him under Lady Logan's marriage settlement. Her family owned a good deal of land in this district at one time."

"Then"—Johnny stared at him—"how is it that *I* now own them? If they're not entailed and originally belonged to Lady Logan's family, surely they should have gone to her, instead of coming to me?"

Mr. Menzies smiled. "They come to you

155

under the late Earl's will, which I drew up for him four years ago. The will was, of course, made when both Viscount Chisholm and his brother, Mr. Hamish, were alive. In anticipation of the charges which would fall on the estate when he died, the late Earl—on my advice—specifically willed the properties I have mentioned to his heir. He did this to enable the death duties to be met."

"I see." Johnny controlled himself with difficulty. This sounded to him like the height of injustice, but he knew it behoved him to go carefully. "And they're worth—what would you say?"

Mr. Menzies gave a cautious and considered estimate. "It is possible that they might fetch more in the open market. If the Ardloch Town Council were to offer for them, you understand, it might be considerably more."

The sum he had first mentioned sounded so vast to Johnny that, for a long moment, he was silent, trying to take it in. "And that would be enough to meet the death duties?" he asked at last.

The solicitor smiled. "Oh, yes, Lord Logan. It should be more than adequate for the purpose. That was the late Earl's intention."

"And I am free to dispose of all this as I see fit?" Johnny pursued, gesturing to the plan with its neatly written annotations. An idea was born in him, startling in its simplicity. He added, seeing the lawyer's frown: "I mean I'm allowed to sell any of this property at any time?"

"Well"—Mr. Menzies hesitated, clearly puzzled by the question—"yes, if you put it like that. But as I have endeavoured to explain, his late lordship intended it to safeguard his heir, to—"

"I understand that. He meant the proceeds to cover his death duties."

"Exactly so. If I may express my opinion, it was a wise precaution. As a result of it your inheritance comes to you intact. You will be able to enjoy the entire income from the entailed estate, keep up the Castle as it has always been kept up and live in the manner in which your predecessors lived."

"Mr. Menzies," Johnny put in quickly, "what *is* the income from the entailed estate? And what does it cost to keep up

157

the Castle? You've never given me an exact figure."

Mr. Menzies pursed his lips. He consulted a number of the documents piled in front of him, jotting down figures.

"I really need more time to answer these questions, I'm afraid. I could only give you an approximate estimate now. Prices fluctuate, wages are constantly going up and the incomings from agricultural rentals must, you understand, be assessed in—"

"Look," put in Johnny, scarcely able to contain his impatience, "I only need an approximate estimate."

"Well . . ." the solicitor sighed. "It's *very* approximate but . . ." Again the sums he mentioned were so enormous that Johnny drew a startled breath.

He got to his feet. "Mr. Menzies"—he was aware that what he was about to say would shock the cautious solicitor, knew also that it would displease Elizabeth, but his sense of justice was outraged—"I don't want to live in the Castle, I've no desire to live in the manner in which my predecessors lived, I've never been used to it and I've never possessed a private income in my life. I should like to make over all the property you have marked on this plan to my cousins, Lady Logan and Lady Fiona, as soon as you can draw up the necessary deeds."

Mr. Menzies' startled gasp expressed the astonished disapproval he had expected. "But the estate duty, Lord Logan—how do you propose to meet that? It will have to be met, you know."

"Immediately?" Johnny questioned.

"Well, admittedly some latitude has to be allowed when so large a sum is likely to be demanded. But—"

"It could be met from income," Johnny pointed out, "if I didn't spend any of it and the Castle were shut up, except for a few rooms which could be set aside for Lady Logan. It could even be opened to the public, couldn't it, and visitors charged half a crown to see over it. Other historic houses are—I know, I've read about them."

"Such an idea has never been contemplated by the Logan family before," Mr. Menzies objected. He sounded horrified.

"But it could be done?" Johnny insisted. "Couldn't it?"

"Certainly it could. If it were necessary. But—"

"It will probably *be* necessary. I'd like you to go into it for me, Mr. Menzies. The death duties are my responsibility and I'm not going to use Lady Logan's marriage settlement to pay them with. I want her to have it back—all of it—now."

"I shall require time to think over your proposals, Lord Logan," the solicitor said stiffly. "They have, I confess, taken me completely by surprise. But do not imagine," he added, in a more sympathetic tone, "that I do not appreciate the motives which have prompted you to make them. You wish to provide for your cousins, Lady Logan and Lady Fiona, in such a way as to enable them to have financial independence, without feeling that they are accepting an allowance from you— which Lady Fiona has already stated her unwillingness to accept. Is that it?"

"Not quite." Johnny paused, choosing his words. "The late Earl made a will, leaving these Ardloch properties to his heir. But it couldn't have occurred to him, when he made that will, that his heir would not be one of his own sons. By no possible stretch of the imagination could he have foreseen that *I* should be his heir. If he had foreseen it, do you suppose that he would have left his wife and daughter penniless in order to safeguard *my* inheritance, to enable me to pay the estate duty and live as he used to live? He would not, Mr. Menzies—no man would. My cousin would have been satisfied in his own mind, when he made his will, that whether Alastair or Hamish succeeded him, either would have taken care of Lady Logan and Lady Fiona. And"—there was a wealth of bitterness in his voice—"that whatever provision they made would be acceptable. Lady Fiona wouldn't have refused an allowance from one of her brothers if he had offered it, would she?"

In fairness, Mr. Menzies was forced to nod his agreement. He started to gather his papers together. "Lord Logan, I understand from Lady Fiona that you have recently become engaged to be married. May I take it, then"—he eyed Johnny shrewdly over the tops of his glasses— "that the future Countess of Logan will be fully in agreement with what you propose to do?" When Johnny did not at once reply, he went on kindly: "It would be as well for you to talk things over with your future wife before reaching any definite decision, don't you think? The young lady may hold different views."

Uncomfortably aware that he was right, Johnny nevertheless shook his head. "No," he said stubbornly, "the decision is mine, Mr. Menzies. It's a question of principle, of putting right what I consider to be an injustice. The Earl did not intend me to benefit by a will he made in favour of his sons. Why should Lady Logan have to accept what amounts to charity from me when most of Ardloch ought to belong to her—when, in fact, it *did* belong to her? I didn't know until now that I'd inherited her marriage settlement. But now that I *do* know, I want her to have it back."

Mr. Menzies nodded weightily. "Again I must express my admiration for your motives, Lord Logan, and since it was upon my advice that this will was made, I must take my share of responsibility for its terms. As you say, the testator's intentions should be taken into account, and they may well have been those you have outlined. I think perhaps they were. But

162

in drawing up the will, I obeyed the instructions my late client gave me and made the provisions for the payment of death duties that he wished me to make, on his heir's behalf. Legally you are in no way bound to take your late cousin's intentions into account, and it will leave you in a very strange and difficult position if you insist on doing so. You realize that, do you not?"

"Oh, yes. But my cousin Fiona has made it quite clear that she doesn't wish to continue to live here. And her mother" —Johnny sighed—"seems now to share her feelings, both about this and about the allowance I wanted to make her—to make them both. I think they would both feel differently if they realized that the money I am proposing to make over to them is morally more theirs than mine—that it's not part of the Logan Estate. Perhaps Lady Logan will stay on here. It's possible that I may be able to persuade her to do so, even if we do carry out my plan to open the Castle to the public. And in any case, whether or not I marry in the near future, I don't propose to live here for any longer than I can help in this—this style.

If it were possible, I'd like to go back to Australia."

The solicitor, closing his bulky brief-case, looked up in alarm. "I don't think you should do that, Lord Logan. At least not until we've settled all that has to be settled. And that cannot be done in a few weeks, you know."

"I'll stay for as long as I have to," Johnny promised wearily. "But I don't see that there's a lot to settle. My mind is made up so far as the question of Lady Logan's marriage settlement is concerned. I want her to have it back, with no strings attached, and if that means that I'm to do without a private income for the next few years, to enable the estate to pay off the death duties, then there's only one place where I can be certain of earning a living and that's Australia."

"You are a very impulsive young man, Lord Logan," Mr. Menzies told him ruefully. "But I must confess that I admire you. However, you have set me quite a problem. It's all very unorthodox and nothing quite like it has ever come my way before. I shall have to go into it very care-fully, in consultation with my partners, when I return to Glasgow. If I might venture to suggest a possible solution, it is that you make another attempt to persuade Lady Logan and Lady Fiona to reconsider your offer of an allowance. You would have no difficulty, bearing in mind your own modest requirements, in making both ladies a very substantial allowance out of income. The alternative is a quixotic one and will beggar you for a number of years, since it would involve the whole of your available capital."

"I'm sorry, Mr. Menzies," Johnny objected, "but I can't see it that way. It's not *my* capital—I was never meant to have it. It belongs to Lady Logan and it's to go back to her. That's my final decision and I don't want to argue about it. Nor do I want either of my cousins told that what I'm doing is going to 'beggar' me, as you call it. I'll be no worse off than I was before, shall I?"

"No, Lord Logan," Mr. Menzies was forced to concede. "But I still cannot advise you to do it."

"I'm not asking for your advice now." Johnny's jaw jutted dangerously. "I'm telling you what I want done. Will you draw up the necessary documents for me to sign as soon as you get back to Glasgow or must I call in someone else to attend to it?"

The solicitor spread his hands in a resigned gesture.

"If you insist, Lord Logan, I shall have no alternative but to obey your instructions. But I do beg you to give the matter more thought. Allow me a week, will you not? I am returning to Glasgow this evening—I can go into the whole question of the estate duty there, and you will be able to talk the matter over with your fiancée and Lady Fiona."

"Very well." Johnny saw the wisdom of this suggestion, but, as he shook hands with Mr. Menzies and went with him to the door, he knew that he would not go back on his decision, whatever Elizabeth might say. He felt reasonably confident of his ability to make her understand his reasons for it: if she loved him, she would see that there was really nothing else he could do. The property was his cousin Catherine's, he could see no further than that. And what if his decision did mean that, for a few years, he would be back almost where he had started from? He and Elizabeth were young, they were in love. He would take her back with him to Queensland and together they would build up the foundations of their life together.

But he would not say anything about all this to Fiona. She, he decided grimly, should be offered no chance to interfere. This matter was between his cousin Catherine and himself: it was simply a matter of fundamental honesty, of returning to her that which was morally hers. The fact that it represented his only available capital needn't be mentioned. He would merely tell her—as she would probably already know—that it was her marriage settlement and that, as such, he couldn't touch it. So long as he prevented old Menzies from seeing her until the necessary documents were signed and sealed, he did not imagine that Cousin Catherine would question his decision. She trusted him and already a strong bond of sympathy had sprung up between them. He spent as much time as he could with her, reading aloud to her in the evenings, talking, getting to know her . . . they were friends. He sensed that the broken-hearted

woman found solace in his company as—
he sighed—as he did in hers.

But with Fiona it was different. She
made it only too obvious that she resented
and despised him.

Johnny said, as Mr. Menzies made to
precede him into the hall: "I'd be grateful
if you would say nothing at all to Lady
Fiona about the matter we have discussed,
Mr. Menzies."

The solicitor's grizzled brows rose but
he replied quite equably: "Very good, if
that is your wish, Lord Logan. But I hope
that you yourself will ascertain Lady
Fiona's views, and, of course, her
mother's." He again held out his hand.
"You know my office telephone number
and can get in touch with me at any time.
In any case, I shall be back in a week's
time to see you. Au revoir—and I shall
look forward to our next meeting."

"Thank you," answered Johnny, with
sincerity. "So shall I, Mr. Menzies."

Jamieson was waiting in the hall with
the solicitor's hat and coat and Fiona,
hearing the sound of voices, came from the
drawing-room to bid him a subdued farewell. She was looking, Johnny thought,

very pale and wan and her eyes were darkly shadowed, as if, for a long time, she had not been sleeping well. Her evident unhappiness moved him strangely. When Mr. Menzies' car had driven away, Jamieson closed the heavy front door and retired to his own domain, leaving them alone together. They faced each other and Fiona said politely:

"I hope you got everything settled, John?"

"Not quite all. Mr. Menzies is coming back."

"Oh?" She sounded surprised, but then the habitual mask of cold indifference she always assumed in his presence hid her surprise and she asked flatly: "Do you want me for anything? Because I thought of going out."

"Well, I—" Suddenly the need to tear down the barrier she had set up between them became urgent and Johnny said eagerly: "I'd like to talk to you. Where are you going?"

"I'm going to walk up to the Frazers' cottage by the dam. Mrs. Frazer is expecting a new baby and I have some things to give her." She smiled faintly. "I don't imagine that such an errand would appeal to you."

"Why not? Would you object if I came with you?"

"Of course not. If you've nothing better or more interesting to do?" She looked a question.

"I haven't," Johnny said firmly. "And I've never seen the dam. Whereabouts is it and what purpose does it serve?"

"It's up there." Fiona opened the front door and pointed towards the tree-clad summit of a low hill, up which wound a curving, ill-defined track. "There's a reservoir formed partly by a natural loch and partly by the River Logan. My father built the dam about thirty years ago and we obtained our electric power from it. Now, of course, we're on the mains supply and it isn't of much practical use, except for fishing. It's stocked with trout and there's a boat on it, if you should feel like a day's fishing."

"Thanks. I might at that." Johnny fell into step beside her, shortening his stride to match hers. "Is that the only way up?" He gestured to the track. "It looks quite a walk."

"You can get a car up part of the way," Fiona assured him. "David does, when he's visiting the Frazers. The cottage is below the dam, some distance below, but it's very isolated and David isn't anxious for Mrs. Frazer to have the baby there, as you may imagine. That's really why I'm going up to see her—I promised him I'd try to persuade her to change her mind about staying. Several families have offered her accommodation, or there's the cottage hospital, of course—she could go there. But she wants to stay with her husband. He's a keeper and they haven't been married very long, so I suppose it's understandable."

She led the way across the lawn. Johnny sensed that she was telling him about the Frazers at some length in order to avoid any more personal topic, but at least, he thought, with satisfaction, she *was* talking to him, which was a change from the icy indifference she usually accorded him. He didn't interrupt her, and as they reached the track and started to climb, he was conscious of a strange sense of well-being. It was a fine, clear day, in contrast to the heavy rain which had been so frequent of late as to become, for him, almost a part of Logan. The sun was warm on his bare head, the scent of pine trees in his nostrils mingled pleasantly with woodsmoke from a cottage bonfire, and he was glad, after the long hours he had spent cooped up indoors with Mr. Menzies, to be able to stretch his legs.

Fiona walked briskly at his side, pointing out various landmarks which came into sight as they climbed higher. She wore thick, sensible brogues, Johnny noticed with approval, and, despite the speed at which they were walking, did not pause for breath or tire. As—he couldn't help making the comparison—Elizabeth would have done. Elizabeth rode well but she didn't enjoy walking. Her pleasures weren't simple, like his own . . . and Pip's. He recalled the carved wooden doll one of the blacks on the station had once made for Pip, as a child, and the hours she had played with it, the years she had cherished it.

He found himself, without any clear idea of how he had come to introduce the subject, telling Fiona about Pip and then, a trifle guardedly because he wasn't sure if she would be interested, about the station and his work there.

She listened attentively. "The picture you paint is rather different from Miss Anson's," she suggested, and Johnny reddened, instantly on the defensive.

"Oh, I don't know. Elizabeth wasn't there very long."

"No. You loved it out there, didn't you, John?"

"Yes," he admitted, "I did."

"Do you wish you could go back?"

"Yes. At times I do, I—oh, I shouldn't, I suppose. It's just that I don't fit in here, I know I never shall really."

"You could, you know," Fiona said. "All this"—her gesture took in the patchwork of cultivated fields spread out below them and the huddled buildings of one of the farms—"has to be cared for. My father ran the estate himself and Alastair was being trained by the Factor, Keith Macrae, to assist him. It's a full-time job and one that you could learn to do if you set your mind to it. You must get Keith to take you round, now that Mr. Menzies has gone."

"Yes," Johnny agreed, "I will, Fiona.

But—" He broke off, knowing that he couldn't explain to her. Instead he pointed ahead to where, through a gap in the trees, he could distinguish a broad wall of concrete several hundred feet above their heads. "Is that the dam?"

She nodded. "And the Frazers' cottage is at the end of this path. Why don't you climb up and look at the loch while I'm with Mrs. Frazer? There's a wonderful view from the top of the dam—you can see almost to Ardloch. The main road comes down from the Pass of Glenardie with a gradient of one in six, it's quite impressive. I'll probably be about twenty minutes, but don't wait for me if you want to go back."

"I'll wait," Johnny assured her. He felt that his relationship with his cousin Fiona had entered a new and better phase and was elated as, obeying her instructions, he climbed slowly and carefully up the steep hillside to the dam. The view was all that she had promised, and he gazed about him, oddly moved by the majesty and grandeur of the distant mountains. The road, separated from him by a thousand feet of rock, came snaking down from the glen, a white, twisting ribbon of a road and something of an engineering achievement. At one point it actually overlooked the loch by which he stood; he caught a glimpse of a red Post Office mail van coming slowly down in a low gear and wondered, fleetingly, if Jock MacPhail were driving it. He must try to see Jock again if he could, he decided. In fact, he would take the first opportunity of doing so, before Elizabeth returned . . .

He turned his attention to the dam, interested because once he had helped Harry Gilliat to build a dam in an attempt to get water to some of the outlying grazing land. But it hadn't been like this one: no Queensland dam had to withstand the weight of water this had harnessed for thirty years. It was solid concrete, worn and weathered, with a few cracks here and there and a narrow outlet, controlled by an iron-bound lock, which permitted a small fall of water over the top. The loch, swollen by the recent rain, came, Johnny thought, perilously close to the top of the dam. He hoped that the floodgates were as solid as they looked and was about to climb over to investigate when he heard Fiona hail him from below.

He was thoughtful when, a few minutes later, he rejoined her on the path outside the gamekeeper's cottage.

"Well?" Fiona asked, as they started to retrace their steps down the track. "What did you think of it? It's a lovely view, isn't it?"

"Yes. Look, Fiona, that dam hasn't ever overflowed, has it? The loch's very full."

She glanced at him quickly. "No, it's always been perfectly safe. Why? Didn't you think it looked safe?"

"Oh, yes, it looked safe enough. You can't tell much by outward appearances, though. It's certainly having to take a terrific weight of water."

"Well, it always has taken it," Fiona said reassuringly. "Do you know much about dams?"

"I helped to build one once. I think I'll come up again and have a look at that. Tomorrow, perhaps. It ought to be inspected regularly."

"I'm glad," Fiona said, "that you are going to take an interest in it, John. My visit was quite successful too—Mrs.

Frazer's promised to come down within the next day or so, which will be a great relief to David."

They walked slowly back, still conversing amicably, as the sun set in a blaze of glory behind the hills. Johnny felt that he had achieved a measure of understanding with Fiona and when, on reaching the house again, she asked him if he would be in to dinner, he suggested, greatly daring: "Look, Fiona, if we're by ourselves, why don't we go out somewhere? To Ardloch perhaps, to the pictures—"

A trifle brusquely, she cut him short. "I'm dining with David Cameron, thank you. At his house. In any case I should not go to Ardloch, either to dinner or the cinema. You seem to forget I'm in mourning."

Johnny's cheeks burned. It was as if his tactless words had again set up a barrier between them, for Fiona was regarding him with her accustomed thinly veiled hostility.

"I'm sorry," he said. "I hadn't forgotten. It was just that I wanted to take you out, to go on being with you, I—"

Again she interrupted him. "It doesn't matter, I'm sure you meant well. Shall I order dinner for you here? Or would you prefer to go out?"

"I'll go out," Johnny returned, stung by her tone. He had no idea, as he said it, where he would go, but he knew that he could not face eating by himself in the huge, forbidding dining-room, with Jamieson serving him in impassive silence and the portraits of long-dead Chisholms gazing down at him reproachfully from the walls. He was still undecided when he saw a Post Office mail van turn into the back drive and then, recognizing Jock MacPhail at the wheel, he smiled. "I'm going out with a friend of mine," he told Fiona. "If you'll forgive me, I'll go and catch him at the back door, where he's about to deliver our afternoon post. I'll probably be late, so please don't tell anyone to wait up for me—I can let myself in by the side door. Thank you for the walk and for putting up with my company so patiently."

He was conscious of Fiona's unvoiced disapproval as he left her staring after him.

9

ELIZABETH returned a few days later, announcing her impending arrival in a brief telegram which Johnny received with relief. *Mother approves and wants to meet you. Am coming to fetch you. Arriving nine twelve Ardloch tomorrow morning. All my love —Elizabeth.*

Johnny was having tea with Lady Logan when the telegram was brought to him, and he showed it to her, his eyes bright. "It's from Elizabeth," he said. "She's coming tomorrow, Cousin Catherine."

"I'm glad, dear—you've missed her, haven't you?" His cousin's voice was sympathetic. "She must stay here, of course. It's not right for your fiancée to stay at the Logan Arms, and you know I'd like to meet her. So tell Fiona, will you? She will see to everything. And I expect you will want to go in to meet her train."

"Oh, yes," Johnny assured her, "of course I will."

He was suddenly impatient to see Elizabeth again, and filled with an intense longing to discuss his problems with the one person in the world who might be expected to understand and help him to resolve them. He had heard once from Mr. Menzies since his departure—a short note, in which the solicitor had said only that, on the advice of his partners, he was seeking counsel's opinion on the matter of Lady Logan's marriage settlement. Mr. Archibald Farquharson, whose opinion he had asked, was, Mr. Menzies asserted, a man of wide experience and unquestionable repute. He hoped that Johnny would keep an open mind on the subject, at least until he had been given the benefit of Mr. Farquharson's advice.

But, looking down into the pale, lined face of his cousin Catherine, Johnny's resolution hardened. It didn't matter what Mr. Farquharson's opinion might be, he didn't need a lot of lawyers to teach him right from wrong. He owed it to Elizabeth, of course, to explain what he intended to do, but she, he felt sure, would agree with him. She *must*. Her first reaction, which had so bewildered him, had been the result of his failure to explain the situation to her, he told himself: she would have thought better of it now, would realize—as soon as he had made the position clear to her—that he was doing the only thing possible, in the circumstances.

"You are a fine young man, John," Lady Logan said unexpectedly, breaking the little silence which had fallen between them. She reached out and took his hand, drawing him down on to the arm of her chair. "I'm not only saying that because you look like my Alastair—you *are* like him, in many, many ways which I recognize as I come to know you better. You have his gentleness, his generosity, his upright standards and, I am sure, his courage. You must forgive a mother's pride, but I did not think that any young man could be as fine as my two sons. I thought, when you first came here, that it would break my heart to see you in their place. Yet"—she smiled at him—"it has not. You are worthy of the name you bear and I know you won't disgrace it. I hope that when you marry Elizabeth you will find it possible to settle down here. Logan needs its laird, John—your title isn't an empty one, and this estate and the people who live and work on it are your responsibility now. It is not a light task or one you can undertake with half your heart. But Fiona tells me you are starting to take a practical interest in the estate. Tell me, has the Factor taken you round the farms yet?"

Johnny shook his head, ashamed that he must deceive her. "Not yet, Cousin Catherine." He hadn't revisited the dam yet either—when he had mentioned his mistrust of it to Macrae, the Factor, he had laughed and made some joke about Australians not being used to water. "But look"—he bent to kiss his cousin's faded cheek—"I will. I'll start tomorrow, when Elizabeth is with me." He couldn't explain his reluctance to visit the estate farms, could barely understand it himself. He didn't want the place to get a hold on him, perhaps that was it—for what was the use, when he might so soon have to leave it?

"I hope you will, dear. Well"—Lady Logan released his hand—"I mustn't keep you here talking to me all the time, must I? Fiona said you were going out this evening, so I expect you'll want to change."

Johnny mumbled something unintelligible and kissed her again before taking leave of her.

He spent the evening, as he had spent his last two evenings, with Jock MacPhail in Ardloch, at the British Legion Club. Jock, at his behest, simply introduced him as "Snow" and let him make himself at home. He *felt* at home there, Johnny thought fiercely, more at home than he could ever feel at Logan Castle in the face of Fiona's continued hostility . . .

But, letting himself in by the side door long after midnight, he reflected that Elizabeth would soon be coming and then everything would be different. His uncertainty would be ended and, with Elizabeth's help, he would be able to plan his life anew.

. . . The London train came hissing to a halt in Ardloch Station punctually at twelve minutes past nine next morning, and Elizabeth, looking fresh and charming in a lavender-coloured tweed suit, stepped out of the sleeping car and into his arms. Johnny held her to him, the scent of her hair a heady ecstasy and her lips soft and yielding under his. He hadn't, until this moment, fully realized his need of her.

"Darling!" She was all eagerness as she clung to him. "Have you missed me?"

"Yes," Johnny confessed, shaken by the intensity of his feelings. "I've missed you terribly, Elizabeth."

"Then I'm glad," Elizabeth smiled, "that I decided to come back." She released herself from his embrace, turned to the waiting porter. "Shall I tell him to take my cases to the Rolls or are we still travelling by taxi?"

Johnny reddened. "I've got a car outside. It isn't the Rolls, it's one I drive myself."

Elizabeth made a moue at him. "Johnny, you're impossible! But never mind, I'm going to change all that, you'll see—I'm really going to take you in hand and see that you assert yourself. I hope that at least you've arranged for me to stay at the Castle this time? You have? Well, that's a relief, I was awfully afraid you'd expect me to return to the Logan Arms. In fact I shouldn't have been a bit surprised to learn that you were staying there yourself! Has Lady Fiona given you any idea of when she and her mother intend to leave?"

"No," said Johnny, up in arms at once, "of course not, Elizabeth, and—"

"Darling," Elizabeth interrupted quickly, "I must tell you that Mummy is simply thrilled about our engagement. She wants me to bring you straight back to London, but I thought we might go down on Friday and spend the weekend at home. There are simply masses of relations and people I want you to meet . . ." She talked on and Johnny listened with a sinking heart, as the porter put her suitcases into the car and stood holding the door of it for them. "Johnny," Elizabeth whispered reproachfully, "tip him!"

Johnny fumbled in his pockets, finally bringing to light a two-shilling piece. He felt oddly numb and shocked, experiencing so swift a revulsion of feeling that, for several minutes after they had left the station, he couldn't find a word to say to her.

Elizabeth, after a quick, puzzled glance

at his face, went on giving him an enthusiastic account of her doings in London, her mother's reaction to her engagement and her plans for announcing it.

"I had some photographs taken, darling," she said, "by Lawrence Rayne, who is *the* photographer now. Of course, so far I've only seen the proofs, but they're excellent and I think the final result should be most pleasing. I want him to take you when you're down. We're going to need a lot of photos, you know—I've ordered three dozen of mine. And about the announcement, Johnny—Mummy thinks we ought to put it in *The Times*, the *Telegraph* and *The Scotsman*. What do you feel? Ought it to go in any of the Glasgow papers? Or the local one?"

"I don't know." Johnny made an effort to answer her but he scarcely heard what she said. He wondered, with growing despair, how he was going to break the news of his decision to her. Because he would have to break it. But dared he hope that she would understand, in view of the question she had asked him—within a few minutes of her arrival—as to when Fiona and her mother intended to leave Logan?

Oh, surely she would understand—she had to!

It was all so clear in his own mind, and yet, as they drove on and Elizabeth continued to chatter gaily at his side, Johnny could not bring himself to put it into words for fear he should fail to make it clear to her. He knew that if she refused to accept his decision, he couldn't possibly marry her. He had to do what he believed to be right and just, no matter what it cost him—even if it should cost him Elizabeth. He was in love with her and she with him and, heaven knew, he wanted to marry her. Hadn't he always wanted it, ever since he had first set eyes on her and seen his dream girl come to life?

Johnny drew a long, painful breath and braced himself. He couldn't go on like this, letting her speak of their engagement, letting her make plans which might have to be sacrificed. She might not want to be engaged to him when she knew . . .

Miserably he took his gaze from the road and let it stray to the lovely face of the girl at his side. To Elizabeth, if to no one else, he must tell the truth.

"You're awfully silent, Johnny," Elizabeth reproved him teasingly. "Why? Aren't you interested in what I've been telling you?"

"Yes, but I've got rather a lot on my mind, you see," Johnny defended unhappily.

"Have you, darling? Well, so have I. There's so much to be thought of and arranged, isn't there?"

"Yes," he agreed. "Yes, an awful lot, Elizabeth. Look, I've simply got to talk to you." He made to slow down, but Elizabeth, guessing his intention, put in swiftly, a faint edge to her voice: "Do we have to stop by the roadside so that you can talk to me? Surely you can talk and drive, can't you?"

"Not about this. It's important. And I don't know either the car or the road too well—I don't want to go and crash us down the hill."

"And I haven't the least desire to *go* crashing down the hill," Elizabeth told him flippantly, "when I've just got myself engaged to a peer of the realm! But have a heart, darling—I don't want to sit out in the rain for hours either.

Doesn't it ever do anything but rain up here?"

Johnny shrugged. He hadn't realized that the rain had started again. But he had, somehow, to make Elizabeth listen to him. "Elizabeth—" he began and was cut short.

"Can't it wait till we get to Logan, Johnny? What you've got to tell me can't be as important as what I've got to tell you —or as exciting, anyway. Listen—do you know who's actually promised she'll be one of my bridesmaids? You'll never guess —Cynthia Ponsonby. Her father owns Ponsonby Motors and they have a glorious villa at Biarritz which Cynthia thinks her father would lend us for our honeymoon. Oh, yes, and *who* do you think is coming to England? Little Pip—Pip Gilliat, she's coming with the Awkwrights. Her mother cabled me just before I left, asking me if I'd look after her if she came up here, if you please! Johnny, you didn't invite her, did you?"

Johnny turned in his seat to stare at her. "Yes," he said, "I did. Why? Do you mind? It won't be for long."

"Not all that much, I suppose—except

that the poor child has a 'thing' about you. But she's too late, isn't she?" Elizabeth smiled up at him with a hint of complacence. "Didn't she let *you* know she was coming?"

He sighed. "No. I expect she will, though." Pip's visit left him strangely unmoved. He would be glad to see her again, of course, but—Lord, this was awful—they were within sight of the gates of Logan and still he hadn't told Elizabeth of his cousin Catherine's marriage settlement and his decision concerning it. And he *had* to tell her . . . He swung round the last bend and slowed down, looking for a place to park his car out of the rain.

"Johnny"—Elizabeth's tone was sharp —"why are you pulling up, for goodness' sake? I told you—"

"I'm pulling up," Johnny returned grimly, "because I've *got* to talk to you, Elizabeth. It can't be put off and I must tell you before we get to the Castle."

He drew up, the car's wheels on the grass verge, and, applying the handbrake, he switched off his engine and turned to face her, aware that the eyes she turned on

190

him were bright with anger. "Elizabeth," he said, "you must listen to me . . ."

A long way away, on the steep Glenardie road, a car horn sounded frantically, but Johnny didn't consciously hear it.

10

"I'M sorry, Elizabeth," Johnny said humbly as he faced her, "it won't take long."

"Oh, all right," returned Elizabeth ungraciously. "But I hope you really do mean that it won't take long, because I've been travelling all night, you know, and I'm exhausted. Have you a cigarette?"

"Only these, I'm afraid." Guiltily, Johnny took out his tobacco tin and papers. "Shall I make you one?"

She shook her head. "I've got some of my own somewhere. I just thought you *might* have remembered that I don't like those beastly cigarettes of yours. In fact I even cherished the faint hope that you might have realized that it's not done to roll your own in this country. However" —she took a flat, engine-turned silver case from her handbag, selected a cigarette from it and permitted Johnny to light it for her—"thanks." She forced a smile and prompted, more graciously: "Well, what is it that you've got to talk to me about? Go on, darling, tell me! I'm all ears and mad with curiosity."

"Well . . ." Johnny hesitated, searching for words. Now that it had come to the point, it was even harder than he had feared it would be to tell her. She was smiling at him, an odd, half-tender, half-mocking expression in her clear blue eyes, and he thought that she had never looked more beautiful—or more unapproachable. If only she would hold out her hand to him, help him a little . . . diffidently he put out his own hand, let his fingers touch hers. "Look, darling," he managed, after an appreciable pause, "it's like this. I've spent most of this week going into things with Mr. Menzies, the family solicitor. He's an executor and he's administering the Logan Estate, as you know."

"Yes," confirmed Elizabeth, when he again paused uncertainly, "I *do* know. You told me all that before I went away." She glanced at the clock on the dashboard and from it, resignedly, to the teeming rain outside. "Go on. Although, as it happens, I probably know more than you think."

193

"Do you?" New hope burned in Johnny's eyes. "About the estate, do you mean? About my cousin's will?"

She inclined her head. "I think I know within a few thousands how much you've inherited. You"—she sounded suddenly a little awed—"you're awfully rich, Johnny. Almost what one calls *disgustingly* rich. The Logan Estate is one of the wealthiest in the country. My mother's solicitor told me that and he's pretty knowledgeable. You're terribly lucky, but you don't seem to realize it." She laughed. "You're a *very* strange sort of earl, darling."

"Yes but"—he brushed that aside—"there's my cousin Catherine, Elizabeth. And there's Fiona. I told you how I felt about them. I must see that they're provided for—"

Elizabeth's lovely mouth compressed. "You can give them an allowance, Johnny, if that's what's bothering you and if you feel you should. It needn't be a lot, of course, but if they're on your conscience because we're going to turn them out of the Castle, then I see no reason why you shouldn't be generous. And you obviously want to be." Her tone was that of a not

194

unkindly adult, seeking to indulge a dense and rather obstinate child.

Johnny flushed. "It's not just a question of being generous," he corrected, "it's . . ." and now the words he wanted came flowing to his tongue and would not be denied. He talked on and on, willing her to understand, going back again and again to the one all-important point, which was that his cousin Catherine had a much greater right than he had to what he wanted to give her.

"It was the will, you see, Elizabeth. The Earl made it intending to safeguard his son. If he'd had any sort of premonition that I should become his heir, he would never have made such a will, I'm absolutely convinced of that. How could he have imagined that both his sons would be killed as they were—that he *and* Alastair and Hamish would die within a week of each other? No one could possibly have foreseen anything so terrible, and it's quite obvious that he didn't—or Menzies either. I was never meant to inherit Cousin Catherine's marriage settlement. Elizabeth, you *do* see that I haven't any right to it, don't you? No moral right, even if legally it's mine. It's a vast sum, all invested in property in Ardloch and free of the entail. Menzies says that the late Earl left it as he did in order that the death duties could be paid in a lump sum from the proceeds of the sale. And . . ."

He went carefully into all the solicitor had said and then, warming to his subject, he told her about his plan to return to Australia.

"I could, Elizabeth, if you'd come with me. You liked it out there when you were staying with the Gilliats, didn't you? Menzies could scrape together a bit of capital, perhaps, enough to start us off in a place of our own. Or I'd get a manager's job, Harry always promised me one. Darling, I'd make you happy, I swear I would. And it would only be for a couple of years, probably—just until the death duties were paid. I know it sounds crazy to say I'll have no income from the estate for a couple of years, but if I do it this way, we'll clear off the charges in the minimum time possible *and* give Cousin Catherine back what belongs to her."

Elizabeth heard him in silence. She sat at his side, quite motionless, save for the hand in which she held her cigarette. But she was listening intently, Johnny knew, and his hopes rose as he talked on and she made no attempt to interrupt him.

At last, when he had said all that he had to say and exhausted every argument at his command, he turned to her.

"Elizabeth," he said and his voice wasn't steady, "Elizabeth, you do understand, don't you? You do think I'm right to give Cousin Catherine back her marriage settlement?"

For what seemed to him an eternity, Elizabeth made no reply. Then she said, with controlled anger that was more telling than any outburst could have been: "Oh, yes, I understand. I understand perfectly. You're quite crazy, Johnny."

"I'm not," Johnny protested, "honestly I'm not, darling, I—"

"You simply haven't a clue." Elizabeth's interruption was swift, her tone suddenly harsh. "And you're a coward. I think that's at the root of it. You aren't big enough to take the wonderful chances you've been given. You want to run away because you're a coward."

"A coward?" Johnny could only stare

at her in hurt and stricken bewilderment. "Why do you say that, Elizabeth? Why, for crying out loud? I only want to be honest. I'd never be able to look myself in the face again if I took this money from Cousin Catherine when I've no possible right to it."

"You can delude yourself into thinking it's that," Elizabeth told him bitingly. "But it's not. Face up to the truth, Johnny. The truth is that you *want* to run away—back to Australia, where you belong, where they'll let you go on being a nobody. You don't want to be the Earl of Logan, you never did, and you're terrified of the responsibilities it carries with it. You're afraid to accept them. You've let the high and mighty Lady Fiona make a fool of you—don't you see it? And now, because she's played on your inferiority complex and made you feel unwanted, your one thought is to try and escape, and so you've dreamed up this absurd, quixotic way of doing it, in the hope that everyone will tell you how noble you are to make such a sacrifice. You expect *me* to tell you —why, you even expect me to run away with you! Well, I won't. If you want to marry me, Johnny, you'll have to be Lord Logan and take what belongs to you, not give it away."

Johnny looked at her for a long moment without saying a word. All trace of tenderness had gone from her face and her eyes were as cold and hard as ice.

She had lost her temper with him, he realized, and was showing herself to him for the first and only time in her true colours. Pip, then, had been right when she had warned him a long time ago that Elizabeth was hard. As hard as nails, Pip had called her . . .

But had she, nevertheless, told him the truth? Were her accusations justified—was he, as she and even old Menzies seemed to think, a fool, a quixotic fool who failed to assert himself and let people ride roughshod over him . . . people like his cousin Fiona? Was there any real need for the sacrifice he had wanted to make? Or was he, as Elizabeth had just told him he was, using it as an excuse because he didn't want to stay here, didn't want to be the Earl of Logan and accept the responsibilities that went with his new inheritance?

Johnny drew a long, painful breath. It

was true that he had been happy in Australia, happy as . . . what had Elizabeth called him? Happy as a *nobody*. He wanted to go back to his old life, wanted it more desperately as day succeeded day and the cold, alien atmosphere of the Castle made it a prison for his nostalgic spirit. He wasn't at home there. In spite of all Cousin Catherine had said to him yesterday evening, he knew himself to be inadequate for the position into which an ironic fate had thrust him. Oh, he might look like Alastair Chisholm, he might even possess a few of his less outstanding qualities, but the fact remained that he *wasn't* Alastair Chisholm and never could be, whatever Cousin Catherine had said.

Perhaps, he told himself miserably, perhaps he had an inferiority complex. That was one of the things which Australians were supposed to suffer from, although he'd never been conscious of it until now. Back home he had been able to hold his own with any man, and no one, in all his life, had ever had reason to accuse him of cowardice . . . least of all a girl.

His girl—Elizabeth whom he had loved and had dreamed of making his wife . . .

Elizabeth who he had imagined would stand at his side and help and believe in him. Sick disillusion in his eyes, Johnny studied her face, seeing it as the face of a stranger. There was no kindness in it, no pity, no attempt at understanding, only a sort of exasperated, petulant contempt. Perhaps what she had told him about himself had been the truth, but, if she had loved him, she wouldn't have expressed herself in the way she had, wouldn't have made it quite so hurtfully clear that all she wanted of him was the title he him-self hated, the money that made him—in Elizabeth's own words—"disgustingly rich".

He said, his anger suddenly matching hers but under his control: "I expect you're right about me, Elizabeth. I'm sorry if I've disappointed you, but there it is—the leopard can't change his spots, they're imprinted on him for life. I told you this hadn't changed me, that I was just the same bloke as the one you knew at Wahrangi. I should never have come here, I can see that now—I was never cut out to be an earl. What you've just told me has made me see it more clearly than ever."

Johnny's hand sought for the ignition switch. He turned it and touched the starter, slipping into gear as the car's engine sprang to life.

Elizabeth, aware that she had gone too far, turned to him in alarm. Her anger faded and she forced a pleading note into her voice.

"Johnny, all I wanted to do was to make you understand—"

"That," Johnny put in, "was what I was hoping to make *you* do. We both failed, didn't we?" He acknowledged the lodge-keeper's raised cap as they entered the drive. "At least," he added, not looking at her, "it solves the problem of which news-papers should print the announcement of our engagement, doesn't it?"

"What do you mean?" Elizabeth demanded sharply.

"Well—since there isn't going to be any engagement, it no longer matters if it's *The Times* or *The Scotsman*, I suppose."

"You're—Johnny, you're not breaking off our engagement, are you?" Elizabeth caught at his arm. "You can't, you—" she bit her lip and now there were tears in her eyes—"you simply can't."

"I was under the impression that you'd given me an ultimatum," Johnny said. His voice was quiet and, strangely, he wasn't conscious of pain but rather of relief. "You told me that if I wanted to marry you I'd have to be Lord Logan and take what belongs to me, not give it away. I can't avoid being Lord Logan, more's the pity, and I'll have to face up to my responsibilities, I know, but—" his firm mouth curved wryly into a smile—"I *do* intend to give away what belongs to me. Every last penny of it, however much of a fool that makes me. So obviously you won't want to marry me, will you?"

"Johnny darling, you don't know what you are saying." Deceived by his smile, Elizabeth sought to placate him. After all, she reminded herself, this was only Johnny. He had always worshipped her, humbly and undemandingly. He hadn't the least idea how attractive he was. For all his good looks and his physical strength, he was as naïve and innocent of guile as a boy, and never before had Elizabeth experienced the slightest difficulty in winning him round. He was in love with her, whereas she . . . well, she had never let her heart rule her head and she wasn't going to do so in Johnny's case. She had been an idiot to speak her mind quite so plainly, but he had taken her completely by surprise and caused her to lose her temper, with his crazily quixotic notions. Still, she couldn't believe that it had done irreparable harm—in the past, she had only had to lift her finger and he had come back to her. Besides, he was absurdly chivalrous: he would never let her down. She tucked her hand under his arm, flexing her fingers about his as they rested on the steering wheel. "Johnny . . ." she begged.

"Well?" The set of his jaw was uncompromising, his tone far from encouraging. "What is it, Elizabeth?"

They were in sight of the Castle now, its vast grey bulk looming at them out of the misty curtain of rain.

Johnny changed down, seeing as he did so that David Cameron's shabby old sports car was parked a few yards from the front door and, behind it, the Factor's Land Rover. Both men were engaged in earnest discussion and, hearing the approach of Johnny's car, they turned and stood side by side, awaiting his arrival. He glanced at Elizabeth.

"My responsibilities," he said, "look as if they may be about to catch up with me. So I'm afraid we shall just have to consider this discussion at an end."

"But, Johnny—" genuinely alarmed now, Elizabeth continued to cling to his arm. "You're not serious, are you? You don't really mean that you don't want us to get married?"

Johnny inclined his head. He possessed a strange, unfamiliar dignity which added to Elizabeth's rising panic, for it clothed him suddenly in an armour against which her accustomed weapons of tears and charm were powerless. He seemed indifferent to both as he said, still not raising his voice: "I am perfectly serious, Elizabeth. I think it would be a great mistake for us to marry in the circumstances."

"But . . . but you're in love with me," Elizabeth faltered, "we're in love with each other—"

"No," Johnny corrected gently, "not any more. I suppose it was a sort of dream, really—an illusion I had about you that deceived me into thinking I was. And you

—why, I don't believe you even had the illusion. Had you? I don't think you were ever in love with me, Elizabeth."

"I was, Johnny . . . I *am!* Darling, you must believe me. Oh, Johnny, you can't do this to me . . ." The tears were gone now, the lovely eyes widening in shocked surprise as, very slowly, it dawned on Elizabeth that Johnny—*Johnny* whom she had once been able to twist round her little finger—meant what he had said. It was incredible but it was happening and, for perhaps the first time in her life, Elizabeth Anson found herself completely at a loss and bereft of the power of speech. Pride forbade that she continue to plead with him and, it seemed, there was nothing else she could do, save wait in the faint hope that Johnny might come to his senses.

She drew herself up and faced him as they approached the front door of the Castle.

"I hope," she said bitterly, "that you realize what you've done, how much you've hurt and—and humiliated me. I can't stay here now, of course. I—I should like to leave as soon as there's a train."

Her teeth sank into her lower lip as she fought for control.

"There's a train at seven this evening," Johnny told her flatly. He pulled up and Jamieson, warned by the Factor, came to the door. "Please make yourself at home. Jamieson will look after you."

Elizabeth didn't move. "You understand," she said at last, "that I—that I'll be waiting if you should change your mind, Johnny. I didn't mean to quarrel with you. I love you."

"Thank you," Johnny answered politely. He, too, found himself at a loss for words. It seemed unbelievable that this strange little scene with Elizabeth should be the end of all the torturing uncertainty he had endured on her account, of his dreams, his hopes, his love. And yet it was. He knew it, beyond all shadow of doubt, knew that he hadn't loved the real Elizabeth, because the real Elizabeth— seen this morning for the first time—was a stranger to him. He was conscious of no pain, only a sense of bewilderment that her loss should hurt him so little, her pleading and her tears leave him so unmoved. He couldn't even feel sorry for her, since her grief seemed to him unreal, her protestations those of an actress playing a stage part without conviction and without heart.

He looked at her. She was still just as beautiful as she had always been, but she was no longer clothed, for him, in the lovely, fragile magic of his dream. He saw and wondered at the thin, ungenerous lines of her mouth, under its veneer of carefully applied make-up, and suddenly she was just Elizabeth Anson, not his dream girl, not the girl he had loved.

He said, with complete finality: "I shan't change my mind, Elizabeth. I'm sorry, but I . . . shan't."

And then Jamieson was beside the car, holding open the door on Elizabeth's side for her to alight, and David Cameron and the Factor began to move towards him, their faces indicating that both had something to tell him. Johnny raised a hand.

"Forgive me for a moment," he requested, "I'll be back." They both nodded and the doctor glanced covertly at his watch. Johnny followed Elizabeth and the butler into the hall. From somewhere a long way away he again heard the frantic blaring of a motor horn but dismissed it as Jamieson came to him.

"Excuse me, my lord, but there is a cablegram for you from Australia. It was phoned through about an hour ago—just after your lordship left for Ardloch. I understand from the Post Office, my lord, that it arrived at Ardloch yesterday, but that, owing to a mistake in the address, it could not be delivered."

Taking the message from the butler's salver, Johnny smiled as he read the address. It was typical of Pip to forget his new title, to send him a cable, announcing her impending arrival in England, addressed to "John Chisholm".

He thought, reading it with an odd lifting of the heart, that it would be good to see Pip again. And the Awkwrights. He would invite them all to stay—or Pip and Bob and Betty anyway, and . . . he looked up to find Elizabeth's gaze on him. Her eyes were full of malice, her mouth twisted into a bitter, angry line, and he read her thoughts as plainly as if they had been written on her face.

"I suppose," she said accusingly, when

Jamieson had picked up her suitcase and moved out of earshot, "it's from Pip?"

"Yes," Johnny admitted, "it is. Why?"

Elizabeth shrugged. "I think you'd better marry *her*." Her tone was sarcastic. "She'll fit in with all your quixotic ideas, won't she? She might even approve of them."

"She might," he agreed briefly and signed to Jamieson. "Look after Miss Anson, please, Jamieson—I expect she would like tea or something. Is Lady Fiona in?"

"No, my lord." The butler shook his head. "Her ladyship went up to the Dam Cottage with Dr. Cameron, but I do not think she returned with him. I haven't seen her since, my lord. But I believe that the doctor is wishing for a word with your lordship. It has something to do with Mrs. Frazer at the cottage, I understand."

"Right, I'll go and see him now." Johnny excused himself to Elizabeth and hurried back to where David Cameron was awaiting him with ill-concealed impatience. "Good morning, Doctor— Captain Macrae. Did you want to tell me something?"

"Yes, Lord Logan. I'm wanting to bring Mrs. Frazer down to the hospital this afternoon. I think Fiona told you that she—" The doctor got no further, for at that moment a Post Office mail van, its horn sounding urgently, came hurtling round a bend in the drive on two wheels, the driver's hand waving to attract their attention. It skidded to a halt beside them with a harsh screech of protesting tyres, and Jock MacPhail, his face white and beaded with perspiration, jumped from the driving seat to fling himself on Johnny.

"Snow, thank God I've caught ye! 'Tis the dam—" He was breathless, his words falling over each other in his haste to get them out. "Listen"—he gripped Johnny's arm—"you mind what ye said tae me the other night about the dam no' being safe? Well, I've kept looking at it each time I do ma mail run up tae Glenardie—you can see it fine frae the road, you're looking down on tae it, ye understand. 'Tis going, Snow, there's a great crack richt across it. It'll not hold much longer—God alone knows if it's still holding now." He drew a quick, scared breath, glancing swiftly from Johnny's face to those of David Cameron and the Factor, who had come to join them. "I've gie'n the warning where I could—there'll be men up frae the village as soon as they can get here and I told Archie at the West Lodge as I came through. But there's no way to it except frae here—ye canna get tae it frae the road. And there's folk in the cottage— Mistress Frazer's there, is she not? And—"

"And Lady Fiona's there," David Cameron put in. His voice was low and shaken. "She stayed because Mrs. Frazer's near her time and we didn't like to leave her by herself while her husband was out on the hill."

Johnny was silent, his brain racing, cutting corners, leaping ahead of him. He visualized the dam, knew that there would be little likelihood of anyone standing below it being able to recognize the danger. It was overgrown in places and, as Jock went on breathlessly describing the crack he had seen, Johnny realized that it could only be seen from above . . . from the road where Jock had seen it and from whence it was inaccessible, owing to the nature of the terrain. There was only one way up and part of that way was so steep that it must be climbed on foot.

"The overflow lock"—he hurled the question at the young postman, arresting him in mid-sentence—"Jock, was it open, was there water coming through the sluice gates, could you see?"

Jock sighed and shook his head. "I canna remember," he said unhappily, "if there was water coming through, 'twas just a wee trickle."

"The sluice gates are closed," the Factor said quietly. "They've not been opened since we went on mains electricity five years ago. There's just the small overflow gate open at the top."

Johnny's lips tightened grimly. "Then we'll have to get them open," he said. Turning to the Factor, he issued terse orders, aware that all three men were looking at him, awaiting his decision. This was his responsibility because Logan belonged to him and he had to take it . . .

"I'm going up," he added, already on his way to the parked Land Rover, "in this. Cameron, you'd better come with me. We'll need tools—spades, axes, a crowbar, anything we can lay our hands on. Pick up what you can, Jock, and follow us up in my car. We'll have to hurry. Macrae, I'll depend on you to collect as many men as you can, with tools and equipment, and get them up to us. We'll try to repair the dam if it's possible, but the first thing to do is to get those sluice gates opened to ease the pressure and lower the level of water. I'll"—he was in the Land Rover, already starting its engine—"I'll see to that while the doctor gets Lady Fiona and Mrs. Frazer down here to safety. If the dam should go when we're up there, you'll have to use your own judgment about coming after us. And you'd better send someone up to warn them at the farm."

He slammed the Land Rover into gear as Jock thrust a spade into the rear seat and David Cameron leapt into the seat beside him. He drove straight across the lawn, his wheel marks leaving a scar-like track across the smooth, carefully tended turf. As he drove, his foot hard down on the accelerator, he strained his eyes for a glimpse of the wall of concrete that should be above them if the dam were still holding. He saw it, with a gasp of relief, and then set his vehicle on to the steep, curving track, its wheels skidding and churning on the loose, muddy surface, barely able to retain a hold.

The rain poured relentlessly down, obscuring his vision and adding, drop by drop, to the weight of water with which they must soon do battle. He knew that if the dam should fail to hold then it would not be only the Frazers' tiny cottage at its foot which would be overwhelmed—there were farm buildings, other cottages and livestock scattered about the hillside. And there would be the men he had ordered the Factor to summon, on their way up, loaded with heavy tools . . .

But his first consideration must be Fiona and the helpless Mrs. Frazer—at all costs they must be got down.

"Stop here," David Cameron bade him, as the Land Rover skidded dangerously and almost stalled. "We'll get no further in this—only a tank could manage the last bit."

They jumped out and began, desperately, to run . . .

11

IN the small, dark cottage kitchen, Fiona was preparing tea. As she worked, she glanced occasionally at her watch, listening with more than a hint of anxiety for the footsteps which would herald the returning Frazer.

It was now more than two hours since David had gone down to arrange for his patient's admission to hospital and to do his round of sick visits, but she knew that she could not expect him back until well on into the afternoon. When he had left her, young Mrs. Frazer had been her normal, soft-voiced, shyly cheerful self, but since then, as time wore on, she had undergone an alarming change. She said little and continued valiantly to smile, but her face had gradually lost its rosy glow and become lined and ashen, and the beads of moisture gathering on her brow had told their own tale to the watchful Fiona.

As soon as Frazer came, she would send

him down to telephone for David, Fiona decided. Or at any rate to warn him of what might be going to happen. The baby, admittedly, wasn't due for another four or five days, but, unless she had misread the signs, it would come much sooner than that—it might even come before they could get its young mother down the hill. It was a pity she hadn't brought a car with her, but, having come up with David in his, she hadn't thought of it. There had seemed no hurry . . . then.

Fiona sighed and reached for the kettle. From the next room, she could hear Annie Frazer moving about restlessly, humming under her breath, a broken, scarcely recognizable snatch of song.

"Are you all right, Annie?" she called, lifting her eyes from the teapot she was filling in order to glance quickly through the open doorway.

"I'm fine, my lady," Annie answered. "Just fine, thank you." There was a defiant note in her soft Highland voice and Fiona, the tea made, sighed again. Not for the first time, she found herself wishing that she had been firmer with little Annie Frazer, had insisted on bringing her down this morning. Annie was a nice girl, pretty and intelligent, but she possessed a strong streak of obstinacy in her make-up and she had succeeded in convincing David that no harm would be done if she were to wait until her husband returned for his mid-day meal. Even now, although it was obvious that she was enduring spasmodic bouts of pain, she denied it and only smiled and insisted she was "fine" when Fiona asked her how she felt.

Fiona sympathized with her longing to give birth to her first-born in this quiet, lonely cottage that was her home and where she had been happy, but she sympathized even more strongly with David, who could scarcely be expected to welcome the prospect of the long, difficult climb up to it each day, in addition to the other heavy work of his busy, scattered practice. And besides, there was the District Nurse to be considered. Fiona wondered, as she hunted for cups and set a tray, if it wouldn't be possible for Frazer and herself, between them, to get the girl down before lunch. But, as she carried in the tray, her first glimpse of Annie's face told her that it was already too late.

"Annie," she said gently, putting down the tray and going to kneel beside her, "it's started, hasn't it?"

Annie nodded, tight-lipped. "I'm sorry," she managed huskily, "truly I am. I'd not thought . . . 'twould be so soon. And the doctor not here . . ."

"Never mind," Fiona spoke with more assurance than she felt. "We'll get you to bed, shall we? And then we'll send Niall to telephone for the doctor. He'll be back soon, won't he?"

"Not till it's his dinner time," Annie answered, with fierce and gloomy pride. "Niall is not one to be skimping his work, my lady."

Niall was not, Fiona knew, and wished, momentarily, that the stolid young keeper were less conscientious. But it was no use wishing. She rose and, an arm about Annie's shoulders, helped her into the bedroom. It took some time to get her undressed, for her pains were coming more frequently now, but at last it was accomplished and Fiona went to fetch the tea. Annie sipped at it gratefully.

"You know," she volunteered shyly, "'twill be a while yet. The doctor was saying that I'd have a long confinement. And Niall will be back—regular as clockwork, my Niall is—he'll be coming on the stroke of twelve, my lady."

"Yes," agreed Fiona, forcing an optimistic note into her voice, "I'm sure he will. All the same, I wish you'd got your telephone, Annie. Then we needn't have waited for him."

"There is a long waiting list for telephones," Annie returned. "In any case, I wasn't wanting one. Noisy things they are, forever disturbing you. 'Twas only because the doctor was saying we must get one that Niall was putting our name on the list." Her face twisted suddenly and she broke off. Fiona grasped her hand. "Is it very bad, Annie?" she inquired kindly.

Bravely, Annie denied it. She added, two bright spots of guilty colour burning now in her white cheeks: "Your ladyship is not thinking that I might have done this on purpose?"

"Well," Fiona countered, "didn't you?"

"No, my lady. I confess I'd thought of it—I wanted the bairn to be born here, dear knows, for this is my home and to be his, if God grants it. And I wanted Niall beside me, but—" her eyes met Fiona's and they were wide and quite innocent— "I'd not thought 'twould come so soon. On my solemn word, I'd not."

Fiona believed her. Even David had not expected it. But of course, it wouldn't be possible to get Annie to the hospital now. The baby would have to be born here. She looked again at her watch. It wanted another hour before Niall Frazer would arrive for his dinner. A great deal could happen in an hour and she didn't know how, in her inexperience, she could cope with it.

"Perhaps," Annie volunteered, setting down her teacup with a little click that sounded very loud in the silence of the cottage, "perhaps his new lordship may be coming up here in search of you, as he was doing the other day."

"I don't think he will," Fiona said shortly. "He has gone to Ardloch to meet the train. His fiancée is expected here, for a visit."

"That will be Miss Anson, the young lady from London?" Annie suggested. "She who was staying at the Arms a while back?" Her eyes met Fiona's again, this time with a question in them. Fiona nodded and Annie went on: "They were saying in the village that his lordship would marry her. My sister, who is a chambermaid at the Arms, was telling us of the lovely clothes she has—ball gowns and fur coats and the like. But she is a London lady, she will not be used to our ways, will she?"

"No, perhaps not at first," Fiona conceded. She made to gather up the cups but Annie caught at her hand, her eyes suddenly moist. "She will not, as you do, concern herself with the people on the estate. She would not come here to sit with me, as you have done, climbing the hill each day with the rain streaming down and yourself soaked to the skin getting here. My sister is saying that Miss Anson is not that kind of lady at all, that she is thinking only of how she looks and that she was not treating those who work at the Arms with consideration but giving them orders, as if indeed the place belonged to her already. It seems a pity, does it not, my lady, that his new lordship should choose to marry such a one as that?"

Fiona reproved her mildly, without

conviction. She rose, freeing her hand from Annie's clasp, and picked up the tray. But as she went into the kitchen to wash up, she thought, ashamed of herself for thinking it, that Annie was right. It *was* a pity. Elizabeth Anson had made the worst possible impression on her. But still, she reminded herself, running water into a bowl, her cousin John's choice of a wife was no affair of hers. Very soon Logan itself would cease to be her affair. She would be leaving it and it would no longer matter to her if Annie Frazer had her babies in this cottage or in hospital.

The water was cold and, suppressing an exclamation, she fetched the kettle and added its contents to the washing-up bowl. She had better start to boil some water now, for David would need it when the time came. And there must be a clean pan put ready, in case he wanted to boil up any instruments.

She thought about David as she busied herself with these primitive preparations, her brow anxiously furrowed and her ears alert for any sound from Annie. David was a dear and she valued his friendship enormously, but . . . she wasn't in love with him. He had again asked her to marry him last evening and she had again refused him. She wished, rather sadly, that she could fall in love with David because she hated hurting him. For his sake, anyway, it would be a good thing when she left Logan. If she were not there, he might find someone else: he was popular in the district, his patients loved him, and once or twice, during the past few weeks, Fiona had thought that Elspeth Macrae—the Factor's twenty-five-year-old daughter, who taught physics at a Glasgow girls' school—was showing a more than ordinary interest in him. Elspeth would make David a good wife, she was an exceptionally nice person.

The water boiled and a selection of pans scoured and ready, Fiona returned to Annie's bedroom. The girl, she was pleased to see, was lying quietly with her eyes closed, and she crept out again. It was twenty minutes to twelve. Perhaps after all, Niall Frazer would be here in time.

She sat down by the living-room fire, stirring its glowing peats to fresh life. Outside it was still raining, coming down in a heavy, depressing stream which beat against the windows of the dark little room. Elizabeth Anson would have installed herself in the Castle by this time, Fiona thought. Probably John would insist on introducing her to Fiona's mother.

"Oh, dear!" Fiona said aloud. Her mother liked John, but she wouldn't like Elizabeth. It was impossible to like Elizabeth—she was so self-centred, so ill-mannered and conceited, so mercenary and . . . hard. And she wasn't in love with John, Fiona was convinced of that, she was simply marrying him for the title, the money he had inherited.

Her expression hardened. Perhaps John deserved no better. He was an upstart, completely unsuited to take Alastair's place . . . and her father's. She had hated him, Fiona reflected, hated and resented him from the moment of his arrival at Logan. No, before that. She had hated him when she had first seen his face on the television screen, when he had been interviewed on the *In Town Tonight* programme . . . hated him because he looked like her brother Alastair. Which— she stifled a sigh—was the reason her mother had accepted and taken him to her

225

heart. It was odd how the likeness had affected each of them in a different way. And yet—Fiona's shapely dark brows came together—perhaps she had not been fair to her cousin John. He had once accused her of having judged and condemned him long before they had ever met, and it was true, she had. Whatever he had been like, whatever he had done, she would have hated him because he was —who he was. The heir to Logan—the last of the Logans, to whom must be given all that should have been Alastair's, all that had been hers and that, all her life, she had loved. Logan, that great proud house, the wide acres of moor and mountain, the farms, the crofts . . . the people, like little Annie Frazer whom, on such occasions as this, it was her duty to help and serve and care for because she was their mistress.

John's wife, his future wife, would—as Annie had seen—have no such conception of ownership, and John himself had little more. How could he have? He hadn't been brought up to it or trained for it, he had lived all his life in the Australian outback, working as a hired hand. And his likeness to her brother Alastair made it, for Fiona, even harder to accept him. Because of the resemblance between them, there were moments when, off her guard, she experienced a feeling of agonized tenderness for John. Seeing him cross a room towards her, facing him across the dining-table with the portraits of their ancestors looking down on them, every instinct she possessed impelled her to hold out her hand to him, to smile. Until she remembered who he was and why he was there and hate returned to fill her heart, smothering that instinctive tenderness to which, from her, he had no right.

Fiona lifted her head. Running footsteps were approaching the cottage, she heard David's voice call her name.

"I'm here, David!" She called back and moved to the door. Half-way to it, another voice, calling her urgently, brought her to a sudden halt.

It was Annie and there was no mistaking the fear and agony in her cry. "All right, Annie," she said, "I'm coming and the doctor's here."

She opened the door and saw David and her cousin John struggling up the path towards her.

It was Johnny who was the first to regain his breath. He said in a brusque, taut voice which Fiona scarcely recognized: "We're going to have to get you out of here—you and Mrs. Frazer. There's a possibility that the dam may go, you see, and . . ." Something about her expression made him break off. He looked at her in growing dismay. "Don't tell me we're too late?"

"Yes," Fiona said, "I'm rather afraid you are. But—" She turned to David, a mute question in her eyes. He braced himself, bent to pick up his bag.

"I'll go and have a look at her. Where is she?"

"I put her to bed."

The doctor's mouth compressed but he said no more, simply made for the door of the bedroom, leaving a trail of damp footmarks in his wake. Johnny called after him softly:

"Let me know how long we've got—if you can."

"If I can," the doctor promised. He vanished into the bedroom, closing the door behind him. Fiona hesitated.

"I boiled water and got everything ready

228

for him. I'd no idea about the dam, of course . . ." Her eyes searched Johnny's face. "How bad is it, John?"

"I don't know. It's cracked right across, according to Jock MacPhail. He spotted it from the Glenardie road and came to give us warning." He explained briefly what preparations he had made to deal with the crisis. "I think you ought to go down, Fiona. There's no reason for you to stay, even if—"

"Even if Annie Frazer has to—and David?" she put in quickly and shook her head. "No, John, I'll stay if they do. David will need help. I'm not a nurse but I—" she smiled faintly and there was no trace of fear in her eyes—"I can do as I'm told."

"I think you should go down," Johnny objected, but she only repeated her head-shake, not bothering to argue.

He sighed. "I'm going up to the dam now, to take a look round, see how bad it is. I think if we can get the main sluice gates open, we may be able to reduce the pressure and lower the level of water below the crack. There's a channel, isn't there, to take the overflow?"

"Yes. But it's been out of use for five years. And the gates haven't been opened since we went on to mains electricity. They'll be rusted, John—you won't be able to do it alone."

"Jock should be here soon—he's bringing tools. We'll open those gates somehow. But"—he glanced anxiously at his watch, admiring her calm courage—"I'd better get cracking. Does Frazer keep any tools up here, do you know? I want a crowbar."

"We can look," Fiona said. She led the way to a small outhouse, disregarding the rain. Johnny unearthed a worn pickaxe, but apart from this and some garden implements, there were no tools. There were, however, some sticks of dynamite, of the type used for blasting, in a corded box and, acting on impulse, he picked it up. There was no detonator, only some lengths of fuse.

He shouldered the pickaxe. "Right— you'd better get indoors, Fiona. If it *is* possible to move Mrs. Frazer, can I depend on you and Cameron to start down the hill with her at once?"

Fiona nodded. "And if it's not?"

"Send someone to tell me. And"—his eyes pleaded with her—"go down yourself. Please, Fiona. Why deliberately ask for trouble?"

She smiled at him suddenly, the lines of strain in her face smoothed out. "What are *you* doing? I don't matter much but you do—you're the last of the Logans, you know."

Johnny grinned. "That's right," he agreed, a derisive note in his voice. "I am. And a hell of a lot that matters now!"

Dr. Cameron was at the door of the cottage as they returned to it. One glance at his face was sufficient to tell Johnny all he wanted to know.

"How long?" he asked, all trace of the smile wiped abruptly from his lips.

David Cameron spread his hands. "Perhaps an hour, if we're lucky. But I don't awfully like the look of her. There may be complications. I can't tell yet."

"It's impossible to move her?"

"Nothing's impossible. It would cause her a great deal of pain, perhaps endanger her life and the child's. I'll do it if I have to, if it's the lesser danger. I'd rather not, if the dam's going to hold."

"Right. I'll go and see and—ah, here's Jock. I'll send him back to report. Come on, Jock, let's get up there."

Jock MacPhail, a crowbar and an axe under one arm, a spade under the other, nodded briefly and fell into step beside him. They were silent as they clawed their way up the steep slope, impeded by the intertwining brambles and loose stones which littered their path, the rain driving into their faces, half blinding them. Reaching the top, breathless and spent, they turned their gaze to the dam. Water was lapping against it and rain ruffled its surface, so that it was difficult to discern the extent of the crack until, standing at last by the overflow lock, they were directly above its widest part.

Jock pointed. "It's richt across, Snow. It'll not hold."

"No. But"—Johnny was on his knees, peering down—"it's high up. We only need to reduce the level by a few feet and we'll be able to get at it. And I think we've got a bit of time, it's not going just yet. How you managed to spot it from the road I don't know."

"I've good eyes. And it wasna raining. The watter was clear."

"Thank the Lord it was. Come on, let's go over to the sluice gates and see if we can open them."

Jock followed him across the flat surface of concrete. It felt unyielding enough, Johnny thought, but knew that, despite his optimistic estimate, they hadn't much time. Concrete was peculiar stuff and hundreds of smaller cracks were starting to spread out from the large one Jock had noticed. The pressure of water, ceaseless and unrelenting, must eventually complete the damage it had started. The reservoir, swollen by the heavy rain, was rising with every hour, the small overflow lock quite insufficient to reduce its level.

At the centre of the dam stood the great sluice gates, built of immensely thick, metal-reinforced timber and controlled by a winch-operated lock. Once these gates had released thousands of tons of water, concentrated in a single fall the height of the dam, which had provided electric power for the Castle and the nearby farms. The water, Jock explained breathlessly, gesturing below them, had flowed off in a channel specially constructed to take it, from which, eventually, it rejoined the Logan River at a lower level. But, after five years of disuse, the channel was overgrown, its outlines impossible to pick out in the driving rain.

Johnny looked down, trying to follow its course, cursing the rain beneath his breath. Then, with a grunt, he straightened himself and turned his attention to the winch.

It was, as Fiona had warned him it would be, heavily coated with rust, and for ten minutes, whilst he and Jock pitted all their strength against it, the lock resisted their efforts to force it open.

They faced each other, breathing hard, rivulets of sweat joining the rivulets of rain already coursing down their cheeks.

"It needs more of us, Snow," Jock said at last, despairingly. "Will I go down and fetch some more of the men?"

Johnny shook his head. "They're on their way, they'll be coming as fast as they can—Macrae will see to that." He dropped once more on to his knees, gazing intently down at the flat surface of the gates. "You know," he said, after a careful scrutiny, "I believe it'd be possible to smash open those gates from below if the winch won't shift them. I reckon I could do it."

"Ye'd need dynamite to make ony impression," Jock objected.

"I've got a dozen sticks of dynamite. Frazer had them in his toolshed. I could use each as a double charge."

"Oh, aye, he had them for blasting rabbit burrows." Jock still sounded doubtful. "How would you get doon tae fix them?"

"On a rope. There's one in the toolshed —I saw it."

"Well, maybe ye could do it like that. But what way would ye get back? There'd no' be time tae haul you up, would there? Yon gates will go fast, when they go, wi' that pressure behind them. And you'd need—"

"There's a ledge," Johnny pointed out, "look—down there at the level of the lower edge of the gates."

Jock peered with him. "It's ower wee tae tak' a man's feet," he said flatly, "and him leaping for it. And 'tis overgrown wi' moss, as slippery as ice. Ye'd not make it, Snow. Let's try the winch again. The damned thing ought to work!"

They renewed their efforts, but still the rusted metal defied them. Johnny worked stripped to the waist, straining until his muscles ached mercilessly. If they couldn't get the sluice open, he thought desperately, then he would have to send Jock down to tell David Cameron that he must carry his patient down to safety. And Fiona must be made to go . . .

"Your lordship—Lord Logan!" Someone, Johnny realized, was hailing him from below. He let the crowbar he was wielding slip from his raw and blistered hands.

"Who's that?" He crouched down, could just make out the figure of a short, broadshouldered man in a sodden raincape, standing at the foot of the dam.

"It's Frazer, sir—my lord. Dr. Cameron sent me to tell you that Annie—my wife—she's in a bad way. He's thinking—my lord, he's thinking that it would be dangerous if we tried to move her now. I don't know, he hasn't said, but I am fearing it is a haemorrhage she has."

"I see." Johnny stood up. He reached

his decision then, knew that it was the only thing to be done, for he dared not hazard a guess as to how long the dam would continue to hold. It might be hours but it might, equally, be minutes. And because Mrs. Frazer couldn't be moved, Fiona and David Cameron would stay with her. The winch was useless, its cable rusted and suspect. They could wait no longer, it was a waste of time struggling with it now. "Frazer," he shouted, "go and get the rope from your toolshed and bring it up to us here. As fast as you know how, man—we've got to get these sluice gates open! Hurry—or we may be forced to move your wife."

Frazer needed no second bidding. Jock said, as he disappeared from sight: "You're no' going doon there, Snow. If anybody goes, let me."

Johnny didn't answer him. He picked up his crowbar and inserted it again into the winch. With a dull crack the worn-out cable parted and with it went their last hope of operating the lock from above. He and Jock looked at each other.

"If we'd got it to move, yon cable would have parted."

"I reckon it would, Jock. I was afraid of that from the start."

"Ye'll let me gang doon on the rope?" Jock pleaded. "I'm smaller than you, I'd have mair chance of getting ma feet on yon ledge."

This time, Johnny shook his head. "No, Jock. I know how to handle dynamite—you don't. And besides, this is *my* responsibility." He smiled as he said it, recalling Elizabeth's words, her accusations, and wondered, fleetingly, whether *she* would have stayed with Annie Frazer, as his cousin Fiona had so unhesitatingly decided to do, a little while ago. It was strange, he thought, how swiftly disillusionment had come, how quickly and easily he had fallen out of love with Elizabeth. Or perhaps the truth was that he had never really been in love with her . . .

He cut short Jock's protests. "We'd better have a look at our blasting equipment," he said, "and get everything ready. And we need something to anchor the rope to—come on, Frazer will be back before we've got ourselves organized."

Jock flashed him a sidelong glance. "You've changed, Snow, since Korea.

There was a time when you used tae let me tell *you* what tae do."

"Was there?"

"Aye, there was that. I'd a stripe mair than you had. But now—" Product of a Glasgow slum, he was puzzled.

Johnny scarcely heard him, his hands busy with a length of fuse. How to keep it dry was the problem. Jock went on: "Now you're the Earl of Logan and this"—he waved a wet and grimy hand in a comprehensive gesture—"is yours. All of it your responsibility. And by gosh, Snow, you're man enough tae tak' it!"

"Thanks," Johnny said briefly. "I hope you're right."

They didn't speak again until Frazer joined them. He had three other men with him, sent by the Factor ahead of his party. One of these, a stonemason, after a careful inspection of the cracked concrete, gave his opinion that the dam might last another hour—two at the outside. Johnny stationed him as look-out, with orders to give instant warning should the danger of collapse appear to be imminent. He kept Jock and another man with him, sending Frazer and the third back to the cottage, so that—if the warning came—they might evacuate it at once. The farm, the mason told him, was already being evacuated, and Captain Macrae was not far behind with the rest of the men. Johnny left orders for them to start on clearing the stream-bed beneath the dam as soon as they arrived.

He looped the rope about his chest, donning his jacket again, and then waited impatiently for Jock and his companion to take up their positions. Since both would be above him and unable to see what he was doing without slackening their hold on the rope, they arranged a system of signals. Two sharp tugs would mean that they were to stop lowering, three that they were to continue and a single tug would indicate that his task had been completed.

He decided to set his charges in one side of the sluice gates only, depending on the pressure of water to complete the damage he had wrought. Normally the gates were raised, the water escaping underneath them, but he knew that his best chance of shifting them would be if he could blow one side away from its concrete bed.

As, at last, he was lowered slowly over the edge, he saw that rust had also attacked the metal reinforcements of the massive gates, and his hopes rose, only to fall again as he struck the first blow with his pick. The gates might be rusted and worn, but, unlike the winch, they were still solid and good for many more years of wear. His blow, delivered awkwardly owing to the fact that his body was swaying pendulum-like at the end of the rope, made not the smallest impression on the heavy metal. He tugged twice and gasped as the rope cut into him. Then, swaying close to the face of the gate, he managed to steady himself, bracing his feet against it. The next blow, on timber, had more effect, but the third all but splintered the wooden handle of his pickaxe. It was like attacking a steel-sided battleship with a tin-opener, he thought grimly, and went on attacking it with savage obstinacy.

He was exhausted long before he had hacked a space deep enough to take the first charge and, when he had inserted it, he clung to his rope, fighting for breath and staring incredulously at the shattered woodwork, amazed that, after all, it should have yielded to his puny and despairing efforts. The rain had ceased momentarily, he realized, which was all to the good. He lit the end of the dangling fuse. It spluttered and went out, so that he was forced to waste precious seconds lighting it again, struggling to keep his balance, the pick impeding him and slapping against his legs.

The next two charges were inserted with less difficulty than the first, for he was learning by experience how to work with his primitive equipment, and the concrete in which the gate was embedded was chipped in places and proved less of an obstacle than the thick, seasoned timber of the gate itself.

There remained three more charges. Johnny bit his lip, tasting blood as his teeth sank into it. He knew that it would be a miracle if the fuses stayed alight: he had had to attach long fuses to the first three charges, to give himself time to set the others and—he had had to guess at the time each would take to burn through. His experience with dynamite had been when detonating it electrically, which was practically foolproof, and this decidedly wasn't. But there was nothing he could do except trust to luck and pray that the rain would hold off for just a little longer. Wearily, a red mist floating in front of his eyes, he gave the prearranged three tugs on the rope and again was lowered a few feet.

He was preparing to insert his last charge of dynamite at the foot of the gate when a muffled roar told him that the first had exploded. The effect was disappointing, for, glancing up, he saw that only a small trickle of water was seeping through the aperture he had created. None of the other charges had gone off yet, and the rain, he realized despairingly, had begun again and might extinguish the fuses. It was hopeless, he had failed. With angry bitterness, Johnny struck again and again at the tough, unyielding surface of the gate. With the final blow, he felt rather than saw the handle of his pick split for almost its entire length and knew that he could do no more. He let the pick fall from his numb grasp, heard it fall with a dull thud on the ground below him.

Then there was a second explosion, a third and a fourth coming immediately after it, the noise all but shattering his eardrums, and a shower of debris came hurtling down on to his head. But that was all, there was no water and the echoes died into silence. Johnny tugged hard on the rope. It didn't move, and a moment later he heard Jock hail him and looked up to see his face peering anxiously down. He held up the last charge, too spent and dispirited to speak.

"Snow—on tae the ledge, man, for God's sake! Ye've done it—the gate's going! Jump clear, Snow—jump, we'll keep a hold on ye . . ."

Johnny stared up at him helplessly. Jock, he realized dimly, must be shouting to him at the pitch of his lungs, but he couldn't hear a thing and Jock's gestures made no sense to him either, he was too exhausted, his brain too weary to take anything in. Something was going but he didn't know what. The sluice gates or . . . from Jock's agitation, it might be the dam. Oh, God, not the dam! Surely not the dam . . . and yet it couldn't be these gates, on which he had been battering vainly for what seemed an eternity.

A fifth explosion, nearer and much louder than the previous ones, sent him reeling. Where should he go—Jock was gesticulating wildly downwards. Johnny looked down and shuddered. The sheer drop of the old waterfall lay just beneath him, dry now and grown over, in places, by moss, vanishing into a thick clump of brambles where once there had been a man-made stream. The stream into which, if only his desperate plan had succeeded, the great mass of water beating on the faulty wall of the dam might, perhaps, have been safely diverted.

"Snow—Snow—jump, man . . . the ledge . . ."

Jock's voice reached him now, the rope about his shoulders tightened and he was being hauled across the flat expanse of the sluice gates. Johnny felt a splash of water on his upturned face. The rain, he thought, it was the rain. But did rain ever descend in a solid lump like that? He turned his gaze upwards but could see nothing. Even Jock's white, worried face had vanished now. So it must be the dam. He had failed. The dam was going, the cottage would be overwhelmed, swallowed up in a welter of leaping flood water, and Mrs. Frazer and her baby, David Cameron and Fiona were there—they were in the cottage, trusting him, depending on him to save them.

And he hadn't. It had been his responsibility—his because he was the Earl of Logan—the first responsibility he had taken and he had failed.

His cousin Fiona would be drowned. She had stayed because she had trusted him and he had let this terrible thing happen to her. She had been right, Johnny thought bitterly, to despise him. He had let her stay, when he ought to have insisted on her going. And there was the Frazers' baby, a new life, so swiftly and horribly to be taken away, because he had failed to avert the disaster that threatened it. "*Oh, God*"—his lips moved, in a silent and despairing prayer—"*keep them safe. Save them, this mustn't happen, not to Fiona, not to that baby, please God . . .*"

A great wall of water struck him. The rope parted, he felt the crack as it broke and then he was falling, falling into blackness, into oblivion, head over heels, his limbs flailing wildly against the empty air.

As he fell, the sluice gates opened, the water was released, the shattered gates crumbling like matchwood. Just for an instant in his headlong fall, Johnny glimpsed this and knew in that instant that he had not failed, that disaster had, by a miracle, been averted.

Then his body hit the ground and all the breath was driven from it. Blackness closed about him and he remembered nothing more.

Above, bare-headed in the rain, Jock MacPhail stood with the broken rope in his hand. The man beside him pointed downwards. He said hoarsely: "Yonder, Jock—in those brambles. They've broken his fall and he's clear of the water."

Both men raced to the end of the dam and flung themselves down the steep, overgrown slope.

12

FIONA felt very tired, but as David put the tiny, fragile creature that was Annie's baby son into her arms, her weariness vanished and she looked down into the pink, contorted little face with a strange, yearning tenderness that surprised even herself. He was so very small and frail and perfect, with the faint cloud of fluffy down on his head and his big, wondering eyes, opened now to a world into which his arrival had been so dangerously ill-timed.

He was crying lustily as she carried him into the living-room and, at the sound of his cries, his father came from his tense vigil by the door to stand looking down at him, his expression a mixture of apprehension and pride.

"Take him, Niall," Fiona invited gently, "he's yours."

The young keeper hesitated. "His lordship said for me to keep watch, my lady, in case Willy Macfarlane should be signalling us from the dam."

Fiona smiled, holding the baby close to her.

"Only for a moment, then. I'll take your place at the door."

"Oh, thank you, my lady." Niall Frazer's eager arms were extended and very carefully Fiona put the baby into them. She left them together and crossed to the door. Standing there, she could just discern Willy Macfarlane, shoulders hunched against the driving rain, silhouetted against the skyline on top of the dam. He was staring intently to his left but he made no sign and she waited, watching him. The dam, it seemed, was holding, but as yet there was no water coming through the sluice gates, and so the danger that had been threatening them all this time still remained, perhaps now more serious than before. Fiona let out her breath in a deep sigh. Until this moment, she hadn't consciously thought of it, she had been too busy helping David fight for Annie's life and that of the child which Niall was now holding.

It had been a difficult birth but it was

over now, and Annie, David had said, was safe: they could move her, if it should be necessary, and Fiona had given this news to Niall ten minutes ago, so that he could take the cottage gate off its hinges and cover it with coats and blankets, to be ready if the signal came. The improvised stretcher lay on the floor behind her, and, as she strained her eyes in the direction of the dam, Fiona wondered if they would have to use it or not . . . whether, if the signal came, it would come in time for them to carry Annie and her child to safety.

Hearing a murmur from Niall, she left her post and took the baby from him. "I'll put him in his cot, shall I? It's all ready for him."

"Aye." Niall's grave young face was lit by a smile. "He's a fine pair of lungs on him, has he not?"

"He has indeed." Fiona tucked the shawl about the baby, laid him in his cot by the fire and, gradually, the frantic cries faded into silence and the shell-pink eye-lids drooped.

"Annie's still doing well, my lady?" Niall asked, anxiety returning.

Fiona nodded. "So the doctor says." She explained, as simply as she could, the condition which had given rise to David's alarm, not fully understanding it herself. It was the first time in her life that she had seen a baby born and the shock of it still lingered. Looking down at the sleeping baby, she said: "He's lovely, isn't he? What will you call him, Niall?"

"We'd not thought, my lady. At least we . . ." Niall's voice trailed off and he stiffened. "My lady—" His tone was urgent.

"What is it?" Fiona came to stand in the doorway with him. "It's not the signal?"

"No." He gestured. "Up yonder, in front of the sluice gates. Do you see anything, my lady?"

Fiona looked. The rain made visibility poor but, against the dark and massive bulk of the sluice gates, she could make out something moving. "It's a man," she said at last, "a—a man at the end of a rope."

"'Tis his lordship," Niall supplied. He tensed as a faint, muffled explosion reached them, followed by several others. Fiona counted four. She stared at Niall in shocked surprise. "His lordship?" she echoed. "But how do you know—you can't possibly see who it is from here. And what is he doing there? What were those explosions?"

"His lordship was going down as I left him, my lady. To try and blow up the gates. He's been there this half-hour and more and he's done it. Look"—he pointed again, his big hand not quite steady—"do you see, there's water—water coming through! He's done it, my lady, he has the gates open, I am sure, for there was no water there before."

Icy fingers of fear came to clutch at Fiona's heart.

"But he's still there, in front of the gates —he'll be trapped! Oh, why don't they pull him up, why don't they warn him?" Her voice was brittle with strain and she dashed through the open doorway, Niall pounding at her heels.

From all directions, men were running —from the top of the dam itself, from the stream-bed, where a dozen of them had just started working, from the cottage garden.

Fiona cried out in agony: "John—John,

look out! The gates are opening. You must . . . get . . . out . . . of . . . the way!"

The wind, swirling rain into her face, took her words and flung them soundlessly away. She knew that John could not possibly hear her from that distance, but, powerless to resist the urge to reach him, she called again, until horror gripped her throat, strangling her cries.

At her back, Niall emitted a sobbing gasp. Even as they watched, the great sluice gates crumpled up under the weight of water behind them, as if they were toys crushed by the toe of a giant, and the swaying figure at the rope's end, caught by the first wave, was swept aside. The rope broke and it fell sickeningly downwards.

Fiona paused in her headlong dash, covering her face with her two trembling hands. She could not watch, could not be a witness to this terrible end to a gallant deed. Her cousin John, whom she had hated and despised, whose coming she had so bitterly resented, had saved all their lives. But at what a sacrifice, for it must have cost him his own. It must have—for no one could fall from that height and live. It was impossible.

Was there, she wondered dully, a curse on the house of Logan? First her father and her brothers and now . . . John. John was the last of the Logans, he . . .

Niall's hand closed gently about her arm.

"My lady—"

Fiona made an effort to answer him but her voice was a stricken whisper. "What . . . is it, Niall?"

He urged her forward. "The brambles at the foot of the dam—they've caught and held him, my lady. We must get to him."

Fiona withdrew her hands, forced herself to look in the direction in which Niall was pointing. The long habit of control and self-discipline restored to her a measure of calm. She saw that John lay, as the young keeper had told her, on a clump of trailing brambles. He lay ominously still, but at least the thick, knotted undergrowth had to some extent broken his fall. There might be a chance that he had escaped serious injury—a faint chance but . . . a chance.

She ran to where her cousin lay and Niall said, as they reached the edge of the bushes: "Let me go, my lady—the bushes are thick and will tear your hands. Wait here, will you not? There are others coming."

Fiona shook her head. It was true that there were men coming, but they were still quite a long way away, the nearest Jock MacPhail, still in his sodden, mudstained postman's uniform, who was running, with a reckless disregard for his own safety, down the slope towards them, his face chalk-white.

Fiona signed to him to slow down. She turned to Niall.

"If you could lift me, Niall, I think I could reach him."

"He may be badly hurt, my lady," Niall warned her, but, obediently, he stooped to lift her in his arms.

The brambles tore at her, but Fiona, intent on the work of rescue, was scarcely aware of them. She reached the still, motionless form of her cousin at last and, very gently, lifted his head. He looked, she thought with a pang, very young and strangely, heartbreakingly vulnerable and so like her brother Alastair, in that moment, that a sob tore at her throat and she found herself looking at his face through a mist of tears.

But—he was alive. Her fingers, feeling for it apprehensively, found a pulse which beat strongly under them.

And then Niall was beside her, putting out thorn-scratched hands to relieve her of her burden.

"Let me, my lady—I can lift him."

"Careful," Fiona begged, "he may have broken bones."

"I'll take care, my lady."

"Wait—" It was Jock MacPhail, breathless and gasping, and Fiona struggled out of his way, relinquishing her place to him. Together he and Niall, tender as women, lifted their unconscious burden out of the undergrowth and laid it carefully on the ground. They were kneeling beside him when the other men arrived.

"I'll away and get the doctor," Niall offered. "And the stretcher we had prepared for Annie."

The men made way for him; two, after a low-voiced conference, hurried after him. The others waited, standing in a small, hushed group, their faces concerned. In the silence, the sound of water rushing in a headlong stream down the face of the dam seemed very loud.

Fiona heard it and looked up. "What about the dam?" she asked. "Is it safe now?"

A chorus of voices answered her. "Aye, my lady, 'tis safe enough now."

The head forester added: "Captain Macrae is up there and will have a gang already at work."

"Won't he need you?"

"I was to clear the stream-bed, my lady. 'Tis done. What we were not able to do, the water has done for itself—it is running away now, thousands of gallons a minute. His lordship knew what he was about, opening the big gates." The forester's tone was admiring and a little awed. "God grant no serious harm shall have come to him, for 'twas a fine brave thing that he did."

Fiona silently echoed his pious wish. She bent again over her cousin John. He *was* alive. In the first flush of relief at finding him to be alive, she hadn't thought beyond the fact that he was, hadn't dared to imagine what injuries he might have sustained, apart from broken limbs.

His face, she saw, was frighteningly pale

and his lips had a bluish tinge that worried her. Several of the men had taken off their coats to put over him and she could see no more than his face, lacerated by the brambles, white and shuttered and remote. Its boyishness moved her deeply, brought tears to ache again in her throat. She had been so unjust to him, so cruel, and he hadn't deserved that of her. He had done his best: it was not his fault, heaven knew, that a strange, unwitting fate had sent him here. As well blame him for her father's death . . . or Alastair's or Hamish's. He had come, because he had felt it his duty to come—not, as he had told her very soon after his arrival, because he wanted to take from either her mother or herself the things that belonged to them.

It was not even his fault that he looked like her brother Alastair. And today he had behaved as Alastair might have behaved—perhaps even better, more decisively than Alastair would have done. He had risked his life without the smallest hesitation: he had known what had to be done and he had done it.

Crouched there, with her cousin John's limp hand clasped between her own, Fiona reproached herself bitterly. Behind her, as background to her agonized thoughts, Jock MacPhail, who was a postman and her cousin's friend, told the men grouped about him the story of what had happened.

"He wouldna let me go, he wouldna hear of it. 'Nay, Jock,' he said, ''tis my responsibility, I'll gang ma'sel'.' And gang he did, I'm telling ye . . . gang he did . . ." The strong Glasgow accent sounded odd against the low, soft murmur of the Highland voices of the Logan men, but Fiona listened, until she felt that every word Jock MacPhail said was written on her heart.

She wished, feeling again for the pulse at John's wrist, that David would hurry. Surely, by this time, he would be able to leave Annie Frazer's bedside? Didn't he realize the urgency? Hadn't Niall told him how badly John might be hurt?

The murmur of voices faded, the men moved.

The head forester said: "'Tis the doctor, my lady. He's on his way up and Niall with the stretcher beside him."

At last, Fiona thought, at last David had come and they would know. She made to rise to her feet, but the hand she was holding seized hers suddenly in a strong clasp and looking down, startled, she saw that her cousin John had opened his eyes, was regarding her with a hint of mockery.

"*You*, Fiona—you're holding my hand?" His voice was weak but she heard him.

"Yes," she admitted, colouring faintly, "I was, I—"

"I thought you hated the sight of me," he said wonderingly.

"I don't, John. I'm sorry if you—if you thought I did."

"Well—didn't you, once? Don't tell me you've changed your mind about me!"

"Yes, I have, John." Fiona's colour deepened. "I'm afraid I misjudged you. I —I am very sorry. I regret it with all my heart." She took a deep, painful breath. "How do you feel?" she asked gently.

"Feel? *Me?* Oh, I'm fine—why wouldn't I be?" He attempted to sit up but Fiona prevented him. "Lie still, John —David Cameron's just coming and he's got a stretcher with him—we'll get you to the cottage in a minute or two."

"But what's wrong with me, for crying

out loud? I feel fine, I don't need David Cameron or his stretcher—I can walk."
He was openly bewildered, at a loss to understand her.

"You had a fall," Fiona told him. "You fell from the dam."

"The dam?" Memory returned, flickered in his eyes and with it alarm. "Oh, gosh, yes, the dam. Fiona"—his fingers tightened about hers urgently—"is it all right? Is it holding?"

She reassured him. "You blew open the sluice gates, John—you risked your life to get them open."

Johnny brushed that aside. "But the dam itself," he wanted to know, "are they working on it?"

"Yes. Keith Macrae is up there now. You needn't worry. You did what had to be done."

"What about Mrs. Frazer?"

"Oh"—a smile lit Fiona's tired, rain-wet face—"she has a son. A lovely little son, with big blue eyes and golden down for hair. Just wait till you see him."

"You sound as proud of him as if he were your own, Fiona." He was speaking quite normally now, Fiona realized, and her spirits lifted.

"I *am* nearly as proud of him as if he were my own. After all, he's the first baby I've ever helped to bring into the world." She broke off as David reached them and touched her arm. "Oh, David," she said, in a low voice, shaken with the intensity of her relief at having such good tidings to give him. "I don't believe John's badly hurt at all. It's a miracle, but I don't believe he is."

"We'll have a look at him," David said, setting down his bag and drawing back some of the coats covering his patient. "Now, then, Lord Logan, we'll see if you've broken any bones first, shall we? Does this pain you? No? And this . . ."

His examination was brisk but thorough and when he rose to his feet, he was smiling.

"Bruises, lacerations and a sprained left wrist. I can't find anything else. You'll be pretty stiff for the next few days but it'll wear off. Your hands are a bit knocked about—I'll dress them when we get back to the cottage. After that, there's no reason why we shouldn't let you go back to the

Castle. I imagine Miss Anson will be worried about you and you'll want to set her mind at rest as soon as you can."

"Elizabeth?" Johnny sat up. His eyes met Fiona's unexpectedly. "Elizabeth is leaving Logan—this evening, by the seven o'clock train. We broke off our engagement by—by mutual consent this morning."

Fiona stared at him in wide-eyed, helpless astonishment. And then, for some inexplicable reason, her heart began to quicken its beat.

Johnny added, turning now to David Cameron: "Look, Doc, I'd be awfully grateful if you could patch me up by Monday. There's a friend of mine arriving from Australia and I'd like to go down to London to meet her. Pip," he went on, to Fiona, "Pip Gilliat. Perhaps you remember my telling you about her?"

"Yes," Fiona answered, after an almost imperceptible hesitation, "I remember your telling me about Pip, John. I remember perfectly."

She turned her head away from him, shocked and bewildered to feel tears burning at her eyes.

David motioned to the men to bring the stretcher, ignoring Johnny's protests. Fiona's tears had gone by the time they started on their way back to the cottage.

13

THE atmosphere at Logan Castle seemed to change, so far as Johnny was concerned, from the moment when—stiff and bruised but disdaining David Cameron's proffered arm—he limped into the great hall a little over two hours later.

Jamieson greeted him with new deference. He was an excellent and well-trained servant who had never given any sign of resentment in the past, yet Johnny had sensed it beneath the smooth correctness of his manner, had guessed that, for Jamieson, to accord him the title he had given to his old master went against the grain.

Now, he supposed—as Jamieson hurried forward with solicitous offers of whisky and suggestions that he might wish to retire immediately to bed—rumour had, as always, exaggerated. No doubt a very garbled account of the happenings at the dam and his own part in them had filtered down to the Castle, carried perhaps by the volunteer helpers from the village on their way home. He could not believe that Fiona, who had preceded David and himself, would have said anything calculated to make him the object of hero-worship by the dignified butler, and, his tone brusque and matter-of-fact, he refused both the whisky and the suggestion of retiring.

"I'm perfectly all right, Jamieson, thanks. There's nothing wrong with me that a hot bath and a change of clothes won't put right. But I can't speak for Dr. Cameron—" He looked at David inquiringly.

The doctor grinned. "I'd not refuse a dram," he confessed. "And then I'll have to be making tracks—I've still three calls and a surgery to do, plus anything else that may have come in during my absence."

"Won't you let us offer you a bath and a change of clothes before you go?"

David shook his head. "I'm comparatively dry, you know—my job being mostly an indoor one. And I honestly haven't time, thank you all the same—I want to pop into the hospital before surgery starts, just to make sure that Annie Frazer and her bairn have stood the journey down without any ill effects." He smiled again, holding out his hand and lightly touching Johnny's bandaged one. "But I'd prescribe the hot bath for you, Lord Logan, just as soon as you can get into it. We don't want to have the hero of the hour falling victim to a dose of pneumonia, do we?"

Johnny reddened. "Look," he pleaded, "come off it, Doc, please! Even in jest I don't want that sort of label. I'm no hero. All I've done is wreck a perfectly good pair of sluice gates which are going to cost the estate a small fortune to replace."

David's laugh was friendly. "You'll have a hell of a job convincing the people here that the label isn't merited. And, you know—however little you may like it—it's not a bad thing to have that label. They were doubtful about you to begin with and —how can I put it? Mistrustful, because you were a stranger and they didn't know what they could expect from you. Now they know. You've won their respect and—" Jamieson brought him his dram and he took it, raising the glass in salute

—"and mine, if you'll allow me to say so. It was a damned fine effort, Lord Logan. I couldn't have done it myself, I tell you straight."

"Oh, for crying out loud, Doc, of course you could!" Johnny was deeply embarrassed by the unexpected turn their conversation had taken. The doctor drained his whisky and set down the glass.

"No," he said flatly, "I couldn't. You ask Fiona."

"Fiona?" Johnny was puzzled. "Why Fiona?"

"I'm talking out of turn," David evaded. "It's drinking whisky on an empty stomach! But . . . *in vino veritas*. I've wasted two years of my life trying to make Fiona fall in love with me. I finally realized this afternoon that it was hopeless. Make what you like of that, John Chisholm! And now it's high time I got back to my neglected practice. As your current medical adviser, I can't urge you too strongly to go and take that bath at once and get into some dry clothes—but I'd avoid drinking anything stronger than tea if you insist on not going to bed—where you ought to be if you'd heed my advice.

You may think you're a hundred per cent, but, let me tell you, you'd the very devil of a narrow escape and you're still suffering from shock. Take it easy for a few days. I'll be along tomorrow to have a look at your hands. Good evening to you, Lord Logan."

He was gone before Johnny could collect his scattered wits sufficiently to think of a reply. But he reflected, as he climbed slowly up the long, curving staircase to his room, David Cameron was one of the most likeable men he had ever met in his life. It was strange that Fiona hadn't fallen in love with him and, perhaps, stranger still that David should have told him she hadn't . . .

But he was too tired to try and puzzle it all out now. There was still Elizabeth to be faced, he reminded himself ruefully: common courtesy demanded that he bid her farewell, since she was still his guest. And he ought also to spend a few minutes with Cousin Catherine, who might be in need of reassurance—though probably Fiona would, by this time, have told her that all was well.

He went into the bathroom and turned

on the hot tap. Then, wearily, his fingers awkward because of the dressings that David Cameron had insisted on applying to them, Johnny stripped off his sodden, mud-encrusted clothes and relaxed with a deep sigh of exhaustion in the steaming water. He wondered, as he lay there blissfully, where Elizabeth was and how she had filled in her time since he had left her, with scant ceremony, more than four hours ago, and then, because it required too much effort to think, he closed his eyes and forgot about Elizabeth. It was as if already she had gone out of his life, and he was again conscious of surprise that her going should occasion him so little regret. So much less regret than David had shown at the loss of Fiona . . . but then . . . Johnny sat up, shocked into wakefulness. To lose Fiona would be to break a man's heart: to love her, unendurable agony if that love were unrequited, because Fiona was . . . Fiona.

Johnny drew a long, startled breath, remembering how Fiona had knelt at his side a little while ago, bare-headed in the rain, his hand clasped in hers and—had there not been tears in her eyes, tenderness as well as concern in her smile? He had imagined himself to be dreaming, he hadn't been able to believe what he saw, because it was so incredible that Fiona should weep for him. Until that moment he had been convinced that she hated him, that whether he lived or died was a matter of supreme indifference to her. Had she not, a dozen times since his coming to Logan, lashed him with her scorn, rejected contemptuously his clumsy attempts to help her, his well-intentioned overtures of friendship?

And yet it had mattered to her that he was hurt. She had minded, she had been moved, she had wept for him! She had even admitted, when he had taxed her with it, to having misjudged him. Why? Because he had risked his neck in a foolhardy, desperate gamble to save the dam? He had been aware at the time that it was a gamble but he hadn't consciously risked his neck, hadn't really thought about that side of it at all. His one thought had been that the dam was his responsibility and that there wasn't anything else to do but what he had done. There had been so little time, and with Annie Frazer helplessly trapped in the cottage, he had really had very little choice. And, after it was done, he had been worrying over the cost to the estate of repairing the gates he had destroyed, obsessed by the fear that Menzies would reproach him for his impulsiveness! He laughed, recognizing the grim irony of this. Had he bought Fiona's respect, as well as Jamieson's deference, at the expense of a pair of outworn sluice gates, some bruises and a sprained wrist? Surely Fiona was not the sort of girl to be impressed by a display of what really only amounted to physical strength, coupled with the knowledge—acquired in his outback days—of how to handle dynamite?

Johnny got out of the now cooling water and started gingerly to towel his bruised and battered body. The soaking had taken some of the pain from his muscles but it had brought out the bruises and induced in him an almost overpowering desire for sleep. He knew that it was no use trying to work out the answers to the questions he had asked himself whilst his brain refused to function and his head felt as if it were filled with cottonwool.

And besides, there was Elizabeth. He *had* to say goodbye to Elizabeth, it was the least he could do.

The towel wrapped round him, he returned to his dressing-room. Jamieson had laid out dry clothes for him and—having evidently ignored Dr. Cameron's parting injunction—had also placed a decanter of whisky, together with soda and a glass, on the dressing-table where it couldn't possibly escape his notice. Johnny smiled. He needed some Dutch courage before meeting Elizabeth, he decided. Pouring out three fingers of whisky, he gulped it down neat, making a wry grimace at the taste.

But the spirit warmed him and drove the muzziness from his head. He drank a second tot. Feeling a great deal better, if a trifle light-headed, he dressed and went in search of Elizabeth.

The gong boomed a muffled summons as he descended to the hall and Jamieson told him, still very deferentially, that he had served tea in the morning-room. Taking it for granted that Elizabeth would be there, Johnny crossed the hall to the small, pleasant room which Fiona used when she was alone. He hesitated at the door, wondering uneasily what he could say, but, to his surprise, when he pushed open the door, it was to see—not Elizabeth—but Fiona waiting for him.

"Oh, John, you're down. How do you feel?" Her tone was warm and completely devoid of hostility, but she avoided his gaze and he was again conscious of a change in her manner towards him as he moved to join her. She seemed, in some curious way, to be holding herself aloof as if—his brows furrowed—as if she were already regretting her emotion of a few hours ago.

"I'm feeling fine." He paused, his hand on the back of her chair. "Where's Elizabeth, do you know?"

She looked at him then. "She left. I ordered a car for her before you came back and Jamieson rang up Ardloch Station to reserve a sleeper. She left this for you." Fiona offered him a sealed envelope, which she had propped up against his cup. Johnny took it, puzzled but aware of a certain relief, thrust it, unread, into his pocket and sat down.

"The train doesn't go till seven. I wonder why she decided to leave?"

"I gathered," Fiona returned, without expression, "that she did not want to see you again in such . . . painful circumstances."

"Oh." There was nothing else to say.

"She seemed very upset."

"You . . . talked to her?"

"Well . . ." Fiona hesitated. "*She* talked to me. She told me a number of things about you that I didn't know."

Johnny could read nothing from her face, which was unsmiling, even grave, but expressive of neither approval nor disapproval. He wished that he knew what she was thinking and what Elizabeth had said to her but, as he opened his mouth to ask her this, she smiled at him. "Here's your tea. And do eat something, you must be starving. You've had nothing since breakfast."

"No." He supposed he hadn't, but it was a matter of no importance and he wasn't hungry. An appalling thought struck him—had Elizabeth told his cousin about the marriage settlement, what he proposed to do? Oh, surely, surely not—

however angry and bitter she might have felt about him, surely she would never tell Fiona that? He looked at her miserably.

"Fiona—"

"Yes, John?"

"What did Elizabeth tell you?"

Fiona set down her cup. It was empty but she didn't refill it. "I wish you'd eat something. Look, there are sandwiches—I ordered them for you, I thought you'd be hungry."

"I'm not. Fiona, I want to know. Please tell me."

"She told me why you'd broken off your engagement," Fiona said quietly. Her cheeks were a little flushed.

Johnny, his cup half-way to his mouth, lowered it, to gaze at her in shocked and open dismay.

"She told you . . . *that?*" He could hardly get the words out. The worst had happened, he thought—Fiona knew—Elizabeth had told her, he could only presume in a spiteful attempt to revenge herself on him. Even from Elizabeth, he hadn't expected this: he was no longer surprised that she had left without waiting to bid him farewell. In view of her betrayal of his carefully guarded secret, she had been afraid to stay and face him. And now, of course, the harm was done. Fiona would reject his offer, would see it—as she had seen all his previous offers—as an insult to her pride, as charity. He had meant to give her mother the signed deeds, without saying a word about his intentions until he had carried them out, so that it would be too late for argument or refusal, too late for anything save acceptance.

He made a great effort to control his voice, aware that his cousin was watching him, waiting for him to speak:

"I'm sorry she told you," he managed at last and saw Fiona's shapely dark brows lift in surprise. And then her face receded, disappeared into a wavering mist, and then appeared again. His head went muzzy. It was the whisky, he thought, cursing himself for having taken it. As Fiona had reminded him, he hadn't eaten since breakfast, he was an idiot to have drunk so much of the stuff when he wasn't accustomed to it. He made a second attempt to drink some of his tea, hoping it might steady him, but his hand shook and he was forced to put the cup down again, spilling some of its contents in the saucer.

"Fiona—"

"Yes, John." Her voice seemed to be coming from a long way away and there was a note of anxiety in it. "John, you're all right, aren't you?"

"I'm perfectly all right," he insisted stubbornly, his words a little slurred and sounding rather faint, even to his own ears. He wished his head would clear when he needed so desperately to concentrate. Fiona's reaction—or what he could make out of it—bewildered him. She wasn't angry or up in arms against him, as he had expected her to be. Either she was exercising iron self-control or . . . she wasn't angry. He was again conscious of her aloofness, though, could almost feel the new barrier which she had set up between them, a sort of impersonal, protective armour that hid her feelings from him as completely as if they were strangers, meeting now for the first time.

He swallowed hard. "Fiona, you aren't angry about it, you don't mind?"

"Angry?" Her tone was mystified. "No, why should I be angry? It's your life, you must do what you want to do with it. Your . . . future plans are no concern of mine, I—"

"But your mother? Do you think she will approve?"

"Why not—if you tell her about it, ask her yourself? She would like you to tell her, I think."

"Oh, well then, I will, if you say so, if you think I should." He paused, trying to search out her face from the mists which surrounded it, so much at a loss that he scarcely knew what to say. That Fiona should take this so calmly was the very last thing he had anticipated. "I want your mother to stay on here," he said awkwardly, "I want that more than I can begin to tell you, Fiona. I want you to stay too. It—it means a lot to me that you should."

"Then we will," Fiona assured him. "Until you get married."

"But I'm not going to get married," Johnny protested indignantly. "My engagement to Elizabeth is broken off. I thought you understood that, I thought you said she'd told you *why* it was broken off—"

"She did. But"—his vision cleared momentarily and he saw that she was frowning—"John, are you quite certain that you feel all right? You're awfully white and, honestly, you're not talking sense, you know. Do try to eat something and—look, your tea's getting cold. Shall I pour you some fresh?"

Johnny shook his head so violently that the room started to whirl about him in crazy circles. He got to his feet, gripping the arm of his chair for support.

"Exactly what did Elizabeth tell you?"

"She told me about Pip," Fiona said. "About how sweet she was and . . ." Johnny lost a few words then. He saw his cousin's lips moving, knew that she must be talking to him but couldn't hear what she was saying. It had been like that this afternoon at the dam, just before the gates collapsed, he remembered. Jock had shouted to him and he hadn't heard a word, only a wind rushing past his ears and afterwards a faint, muffled explosion. Perhaps he'd been too close to the exploding charge and the concussion had affected his hearing. It must have been something like that. And now it was happening again . . .

". . . I think you should invite Pip up here to stay . . ." Fiona's voice reached him quite clearly now.

"Yes," he agreed thickly, "I will, I'd . . . like to, Fiona. I'm awfully fond of Pip." He wondered why they were talking about Pip, instead of about Cousin Catherine's marriage settlement, but he suddenly felt very tired and couldn't summon enough energy to argue. It was enough that Fiona had apparently accepted the idea of what he planned to do, without —as he had been so afraid she might— objecting to it. "Pip's due at London Airport on Tuesday," he said, thankful that this, at least, was a fact and made sense. "I'll go to London, take her around a bit and then bring her back here, with —with the people she's travelling with. They're nice. I used to know them at Wahrangi."

"John, you aren't well." Fiona's voice was high pitched, sharpened by anxiety.

Johnny knew that she was right. "I'm rather afraid I'm going to pass out," he told her, trying very hard to say it slowly and clearly, so that she would understand. He moved away from his chair, began to grope vaguely in the direction of the door and, reaching it somehow, he flung it open, only to stand there helplessly, both hands gripping the jamb to keep himself upright. He felt rather than heard Fiona come to him, felt her arms go round him and was suddenly aware of nothing save the sweet, lingering scent of her hair in his nostrils and her face, frightened and concerned, very close to his.

"Fiona," he whispered, "Fiona, I . . ." He held her to him, his heart racing, the blood throbbing in his ears. Once before, he recalled dimly, he had held her in his arms and had experienced this same strong, surging emotion that had sought to draw him to her against every instinct that cried out to him that it was madness. His mouth found hers, crushed down on it relentlessly, silencing her little cry of shocked, bewildered protest. For an instant, taken by surprise, Fiona did not resist him. Johnny felt in that instant a heady ecstasy he had never before known, compared with which his feelings for

Elizabeth had been the vapid gropings of a boy, imagining himself in love.

And then Fiona released herself. Her face was very pale, he saw, and he flinched before the blazing contempt in her eyes.

"I can only think you're ill, John. And —and that you've been drinking. It's . . . the only possible excuse. Please don't touch me again, ever—" she choked on a sob and Johnny stared at her, horrified by what he had done, unable to understand what madness had seized him. He had always known, he reminded himself dully, that Fiona hated him—why had he been so great a fool as to imagine that she could have changed? Because, of course, she hadn't. It was only he who had changed. He had fallen in love with his cousin Fiona. As . . . as David Cameron had. He was to know and endure the agony of an unrequited love, as David was enduring it . . .

Fiona said, her voice colder than he had ever heard it:

"I'll call Jamieson and ask him to help you to bed. You're shocked—David warned me that you might be and you ought to be in bed. We'll forget this. I realize that you weren't yourself, that you didn't mean it."

"I did mean it. That is—"

"Please don't say any more, John." A spasm of pain flickered across Fiona's white, strained face. "You behaved with great gallantry this afternoon. I can't forget that. But you mustn't hurt Pip Gilliat again, you simply mustn't."

"Hurt . . . Pip? But—" Once again the room whirled about Johnny's head and Fiona's face vanished into the mists, her voice faded into silence, complete and absolute.

Jamieson, summoned by Fiona's frantic cry, just caught him as he fell.

When Johnny recovered consciousness, it was to find himself in his own room, with his cousin Catherine sitting in a chair at his bedside, a shaded lamp on the table behind her.

He stirred restlessly, finding it difficult at first to remember what had happened and why he should be in bed.

Hearing his movement, Catherine Chisholm raised her head. "Lie still, John dear," she cautioned him gently. "Everything is all right. David Cameron is coming out to see you as soon as he's finished his surgery, but until he gets here, I think you should try to sleep if you can."

"What happened, Cousin Catherine?" Johnny asked.

"You fainted a little while ago."

"Downstairs—in the hall?" Memory was returning, a confused memory which, for some reason, worried him. His cousin nodded. "Yes, in the hall. Jamieson caught you."

"Jamieson? Was—was Fiona there as well?"

"Yes, dear, she was—you'd been having tea together, in the morning-room. She told me she thought that you must have drunk some whisky and, as you'd eaten nothing and were shocked—with, per-haps, slight concussion from your fall—you collapsed. It's nothing to worry about: I believe that alcohol does have that effect sometimes. You'll be quite all right in a day or so, I'm sure you will. But now"—she bent over him, smoothing the untidy hair back from his brow with a slender, affectionate hand—"couldn't you try to sleep a little? I don't think it's good for you to talk."

"Please, Cousin Catherine," Johnny pleaded, "I only want to get things straight. Did—did Fiona tell you anything else?"

Lady Logan looked puzzled. "No. Nothing—except of course, about what happened at the dam this afternoon. And that you weren't going to marry Elizabeth Anson after all." She continued gently to stroke his forehead. "You behaved very well this afternoon, John. We're all very proud of what you did."

Johnny waved an impatient hand. He remembered every detail of what had happened this afternoon, remembered the tense, unhappy little scene which had ended his engagement to Elizabeth on their return from Ardloch earlier in the day. He even remembered coming back to the house with David Cameron in his car, after Annie Frazer and her baby had been packed off to hospital in the Land Rover and after Macrae, the Factor, had told him that the dam was safe. But after that, save for odd flashes, he could recall very little. He had bathed and changed. He had drunk the whisky that Jamieson had left out for him. And then he'd gone downstairs to have tea with Fiona—at least, no, that was wrong—he'd gone expecting to find Elizabeth, but she hadn't been there. She had left him a note and shaken the dust of Logan from her feet. But, before leaving, she had told Fiona the reason for their broken engagement. He glanced anxiously at his cousin Catherine.

"Elizabeth," he said, "you know about Elizabeth, Cousin Catherine?"

"Yes, John dear, I know what Fiona told me. It wasn't much, just that you'd decided to break off the engagement." She eyed him kindly. "From what I saw of Elizabeth, I believe you did the right thing. I shouldn't be too upset about it: I do not think she is deeply hurt."

"You talked to her?"

"Only for a few minutes. She was all alone, you see, and although I haven't felt like meeting strangers lately, I—well, I thought it was rather unkind not to speak to her. We had coffee together in my sitting-room. She wept a little, but, you know, I don't think her tears came from her heart. She wouldn't have been the right wife for you, John."

"No." He knew it now, there was no point in denying it. "She didn't mention anything about the estate, did she— anything about my plans for it or—or for you?"

Lady Logan shook her head with emphasis. "Oh, no. If she had, I should not have listened to her. What plans have you for me, John dear? Surely you don't have to worry about me? I don't want you to."

Johnny sought for her hand, held it against his cheek. He was unutterably relieved. Cousin Catherine obviously knew nothing, whatever Elizabeth had told Fiona. He said pleadingly: "It's only that I don't want you to leave Logan, Cousin Catherine. I'd like you to consider it still your home, as long as it's mine. Please, won't you promise me you'll stay?"

The lovely, pale face was lit by a smile of dazzling radiance. "I'll promise you this, John," Lady Logan said softly, "that I'll stay for as long as you want me to."

"I shall always want you to, Cousin Catherine. There'll be times when I'm away—I might even go back to Australia for a while—and if I knew you were here at Logan, looking after it for me, I'd be free to go, I wouldn't worry."

Lady Logan bent to kiss him. "Logan is yours, John. Your inheritance, your responsibility, yours to love and care for. You mustn't leave it. Logan needs you. No woman could take your place or run it for you for very long, you know. Don't worry about it now, but think about it when you're feeling stronger. In time you will find the right wife to share it with you and then you'll be able to settle down here, bring a son into the world to whom, one day, in his turn Logan will belong. This Castle is part of us, its history and ours goes back eight hundred years. The land on which it stands was won and held and cherished by a long, unbroken line of Chisholm men who sacrificed their lives to keep it. You can never be free of Logan, John. You are a Chisholm, and in the end you'll find that you do not want to be free, because Logan will be in your heart, as it is in your blood."

Her voice was very quiet and calm, but it beat in Johnny's brain long after she had left him alone. He could not forget what she had said, but when at last he fell asleep, it was to dream, not of her or of Logan but of Fiona, and in his dream, which he knew was madness, he kissed her and, bemused with wonder, heard her say she loved him . . . He woke, startled, to find David Cameron bending over him. A dazzling light shone into his eyes, making him blink stupidly.

"It's nothing," the doctor said, "just a slight concussion. I'm sorry I had to wake you up, but Fiona was worried about you. Take a couple of these"—he dropped two small, white pills into Johnny's palm—"and you'll sleep the clock round. A day or so in bed and"—he smiled—"you'll be as good as new, I give you my word. Fit, at all events, to go off to London on Monday as I understand you'd like to. Only this time"—his smile widened—"no whisky, Lord Logan. That was what caused the trouble. But it's an ill wind—at least it's got you to bed and I hope you'll stay there. Well, I'll leave you to sleep. Pleasant dreams and—to add to them—you'll be glad to know that Annie Frazer is doing fine and she and her husband have decided to name the bairn John, after you! Goodnight, Lord Logan."

"Goodnight," Johnny echoed weakly, "and thank you—thank you very much."

"Think nothing of it," the doctor besought him. "We'll have you up and doing again in a couple of days."

He was as good as his word. Johnny fretted during the two days he was kept in his bed, but he felt the better for them when, after a final careful check-up, David Cameron agreed to his resuming his normal life. The two days had passed slowly. He had read a little, his cousin Catherine had visited him regularly and Jock MacPhail, calling with the post, had come up twice for brief visits; and Jamieson had carried up his meals. But Fiona, save for an inquiry made in a cold little voice from the door of his room, had not come near him, and this, more than anything else, caused him to fret.

He still remembered very little of what had passed between them immediately before his dramatic collapse, but Fiona was never out of his thoughts. Had he, Johnny asked himself a hundred times, really kissed her or had it all been a dream, a figment of his imagination? He simply didn't know, and her manner towards him was not such that he could ask her. But he recalled scraps of their conversation as he lay, restlessly, in enforced idleness in his room. It had been about Pip, though why they should have talked of Pip he couldn't imagine. Fiona had started to tell him of the reason Elizabeth had given for their broken engagement and he had been desperately worried, lest the premature disclosure of his plan to return Cousin Catherine's marriage settlement to her should meet with Fiona's opposition. Which, apparently, it had not, despite Fiona's earlier refusal to accept anything from him, even an allowance. But perhaps she hadn't opposed this because it only concerned her mother. It might be that, only he couldn't be certain of it.

He decided, finally, that the first thing he would do when he was allowed up would be to telephone Mr. Menzies and ask him to have the necessary documents prepared for his signature at once—he would call at the solicitor's office in Glasgow on his way to London on Monday, sign the deeds and have done.

He duly telephoned and, cutting short the solicitor's objections, informed him curtly that he would call on Monday afternoon and that he would expect the documents to be ready.

Mr. Menzies said heavily: "This goes against all my considered advice to you, Lord Logan, but if you insist—"

"I do, Mr. Menzies. I'll be with you at three o'clock on Monday and I shan't have a great deal of time because I'll be on my way to London. Some friends of mine are due at London Airport from Australia early on Tuesday morning."

"Very well," the solicitor agreed, recognizing defeat. "I will do as you ask. I trust you have obtained Lady Logan's consent to the gift?"

Johnny ignored the question, bade him an abrupt goodbye and rang off before the old man could think of any further objections to offer. He felt much happier now that his decision had been put into effect, but his spirits fell when, searching for Fiona, he heard from Jamieson that she had gone out with David Cameron.

Disconsolately, he wandered into the morning-room and made an abortive attempt to occupy himself with the day's newspapers. It was here, he thought, that they had talked, he and Fiona: here—unless indeed it had been a dream—here that he had kissed her. He couldn't believe that it was a dream, it was too real, it had made too vivid an impression on his mind for him to have imagined it. He was in love with his cousin Fiona—whether or not he had kissed her—and . . . what had Cousin Catherine said to him, the other night when he had woken to find her at his bedside? *In time you will find the right wife to share this with you and then you'll be able to settle down here, bring a son into the world to whom, one day, in his turn, Logan will belong . . .*

His son—Johnny's throat was tight—his son and . . . Fiona's, whose heritage would be Logan. It was right, it was justice, quite apart from his personal feelings and the fact that he was in love with Fiona. If she married him, then Logan would be hers, to share with him, and it would pass, eventually, to their son. The long, unbroken line of Chisholms of Logan, which had survived for eight hundred years, would go on, through

Fiona and himself; and they could stay here, there would be no need for him to go back to Australia if he and Fiona married. Cousin Catherine would remain here with them, her future assured. The marriage settlement could, after all, be used for the purpose his cousin Roderick had intended, to pay off the estate duty and leave Logan free of debt.

His eyes bright, Johnny got up and began to pace the room. The sound of a car drawing up in the drive outside sent him to the window. He recognized David Cameron's rakish old Lancia and saw Fiona getting out of it. She was wearing a kilted skirt of gay Chisholm tartan, with a dark green cardigan which displayed to advantage her slim, lithe beauty and lovely figure. Head thrown back and dark hair ruffled by the wind, she was bidding a smiling farewell to David, quite unaware of the fact that Johnny was watching her from the window.

He drew a sighing breath, his pulses quickening. She was so beautiful, so desirable, her pride a challenge. Had he been blind until now, Johnny asked himself in wonder, not to know that in all the world there was for him only one woman, only one Fiona? It seemed incredible that any man could have been so blind . . .

He waited, his heart pounding, scarcely able to contain his impatience for her to come to him. He saw David's car drive off and heard Fiona's voice in the hall, speaking to Jamieson. He knew that she would come to him: this was the room she always used and—surely she must feel the urgency of his longing for her, surely she must sense his need, his burning desire to take her again into his eager arms?

The voices came nearer, Fiona's light, quick, unmistakable footsteps crossed the hall.

"Is his lordship up, Jamieson, do you know?"

"Yes, my lady. I saw him about half an hour ago. He was asking for you."

"Was he?" Fiona's voice was flat. "Well, will you tell him, please, that I shall be in the morning-room? And perhaps you'd serve coffee there."

"Very good, my lady," came the butler's dutiful response. "MacMichael has taken her ladyship's up to her in her room."

"Thank you," Fiona said. Johnny heard her coming towards him but he didn't move.

The door opened and she stood for a moment framed in it, looking at him in surprise.

"Oh, this is where you are. I was just asking Jamieson if he'd seen you." Her tone was her normal one, quiet, self-controlled, devoid of emotion. "Jamieson said you were asking for me."

"Yes," Johnny admitted, "I was, I—" The words froze in his throat at the sight of her expression. "Is there anything wrong, Fiona?"

"No, John." She shook her head. "I was looking for you too, as it happens. I have something to tell you."

"Something . . . to tell me?" Instinct warned him, before she said it. He took a pace towards her, holding out his arms. "No—no, Fiona, don't tell me. Don't—"

Fiona drew back. "John, I simply don't understand you—I wish I did. All I want to tell you is that I'm going to marry David. I thought you . . . should know."

Johnny's arms fell to his sides. "I see." Blindly he turned away from her. "Forgive

297

me, it's rather a shock, that's all. I never imagined you were in love with David, I thought—"

"What did you think?" There was pain in Fiona's eyes, pain and a strange, reluctant tenderness.

"Nothing. It doesn't matter now."

"No, I don't see any reason why it *should* matter to you now. After all, you are going to marry Pip Gilliat, aren't you?"

"Marry . . . *Pip?*" Staggered, Johnny could only stare at her. Marry Pip—little Pip, who was like a sister to him, a child, a schoolgirl whom he had known all her life? Good heavens, where could Fiona possibly have got so incredible an idea? He opened his mouth, his lips moved but no sound came from them.

And then, startling in the silence, the telephone rang. Fiona crossed to the table on which it stood and picked up the receiver. Johnny heard her answer it in a low voice.

She turned to him, the receiver in her hand.

"It's for you, John. It's Pip Gilliat. She has just arrived in London."

14

JOHNNY left for London that night. Pip's arrival, three days before he had expected her, left him with no choice but to go.

Fiona, when he had discussed it with her, had urged him to travel down at once —had, in fact, booked a sleeper for him on the Night Highlander and, as she had done for Elizabeth two days ago, ordered a car to take him to Ardloch, almost before he had had time to voice his decision to go.

She had seemed, Johnny thought with bitterness, as he paced the Ardloch platform a few hours later, she had seemed very anxious for him to go—as if, for some reason he couldn't fathom, her one desire was to see him reunited with Pip.

"She'll be longing to see you, John— you mustn't keep her waiting. And do bring her back to Logan with you as soon as she feels like coming. She'll want to see it for herself, won't she?"

"Yes, I suppose she will," he had agreed without enthusiasm, his heart as dead as the hopes she had killed. He hadn't said much more, hadn't even asked Fiona why it was that she believed he intended to marry Pip. For one thing it wasn't hard to guess the reason—Elizabeth's parting letter to him had hinted at something of the sort, but until now he hadn't fully understood the barbed innuendoes the letter had contained. And, for another, it was too late now to deny the spitefully aimed suggestion—too late even to wonder why Elizabeth should have made it. Fiona was to marry David. She had said so and . . . that was the end. David Cameron was a decent fellow, the best of fellows, and if Fiona loved him, then, of course, there was no more to be said.

No more that *he* could say, at all events. David was his friend, and Johnny's code —the code of the Outback in which he had been reared—was a rigid one. A man didn't seek to steal his friend's wife or the girl he loved, whatever the temptation to do so, whatever his own feelings. In the great, barren, under-populated bush country, where loneliness and isolation were enemies to be fought almost daily, a man's only security lay in the trust he could place in his friends and in the proven loyalty of his neighbours. This was the basis of the Outback's civilization and, Johnny told himself, it applied equally here. Honour made the same demands in the Old Country as it made under the Southern Cross, loyalties were no different, a friend was a friend . . .

The train came roaring into the station, to halt with a hiss of escaping steam from its two powerful engines, and he moved towards it as the attendant, list in hand, descended from the rear of the sleeping car.

"Yes, sir? Have you a reservation?"

Johnny nodded.

"Your name, sir?"

"Logan."

The man's manner changed at once, became deferential.

"Oh, yes, my lord, this way, if you please. Your berth is number seventeen, second from the end." He took Johnny's suitcase from Mackay's hand, the chauffeur touched his cap smartly and Johnny entered the sleeping car, smiling a little at the contrast between this journey and his last.

A few weeks ago, he had been an unknown stranger, sitting up all night in a crowded Second Class carriage: now, as the Earl of Logan, he went First and was accorded this respectful reception by the sleeping-car attendant, this farewell salute from the uniformed chauffeur he employed. It seemed odd, for he felt no different. But, he thought, as the attendant led him to his berth, he wouldn't really miss all this, when the time came for him to return to what he had been. Money was all right, if one had earned it, but it wasn't necessary for happiness. An hour before, he had tried to explain this to old Mr. Menzies when he had telephoned the solicitor's private residence, to acquaint him with the enforced change in his plans.

"I won't be able to call at your office on Monday as we arranged," he had said. "I shall be in London. But that doesn't mean that I've changed my mind. I still want those documents prepared, and if I should be delayed in London I'd like them sent on to me there. The sooner they're signed, the sooner I can get away. And I want to get away."

"You're still determined to return to Australia, Lord Logan?" Mr. Menzies had sounded incredulous and, hearing the note of doubt in his voice, Johnny had cut him short.

"More determined than ever, Mr. Menzies. I'm certain that I shall be doing the right thing."

The right and . . . the only thing, he thought grimly—now. Fiona's decision to marry David had robbed him of any lingering desire to remain at Logan: even if it had been possible, he wouldn't have wanted to stay there now. He would bring Pip back with him for a short visit, perhaps—if she wanted to come. He had promised to invite her. And, of course, there were the Awkwrights with whom she was travelling: they would think it odd and inhospitable of him if he didn't include them in his invitation. Perhaps, with his own people about him, he wouldn't find it too painful to be with Fiona again. At least in the Awkwrights' friendly, cheerful company, he would be able to put on an act. He wasn't much good at deception, it was true, but—somehow he would pretend. It shouldn't be too difficult: Fiona was indifferent to him, it was unlikely that she would notice anything or suspect how he felt about her. And, as soon as old Menzies could clear up the legal tangle, he would go back to Australia where he belonged . . .

"Will you have morning tea, my lord?" The sleeping-car attendant's voice broke into his thoughts and he forced himself to concentrate.

"What time do we get in?"

"On the stroke of eight, my lord."

"Then thank you, I'd like tea at seven."

"Very good, my lord. And dinner will be served in the restaurant car from seven-thirty. If your lordship would like a reservation, I can see to it."

"No, thanks." Johnny shook his head. He didn't feel like eating, didn't relish the curious glances that would greet his appearance in the dining-car when his identity became known.

"Then if that is all, my lord?" The attendant hesitated, struck by the weary pain in the face of the young man whose strange, romantic story he had read in his

Sunday newspaper. He remembered seeing the new Earl of Logan on television a few weeks ago and, looking at him now, in the flesh, was shocked by the change in him.

It didn't do, the attendant thought, remembering his own experiences, to pitchfork a man out of his accustomed environment into a life that was completely foreign to him. All the money in the world couldn't really compensate for the loss of familiar things, for being uprooted. The young Earl of Logan was about the same age as his boy, George, but George was settled now in a good job and about to get married. He was no longer lost and unhappy, as this young man so obviously was: he was a success, George was, and yet there had been a time when his father had been afraid he never would be.

Impulsively and still with deference, the white-haired attendant said, his tone the gentle, kindly one he might have used to his own son: "If your lordship would care to turn in now, I could bring along a tray —tea and sandwiches, if that would do. I mostly have a bite of supper meself about now, so it wouldn't be any trouble." With the deftness of long practice, he turned back the covers on the sleeping berth and smiled at his passenger. "I was a steward with the P & O in me younger days," he confided. "On the Australian run, before and during the war—Fremantle, Adelaide, Sydney, then up to Brisbane. A grand country, Australia—and grand people too. You'll be missing them, I expect, and finding some of us a bit strange. Though we're all the same stock, you know—branches off the same tree and not so different under our skins, really. Only sometimes, I think, we Britishers find it hard to talk to strangers—we're that caught up in our own affairs and that proud of being insular, we're inclined to forget that they may be lonely and home-sick and in need of a friendly word. As—forgive me taking the liberty—as you are, aren't you, my lord?"

Surprised but deeply touched, Johnny echoed the old man's smile. "Yes," he admitted, "at times. Though probably it's my own fault." He reddened. "When you spoke to me, I was just deciding that I'd go back home, oddly enough." He sighed and fumbled in his pockets, searching for the packet of cigarettes he had bought on the station. "Will you have a smoke?" he invited, extending it.

The attendant shook his head. "If you don't mind, sir—my lord—I always roll me own. It's a habit I picked up in your country. That and"—his smile widened, as he took out a tin of tobacco, extending it for Johnny's inspection—"that and talking to the people I meet. They're friendly folk are the Australians, and not a bit of side to them."

Their eyes met across the battered little tobacco tin and suddenly Johnny started to laugh. "Perhaps that's what's wrong with me," he said. "That's why I don't fit in— and why I'd better go back. Why I *want* to go back."

"Now look, sir," the old man bade him gently, "isn't that admitting defeat?"

"Is it? I wouldn't know."

"Yes, sir, I think it is." He gave Johnny his tobacco tin and papers. "Help yourself, sir, while I just go and fetch you that tea and make sure none of me other passengers wants me for anything. And then, sir, I'll come back and try to prove it to you, if I can—tell you about my boy George. Living in America, he is. Like you, sir, he found it strange at first and wanted to pack it in and come home, but he didn't and he's glad now. He's made a success of things, has George. It never does to let anything beat you, sir. Faith in yourself, that's what you've got to have if you're going to get anywhere. Believe me, sir—my lord—it's the truth."

Was it, Johnny wondered, as the old man went out, leaving him alone—was it? Did he lack faith in himself, was he admitting defeat? And had it needed this kindly, humble old man, whose son George had wanted to come home, to point out to him what Elizabeth had said and he hadn't believed? Had it needed a stranger to show him that he couldn't escape his destiny, couldn't run away, however much he wanted to?

Thoughtfully, he rolled himself a cigarette, his fingers still a trifle awkward because of the dressing on his left hand, which David had insisted he should retain.

Fate had a curious way of working things out, he reflected. It was quite by chance that he had boarded this train tonight: quite by chance, too, that Pip and the Awkwrights had arrived in England three days earlier than they had intended to—the result, Pip had told him, of a last-minute cancellation. He wondered, going to stand in the window as the long train rushed southwards into the night, what fresh surprises lay ahead and what new twist Fate had in store for him before, finally, his destiny should be decided. Or was the decision his own to make? Could he turn defeat into victory by having faith in himself?

Inhaling smoke, he wondered what Pip was doing. It would be good to see Pip again. She was a sweet kid but— Johnny sighed. Pip was only a child . . . the nicest, most adorable child he knew, but still a child. Fiona was a woman. He had held her in his arms, had kissed her and had felt her lips surrender to his for one breathless, ecstatic moment which had changed everything for him, taught him the meaning of love and given him the measure of his own manhood.

Nothing could ever be quite the same for him again. Not—he turned blindly from the window—not even Pip. Perhaps not Australia, certainly not Logan. For what victory could he win, without Fiona to share it with him?

He flung his cigarette away, ground it out with his heel on the floor of the compartment.

It was borne on him suddenly that he *would* go back to Logan. Perhaps alone. He wouldn't admit defeat. Cousin Catherine should have what was hers, but Logan belonged to him and he belonged to Logan. He would . . . what had Cousin Catherine told him his ancestors had done? He would love and cherish the land that was his, alone. Fiona had chosen David and he couldn't fight David, but he wouldn't run away . . .

There was a tap on the door of his compartment.

"Your tea, my lord," said the sleeping-car attendant. He smiled suddenly. "I don't believe you need me to tell you about my lad George after all, do you, sir?"

"No," said Johnny, "I don't think I do. But I'd like to hear about him just the same."

The faded old eyes met his in sympathetic understanding. "You drink your tea, my lord," the sleeping-car attendant suggested, "and I'll tell you."

He set down his tray and, smiling, Johnny passed him the little tin of tobacco.

The Night Highlander sped on through the darkening countryside.

Pip Gilliat returned the telephone receiver to its rest and said unnecessarily: "That was Elizabeth."

"So we gathered," Bob Awkwright returned, with a hint of sarcasm. "Considering you said nothing but 'Yes, Elizabeth' and 'No, Elizabeth' throughout the entire conversation. What did she want, anyway? I thought you didn't like her?"

"I loathe her," Pip assured him, with frankness.

"Then why talk to her? Why leave a message, asking her to ring you up?" Bob's good-looking young face was sullen.

"I had my reasons," Pip retorted. She glanced at Betty. "Perhaps you ought to explain to your brother, Bet."

Betty Awkwright shrugged. "Oh, he knows, he's just being awkward because he doesn't approve, that's all."

"I do *not* know," Bob protested. "You two never tell me anything."

"Well," said his sister patiently, "Johnny has done what we were afraid he'd do—let Elizabeth Anson get her claws in him. He told Pip in his last letter that he was engaged to her and we're terrified in case he marries her."

"I know all *that*. You've talked of nothing else since we left Australia. But I still don't see why Pip has to go and ring up Elizabeth."

"Because," put in Pip, "I want to see her, that's why—before Johnny gets here. I'm going round to see her now."

"But look here, Pip"—Bob reddened and his tone was indignant—"you promised to come out with me this evening. I've got tickets for a show and booked a table at the Savoy for supper afterwards."

Pip's expression softened. Bob, she thought, was very sweet. She found his devotion touching and his possessiveness —if a trifle overdone at times—oddly heartwarming. He needed her so, was unhappy and lost when she wasn't with him, and . . . she was fond of him, really. He and Betty had always been her closest friends, but—there was Johnny. It was on Johnny's account that she had come to England, she couldn't conceivably let Johnny down, not now when she was in sight of her goal.

"Bob, it's only half-past five," she said, "and I'm changed. There's plenty of time. If I go to Elizabeth's now, I shouldn't be more than half an hour. And I absolutely must see her, it's terribly important that I should."

"Why?" demanded Bob bluntly. "What do you expect to gain by seeing her, for Pete's sake?"

Both girls looked at each other and sighed at this fresh evidence of masculine denseness. "I shall find out what's happening," Pip said. "Johnny hasn't told me a thing—I only spoke to him for three minutes this morning and he was so surprised that we'd got here so soon, he couldn't talk about anything else. And Elizabeth was more cagey than I've ever known her to be—there's something brewing, you can take my word for it. She didn't *mention* Johnny—simply asked me to come round for a drink. So I'm going," she ended defiantly, "whether you like it or not. Johnny's due tomorrow morning and we've got to have a plan of action worked out before he arrives."

"I don't think you ought to interfere," Bob told her severely but without much hope that she would heed his warning. "After all, Johnny's free, white and twenty-one. Surely who he chooses to get engaged to is his own affair, not yours? I think you've got an awful nerve, myself."

"Would you want your best friend to marry Elizabeth Anson?" Betty asked, with finality.

"Well . . . she's very attractive and—"

"Yes, *and*—it's the 'and' that matters. You know what *you* said about her when she was at Wahrangi. Johnny's a million times too good for her and she's not in love with him, she never was, and she treated him shockingly when she was at the Gilliats'. But he's too nice to see through her. Men like Johnny Chisholm always put women on a pedestal—they just don't recognize evil because they're so decent themselves."

"A heck of a lot you know about men," her brother told her rudely. But, seeing Pip pick up her bag and gloves, he rose.

"I'm coming with you, Pip"—his tone was pugnacious—"I disagree heartily with what you're trying to do but I'm coming with you."

"You can't possibly." Pip stared at him in dismay. "In any case, Elizabeth only asked me. You—"

"I'll wait for you outside," Bob said flatly. "You've got a date with me tonight and I'm going to see you keep it, because it'll probably be the last I'll have with you, if Johnny's coming." He had the satisfaction of seeing Pip flush. She exchanged an anxious glance with Betty, who sighed and spread her hands. "I'm afraid you'll have to let him go with you, Pip. He means it."

"Oh, all right," agreed Pip resignedly. She went to the door of their sitting-room. "Let me know what happens, won't you?" Betty called after her and she nodded. Bob fell into step beside her and they made their way in silence to the lift.

"Shall I get a taxi?" he asked, as they reached the ground floor. "Where does Elizabeth live, anyway?"

"Eaton Square," Pip supplied. They left the comfortable warmth of the hotel foyer, and the uniformed porter, in response to

Bob's nod, whistled up a taxi and ushered them into it.

Bob said, suppressing a shiver: "Ugh, it's cold, isn't it? What'd you give to be back at Wahrangi, Pip?"

"Back—in Wahrangi?" Pip echoed, startled. She gestured through the taxi window at the busy, crowded street, at the lighted windows of a famous department store, at the hurrying shoppers on the pavement. "But, Bob—this is London!"

"I know it is. And, of course, it's wonderful—the most wonderful city in the world. I'll be glad I've seen it, with you . . . the Tower, Buckingham Palace, Hyde Park, all of it. But I wouldn't want to stay, Pip. Not for ever." He glanced at her in the dim light and smiled. "Would you, dinkum?"

"I don't know," Pip confessed. She thought of the sunshine of her home, the strong, relentless Australian sun, the blue, cloudless skies, the limitless horizon, the wide, rolling acres of the sheep pastures, the gumtrees casting their long shadows across the paddocks as the sun went down in a blaze of glory behind the distant Macgills and then, looking out at the austere greyness of London, felt tears sting at her eyes. "No, I wouldn't, Bob. Not for ever. I'd want to go back."

"Me, too," Bob said, with conviction. He felt for and found her hand, holding it gently between his own strong, calloused brown palms. "There are so many people here," he observed thoughtfully. "You see more in a five-minute taxi run than you'd see in a year at Wahrangi. But I like Wahrangi the way it is and I like my life the way it is, too. I like the people I see to be my friends, not strangers in a hurry, as they are here. And I like a horse to take me where I want to go—or the old station wagon!" He grinned reminiscently at the girl at his side. "Don't you—in your heart?"

"Yes, I think I do. But we haven't been here long, Bob—not long enough to judge. I want to explore it all, talk to people, be one of the crowd, just as if I lived here. I want to go to a concert at the Albert Hall and walk in the Park and see the Round Pond and then go into the English country. And—and to Scotland, too." Pip's voice was soft, her answering smile a plea. Bob responded to it.

"Have your fling," he bade her gruffly. "We'll see it all, Pip—go chasing after the bright lights too, paint the town red and have fun. But we'll go back, you know, both of us, when it's over, and the memories will do to last us a lifetime. Us —and our grandchildren too!"

"*Our* grandchildren?" Pip teased him lightly.

"That's right—ours. You belong to me, Pip. Not to Johnny or anyone else—to me."

His young face was suddenly grave and Pip saw it with a pang. She hadn't realized until now how serious he was about her, she had thought of him as a boy. He was only nineteen but already, she thought, studying him, he was a man, doing a man's job on his father's station which, one day, would be his. And he was very like Johnny. They were cast in the same mould: strong and gentle and chivalrous, putting their women on a pedestal, as Betty had said. Bob had put *her* on a pedestal, just as Johnny had put Elizabeth, and she had no right to his worship. No more right, if it came to that, than Elizabeth had to Johnny's, for was she not, Pip reminded herself guiltily, even now contemplating an act of disloyalty? Wasn't what she was about to do going to hurt Bob unbearably?

She sought to free her hand from his clasp but Bob's lips tightened and he clung fiercely to her wrist.

"Pip," he said, as if she had spoken her thoughts aloud, "don't go on with this, don't go to see Elizabeth. Why do you have to? Let Johnny take care of himself. He's no fool. And if he loves Elizabeth, he won't thank you for interfering, you know."

She stared at him helplessly, biting her lip, torn now between conflicting loyalties. Bob was in love with her, it wasn't just a passing infatuation, his heart was in his eyes as he looked at her and they weren't a boy's eyes but a man's. She didn't want to hurt him. But Johnny was a very special person in Pip's estimation, he always had been and—he was her first love, in spite of the fact that it had never come to anything and Johnny himself had never realized it.

"Bob, trust me, won't you? I must talk to Elizabeth, before Johnny gets here. But

I won't"—her cheeks were pink in the darkness of the taxi—"I won't tell her the —the lies I was going to tell her. I'll just see her and do what I can with the truth. After all"—the taxi was slowing down as she made her final plea—"Johnny's your friend as well as mine, isn't he?"

Bob released her hand, leaned across to open the door of the taxi and, as it came to a halt outside an opulent-looking three-storey house with a cream-painted front door, he got out.

"Yes," he agreed, "that's right, Johnny's my friend too. Go on then—I'll wait for you. And"—he bent swiftly and his lips brushed her cheek—"good luck to you, Pip!"

Pip hesitated for a moment, looking up at him and then, with a brief little nod that was typical of her, she walked briskly up to the cream-painted front door and rang the bell. She looked very small and straight and determined, standing there, Bob thought, watching her. He saw a uniformed parlourmaid open the door, saw Pip go into the house and the door close behind her. He turned to pay off his taxi. She would be a while, he thought, it was no use worrying, and, shoulders hunched under the upturned collar of his overcoat, he started to pace slowly down the lamplit street.

It had started to rain by the time Pip rejoined him, and Bob went to meet her, his expression rueful as a passing taxi, disregarding his raised arm, went splashing past him.

"I'm sorry," he said, "it looks as if we may have to walk a bit before we get a taxi. I ought to have kept the one we came in, but I'd no idea how long you were going to be."

"I don't care," Pip told him recklessly, "let's walk, it doesn't matter." She slipped her arm under his and he saw, to his amazement, that her small, sweet face was lit by a dazzling smile.

"You look as if you'd been successful," he suggested, trying hard not to sound resentful or jealous, although he was feeling both.

She dimpled up at him. "*I* wasn't. Johnny did it for himself, Bob, he's not going to marry Elizabeth after all. Their engagement is broken off!"

"Is it?" Bob was staggered. "Well, stone the crows!"

"You won't have to use those awful Australian expressions here," Pip warned him, with mock severity, "however astonished you are. Although I must admit," she added honestly, "I was pretty surprised too."

"Tell me what happened. Why was it broken off? And who broke it—Johnny?"

"Elizabeth *says* she did but"—Pip chuckled—"frankly, I think it must have been Johnny because she was so much on her dignity about it. And"—she halted, turning to face him—"Bob, you won't believe this, I know, but she's engaged to someone else. The most terrible-looking man, years older than she is, but he has some sort of title and Elizabeth says he's enormously rich. She showed me his photograph. Gosh! He's fat and almost bald. She told me he'd been begging her to marry him for years, but I gather she only agreed to it last night. I must say, I wish her joy. She's got what she deserves."

"What about Johnny?" Bob's heart missed a beat as he asked the question. Because if Johnny wasn't engaged to Elizabeth any more then he was free. And Pip . . . he swallowed hard. "What about Johnny, Pip?" he asked again.

"Oh, that's the best thing of all," Pip said. Her voice was tender, vibrant with happiness, and the eyes she turned on him were bright. "That's why I've saved it till last. Bob, Elizabeth says that Johnny and his cousin Fiona are simply crazy about each other—you remember, the girl he told us about in his letter, the one he thought didn't like him? According to Elizabeth, it was Fiona who was largely responsible for coming between herself and Johnny. She hinted something about having spiked Fiona's guns but I didn't quite understand it. Perhaps I wasn't meant to, I don't know."

"Perhaps you weren't," Bob agreed. They resumed their walk. "Are you getting awfully wet, Pip?" he questioned anxiously. "Would you like my coat round you? I can change when we get back to the hotel—"

"So can I," Pip assured him. "Anyway, I'm too happy and relieved to care a hoot how wet we get, aren't you?"

"Well, yes. But"—he glanced at her in

bewilderment—"do you mean you're *pleased* because Johnny's fallen for this cousin of his?"

She nodded vigorously. "Yes, of course I am. And because he's not going to marry Elizabeth."

"But why should you be pleased about the cousin?" Bob persisted, still puzzled. "I should have thought—"

"Bob dear, don't you see—it lets me out, that's why I'm pleased."

Bob thought about that for a long moment, a succession of swiftly changing emotions chasing each other across his face. Then, firmly stepping in front of a bowler-hatted man who had waved his umbrella at a passing taxi, he handed Pip into it and flung himself on to the seat beside her, reaching for her hand.

"Pip," he said breathlessly, "I know there can't be anything like an engagement between us until we get back home and can ask your folks about it but—Pip, will you marry me, one of these days? Will you be my girl from now on? Will you, Pip?"

Pip was just about to give her consent when the window at the front of the taxi opened and the driver asked, not turning his head: "Where to, sir, if I may ask?"

Bob held Pip to him, his cheek against hers. "In the books I've read about London, darling," he said softly, "they always drive round the Park. D'you mind if we do? Because I should like to kiss you before we go back to the family . . ." Pip nodded and Bob said happily: "Round the Park, please, driver. Three times round."

"Right you are, sir." The driver grinned, slid back the window and let in his gear, humming as he did so. The taxi splashed on through the rain-wet streets in the direction of the Park.

"I wonder," Bob said, after a long silence, "what made Elizabeth tell you all that? It's not like her, somehow, is it?"

"Well, perhaps she was sorry that she'd tried to spike Fiona's guns. Anyway"— Pip stirred in his arms—"I asked her, so she could hardly not tell me, could she? And I suppose, being Elizabeth, she hopes I'll tell Johnny that she's found herself a new beau. Which I shall," she added and then, as an afterthought: "But I won't tell Johnny that he's bald and fat."

"Why on earth not, for crying out loud?"

"Darling, you told Bet she didn't know anything about men," Pip reproached him. "Well, you don't know much about women, do you? I'd be a fool to tell him because he might feel sorry for her. That's feminine logic."

Bob laughed. "I'm beginning to learn something about women, sweet," he told her. "But please don't stop teaching me, will you?"

"No," Pip promised, "I won't." She raised her soft lips to his. "I'm learning too. You're—Bob, you're the first man I've ever kissed like . . . like this."

Bob's arms tightened about her. "And the only one, Pip," he said exultantly. "The only one—from now on!"

15

FIONA was in the drawing-room with her mother when David was shown in. They both smiled at him and Fiona rose to turn off the television.

"Don't let me disturb you," David begged. "I only looked in to see how things were going. Do go back to your programme."

"Oh, we weren't really watching it. I'm afraid we were talking, weren't we, Mother?"

"We were," Lady Logan agreed. "About you, David." Her eyes were very kind as they met his and David went to her and, the gesture a spontaneous one, he took her hand and raised it to his lips. "It's wonderful to see you down here, Lady Logan—watching television or otherwise. I hope," he added, searching her face anxiously, "that the fact that you were talking about me doesn't mean that you disapprove of me as a prospective son-in-law?"

"I could never disapprove of you in any capacity, David dear," Lady Logan assured him, but she sighed and David was quick to notice it. His smile faded. But he said no more, contenting himself with a brief "I see," his fingers feeling automatically for her pulse.

"I'm a good patient, aren't I?" Lady Logan suggested.

"You're wonderful. I wish all my patients took my advice as religiously as you do. I understand"—he looked at Fiona—"that Lord Logan disregarded it. He's away to London, isn't he, by the night train? Jamieson told me he'd gone."

"Yes," Fiona confirmed, "he's gone. Pip Gilliat arrived, three days before he was expecting her, so—he went off at once." Her voice was curiously flat and devoid of emotion and she avoided David's gaze.

"Who is Pip Gilliat to send him on so precipitate a dash?" David wanted to know. His brow furrowed. "He's not really fit to travel—good heavens, I only told him he could get up today and I meant that to include a gentle stroll about the grounds, but not a trip to London. You ought not to have let him go, Fiona."

"I'm sorry. Perhaps I should have dissuaded him. But he was very anxious to go. Pip Gilliat is the daughter of the man he worked for at Wahrangi—I think her full name is Phillipa. Didn't John ever tell you about her?"

"No," David said, still frowning, "he didn't."

"According to Elizabeth Anson, on whose word I am not inclined to place *great* reliance," Lady Logan put in drily, "John treated the poor child rather badly. It was always understood that he was going to marry her, but when he met Elizabeth . . ." She spread her hands in an expressive gesture. "It appears that he changed his mind. It doesn't sound like John, but there it is—Miss Anson insists that's what happened. She told Fiona that she knew nothing about it when she was at Wahrangi—John, she says, saw to it that she did not. He proposed to her and she accepted him: he was engaged to Elizabeth when he came here. And"—she glanced at Fiona—"I'm telling this at second-hand and perhaps not very accurately. It was to Fiona that she unburdened herself. I'm not quite clear whether Elizabeth broke off the engagement because John wanted it or because she'd received news that little Pip Gilliat was on her way to England. Which was it, Fiona dear?"

Fiona said briefly: "Because Pip was coming here, I think. She told me she'd had a cable from Mrs. Gilliat saying that the girl was heartbroken and she felt she couldn't go through with it. And she said she believed John was in love with Pip."

"Do *you* think he is?" David asked, a faint edge to his normally pleasant voice.

"I?" Fiona's fine, dark brows lifted. "How should I know, David? John hasn't said anything to me—apart from mentioning Pip, of course. I'm not in his confidence. But he seemed anxious enough to go, when he heard she'd arrived."

"I see." David crossed to the fire and stood holding out his hands to the glowing logs. He looked tired, Lady Logan thought, and there were lines of strain about his mouth, smudged shadows beneath his eyes. His hands, she saw, square, well-kept, physician's hands, weren't as steady as they usually were. Fiona, too, seemed far from her usual self, tense and strung up but much quieter than her wont. She had told her mother this evening, as they sat watching *In Town Tonight*—or pretending to—that she had decided to marry David, and Lady Logan had tried to feel pleased. But it was difficult: she was deeply attached to the young doctor, who had been a tower of strength to them throughout this difficult time and, of course, she loved Fiona and had always imagined, as mothers do, that she understood her. Yet, no matter how hard she endeavoured to do so, she could not reconcile herself to the fact that they proposed to marry each other.

It was—Lady Logan drew a long, sighing breath—it was *wrong*. They weren't suited to each other. Fiona was too proud, too high-spirited for the phlegmatic young doctor. He was Fiona's good friend and her own but—he wasn't the lover for a girl like Fiona and certainly not the husband her mother had hoped she might find. Besides, here they were, their engagement to each other only a few hours old and both looking acutely miserable, neither looking at the other and David obviously embarrassed for some reason.

But perhaps, if she left them alone together, they would talk more freely, sort things out for themselves. Probably that was why David had come and she must give him the chance he wanted to talk to Fiona.

Lady Logan rose from her chair. "I think," she said gently, "that I'm rather tired. I'll go to my room and read for a little, listen to that concert on the Home Service on my wireless. Goodnight, Fiona dear. Goodnight, David. Perhaps, if you feel like it, we could all go to church tomorrow morning. I should like to go, if you'll come with me."

David met Fiona's gaze then and he saw her nod.

"Of course," he said, "we'll do that. Goodnight, Lady Logan. I hope you'll sleep well."

"I'm sure I shall, David. And I hope *you* will. You look to me as if you're the one who needs a good night's sleep." She accepted Fiona's kiss and, for a moment, held her close. "Goodnight, darling," she whispered softly and added, as they walked together to the door: "Don't come with me. I think David wants to talk to you."

Fiona coloured faintly. "Yes, I'm afraid he does. But—"

They had reached the door and Lady Logan turned to face her. "Tell him the truth, Fiona. He is too good to be put off with less than the truth, you know." Fiona kissed her again without speaking and then, closing the door after her, she returned to David's side.

He studied her face for a long moment in silence and suddenly smiled.

"Fiona," he said, "do you really want to marry me?" She was silent. "Fiona," David said again, very gently, "*do* you want to marry me?"

Fiona didn't look at him. She answered, head averted, her voice quite flat: "Yes. Yes, I do, David. I—I'm very fond of you and—"

David took her by the shoulders, turned her to face him. She had to look at him then and he saw the pain in her eyes. "But you aren't in love with me, are you?" It was more a statement than a question and he made it calmly.

"I never pretended to be—in love with you," Fiona reminded him.

"No," he conceded, "you didn't. I had no illusions about that, really—although this morning, when you said you'd marry me, I—well, I let myself hope that perhaps after all you might have changed. Now I know you haven't."

"You . . . *know?*"

"Of course I do, darling—I know you and I'm not easily deceived. Patients are always trying to deceive me, hide their secrets from me. I get plenty of practice with would-be deceivers. And I love you, so it's impossible for *you* to pull the wool over my eyes. I'm afraid even your mother saw through you, didn't she?"

Fiona bit her lip. There was a glint of tears in her eyes as she nodded. "Yes, I'm afraid she did, David. She told me before you came in that I was making a mistake in thinking I could deceive you."

"You were," David agreed gravely. "It might have worked a while ago, when you were simply fond of me and there was no one else. But it hasn't a hope of succeeding when you're in love with—with someone else."

"You know that too?" Fiona was dismayed. "Am I so transparent? Are all my emotions written in my face?"

"For me they are," David told her. He took her arm and led her to a chair, which he drew up to the fire.

"Sit down, please. I want to talk to you."

Obediently she did so, and David, having flung another log on to the blaze, took his seat opposite her.

"Don't reproach yourself on my account," he said. "I never really believed you were for me, you know: in my heart, I think, I've always realized that your friendship was all I should have of you. I'm awfully grateful for that—I've had two years of it and . . . I hope it will go on, that we'll go on being friends, Fiona— even when you marry the man you're in love with."

"But—"

"Oh, he's in love with you, you need have no doubts on that score," David put in quickly. "They say that the onlooker sees most of the game, don't they? I've been watching both of you, especially during the last few days, and if ever a man broke his stupid, chivalrous heart over a woman, it's his unhappy lordship of Logan—over you. Would it interest you to know the real reason for his break with Elizabeth Anson? Quite by chance, I know it, and, although I was pledged to secrecy by the person who told me, there comes a time, I think, when even a doctor has to betray a patient's confidence. In this case, I'm personally involved, so I'm going to —and to hell with my professional conscience! I think you ought to know the truth."

"The truth, David?" Fiona echoed. "But I thought—"

David passed her his cigarette case. "Listen," he bade her, as he leaned forward to light her cigarette, "you thought wrong, darling. This business about Phillipa—Pip Gilliat was a spiteful invention on the part of our Miss Anson. She did it to save her own face and because, like me, she realized how you and John felt about each other. The truth of the matter is that John broke off the engagement. But perhaps it would be easier to follow me if I began at the beginning."

336

"Perhaps it would," Fiona agreed faintly. Two bright spots of colour flamed in her pale cheeks, and, for the first time in the two years he had known her, David realized that she was experiencing difficulty in hiding her emotions behind the mask of disciplined good manners she habitually wore. The hand in which she held her cigarette trembled perceptibly and, seeing this, he came to the point without preamble.

"Angus Urquhart, the Bank Manager in Ardloch, is one of the Logan Estate Trustees," he said, "as, of course, you know. He's also a patient of mine and he called to see me the other evening, just as I was finishing my surgery—the night we had all the excitement with Annie Frazer at the dam. The evening Miss Anson left here—remember?"

"As if I could forget it!" Fiona shivered.

"I imagine you know much more about the Logan Estate Trust and the provisions of your father's will than I do," David went on. "Angus Urquhart came to consult me about a private medical matter and when we'd dealt with that, he suddenly started to look very worried and said he wanted to ask my advice about an aspect of the Logan Trust. To my astonishment, having told me that he was speaking confidentially, he asked my opinion of the new earl's sanity. He—"

"Your opinion of—*John's* sanity?" Fiona interrupted, half rising from her chair. "But John is the sanest person I've ever met in my life."

"Steady, now—you haven't heard the half of it yet," David cautioned. "I agree with you, of course—your cousin John is one of the sanest people *I've* ever met."

"Then why on earth should Mr. Urquhart question it?" Fiona demanded. "He's a trustee, I know, but that does not give him the right to—to ask you a question like that."

"He asked me because someone asked *him*," David said drily. "Elizabeth Anson, to be precise. She called at the Bank on her way to the station and insisted on seeing him, although, of course, the Bank was closed. He received her in his office and she told him the most extraordinary story which I must confess—as he retailed it—certainly made your cousin John out

338

to be either a madman or"—his expression softened and he smiled—"the most generous, quixotic idiot ever born. It appears—and you must correct me if I've got it wrong—that under the terms of your father's will, his heir inherits some very valuable property in Ardloch, which originally came to the family as part of your mother's marriage settlement?" He looked a question.

"Yes," Fiona confirmed, "that is so. Daddy set the property aside in order to meet"—a shadow clouded her face for an instant—"his death duties. He knew, of course, that these would be heavy and the estate, as you know, is entailed. The Ardloch property is free of the entail, it can be disposed of and the proceeds used to pay the estate duty. That was Daddy's intention, when he made his will. I remember he told us all about it at the time. He"—there was a catch in her voice—"he told Alastair that he was doing it so as to safeguard his inheritance." She hesitated and then added: "The Ardloch property is the only part of the estate that *can* be sold."

"And it was originally your mother's

marriage settlement," David pointed out, "wasn't it?"

"Yes, it was. But—"

"According to the story Elizabeth Anson told old Urquhart, your cousin John intends to deed it back to your mother—every square foot of it. Urquhart rang up Menzies, the solicitor, and he confirmed it. He was as worried as Urquhart, but said that John had made up his mind and couldn't be made to change it. Menzies has had counsel's opinion and God knows what else, he's brought every gun in his legal armoury to bear, but John simply refuses to listen to him. And he wouldn't allow Menzies to mention a word to your mother or Urquhart—or to you."

Fiona stared at him, momentarily bereft of words. The enormity of the sacrifice her cousin had sought to make appalled her, took her breath away and filled her with shame. For *she* had driven him to make it, she with her stiff-necked refusal to accept his charity, her insistence that she must leave Logan. This was her fault, all of it.

"How," she managed to ask at last,

"was John proposing to pay the death duties, then?"

David spread his hands. "Out of income, I gather. That was the craziest part of it. But he'd got it all worked out and not so crazily either, to his way of thinking. He was not going to live at Logan and he wasn't going to take a penny of the income for himself until he'd seen the estate free of debt. He was going back to Australia, to support himself, leaving you and your mother in possession here. If necessary, he was going to open the Castle to visitors."

"I . . . see." Fiona's voice was faint and muffled.

"Elizabeth Anson," David went on relentlessly, "didn't like the idea at all—she wouldn't have any part of it. You can imagine that going back to an Australian sheep farm, instead of queening it at Logan, held no appeal for her. It wasn't your John she wanted, only what he could give her—the title and the money. *That* was why the engagement was broken off and why the charming Miss Anson bearded poor old Urquhart on her way back to London."

"But what did she hope to achieve by doing that?" Fiona demanded. "If she wanted to stop John doing what he proposed, then surely the obvious thing to do was to tell me? She must have realized that if either Mother or I had known of the—the sacrifice John was contemplating, we should have refused to accept it. As we shall refuse now, it goes without saying."

"My dear"—David's smile was affectionate—"you judge people by your own standards. So does Elizabeth Anson. It wouldn't have occurred to her that you would refuse John's gift or his sacrifice. Her sole object in going to see Urquhart was in order, if she could, to stop John making your mother the gift. Had she seen any hope of being able to stop him, she'd have hung on, tried, after all, to marry him. But Urquhart didn't hold out any such hope. He told her straight out that, sane or not, John was perfectly free to dispose of the Ardloch property in any way he wished. So"—his shrug was expressive—"she got out from under, leaving chaos behind her."

"Yes," Fiona agreed sadly, "she did." David could not see her face, for again she had averted it from him, but he sensed that she was crying soundlessly and, his own heart heavy, he held out his hand to her.

"He's quite a man, this John of yours."

"He's not my John."

"Isn't he? I beg to differ. If his sanity is in any doubt, it's because he's lost it over you." David sighed. "Do you remember when he fell off the dam and Niall came to fetch me from the cottage to attend to him? You were sitting beside him, holding his hand. I saw his eyes, as he looked at you, Fiona . . . and I saw yours. No one else existed for either of you at that moment but your two selves. I think I knew then. I knew it was defeat for me but"—David sighed again—"a man clings to hope, doesn't he?"

Fiona's hand moved in his and she looked up at him, the tears shining unashamedly in her eyes.

"I'm sorry, David. Honestly I am."

"You don't have to be," David returned gruffly. "I had my two years and I can't regret any of it." He took her hand in both his own, held it palm upwards and studied it. "Your heart-line," he told her, "is very strong and straight, it makes no deviation from its chosen course. When you love, Fiona, it's for always—one man and only one. I'm sorry that man isn't me, but, if I'm honest, I've got to give John Chisholm best. He's right for you—the proverbial knight in shining armour from the Australian Outback, where, it seems, they still breed them. He has all the virtues—courage, chivalry, honesty and generosity —and he's a hell of a fine chap. But he needs you and what you can give him, you know."

"Haven't you left one or two essentials out of your calculations, David?" Fiona asked gently. "He's not here, he's with Pip Gilliat in London—or he will be, tomorrow morning. And he's never told me he loves me—or at least he . . ." She coloured and David rose abruptly to his feet, to stand looking down at her, an odd little smile curving his lips.

"He'll be back, darling," he said and bent quickly to drop a light kiss on the top of her head. "In any case, I think you'll have to marry him—if only in order to prevent him from upsetting the calculations of the Department of Inland

Revenue by giving his money away! Goodnight, Fiona. I'll look in and have a word with her ladyship before I go—and I can see myself out, so don't move, please. Er—" He paused, eyeing her sombrely now, his smile no longer in evidence. "Fiona—"

"Yes?" she prompted. "What is it, David?"

"Our engagement is off, darling. As from now. If you don't mind."

"Oh, David—" Fiona choked on a sob.

"It was fun while it lasted. I enjoyed, however briefly, having the right to call you 'darling' and—to kiss you. But I won't do either again, you don't have to worry. And I won't tell your mother anything, except that we've both thought better of marrying each other. I think she'd like to know that, she wasn't in favour of it and she'll probably sleep better if she knows we've come to our senses. I'll leave you to tell her the rest, if you want to. She'll have to know sometime, won't she—what John was proposing to do, I mean?"

"You don't think he's done it yet, do you?"

David shook his head. "No. According to Urquhart, he'd told Menzies to have the necessary deeds of gift prepared for him and he intended to call at Menzies' office on Monday to sign them. There's time to stop him—today's only Saturday. Well"—he raised a hand in salute—"I'll be on my way. Goodnight, Fiona. You know where to find me if you want me for anything."

"Goodnight, David. And—thank you. Thank you from the bottom of my heart for . . . everything."

David smiled, touched her hand lightly and left her. He spent nearly twenty minutes with Lady Logan and he was thoughtful when finally he left the house and got into his car. They had been an illuminating twenty minutes, he reflected, as he pressed the starter and his engine sprang to its accustomed noisy life. Lady Logan had shown him Pip Gilliat's photograph and he had learnt, from her, that Pip was only seventeen, a child, scarcely out of the schoolroom. John, it appeared, had talked of Pip quite freely to his cousin Catherine, and as she had recounted to him what the younger man had said, David's last, lingering doubts had vanished. Elizabeth Anson's hints had been without foundation, so far as Pip Gilliat was concerned. She must, as David had suspected, have made them with malicious shrewdness because, like himself, she had realized how Fiona felt about John—Johnny, she called him.

Fiona did not, as a rule, show her feelings, but, returning from those tense, dangerous hours in the Dam Cottage, no doubt she had been caught off her guard: perhaps the fear and the horror and the agony she had endured when she had seen Johnny fall had lingered still in her eyes for Elizabeth to see.

At all events, he felt sure, Elizabeth had known . . . and so she had introduced the innocent Pip as a red herring. He felt certain that she could be no more, for how, he asked himself, from the depths of his own pain, could any man who had known Fiona love any other woman? It was impossible. Well, unlikely in the extreme but . . . he could make sure, David thought. He could telephone Pip Gilliat, now, tonight, at her hotel. He could ask her to tell Johnny to come back to Logan because Fiona needed him. It was as simple as that. If Johnny loved Fiona, he would come.

David sped down the long, curving drive, glancing back once to where the great grey hulk of the Castle of Logan stood outlined in majestic silhouette against the night sky.

This was the end of his own hopes, the final episode in his own ill-starred love for Fiona Chisholm, but he could have no quarrel with his fate. He had had so much and the truth was that he wanted Fiona's happiness more than he cared about his own, a great deal more. Love wasn't only taking, it was giving too. David's foot came hard down on the accelerator. If it were the last thing he did, he would ensure that Fiona found her happiness with the man she loved. The last of the Logans should come back to take possession of all that was his, as tradition decreed. And his bride would be waiting for him . . .

It was nearly midnight before David succeeded in getting Pip Gilliat on the telephone. She had gone out, the hotel receptionist told him: she hadn't said when she would be back so, obstinately, David rang through every hour and, at last, heard an unfamiliar, faintly accented voice on the line.

"This is Miss Gilliat"—the voice was friendly, with an underlying note of happiness in it—"who is that, please?"

"I'm Dr. Cameron, David Cameron from Logan . . ." David talked on, doing his best to explain, but the line was bad and he could not be too explicit. But finally his unknown caller said: "I think I understand, Doctor—you want me to tell Johnny—Lord Logan—to return as soon as he can because his cousin needs him? I'm not sure if . . ."

The line crackled and David, passing a weary hand across his brow, managed to say, above it: "Yes, that's approximately it. Tell him—his cousin Fiona . . ." The pips sounded, the operator's voice cut in and then the line went dead.

David let his receiver clatter back on to its rest. He had done all he could and suddenly he was very tired. If Johnny didn't understand the message, he could ring him up tomorrow. There were limits to a man's endurance and, just then, David Cameron had reached his. He got up and went stiffly into his sitting-room, poured himself a whisky and soda and sat down beside the dying fire to drink it.

Tomorrow, he thought, tomorrow was another day. Tomorrow was Sunday and he had promised to go to church . . .

16

JOHNNY received David's message from Pip as soon as he reached her hotel. An hour later, he was in the train once more, on his way back to Ardloch, with Pip's farewell still ringing in his ears. He had barely had time to exchange greetings with the Awkwrights, but at least, he thought, as he leaned back in his seat, watching the English country-side flash by the train window, at least he had extracted a promise from them to pay a visit in the near future to Logan. And Pip had told him, in the taxi on their way back to Euston, about herself and Bob.

Johnny smiled. He could not help but be delighted by Pip's news. Bob was a good lad, one of the best, as gay and high-spirited as Pip herself but full of character and good sense. He would make little Pip an excellent husband when the time came, and Johnny was sure her people would approve wholeheartedly of the match. Why shouldn't they, when one day Bob would own the Awkwright property which neighboured theirs?

For a moment, sitting there staring out at the unfamiliar fields and woods of England, Johnny experienced a pang of nostalgic envy. Bob and Pip would go back to Wahrangi, but he must stay and, perhaps, never see Wahrangi again. He would never go out to the yard, when dawn was still grey in the sky and the tin-roofed station buildings lay deep in the night shadows, his saddle on his hip, to whistle softly at the gate of the corral for Barney to come to him. Never again, perhaps, would he and Barney lope off on their long, lonely patrol, the rising sun warm on their backs and the fence stretching as far as eye could see in front of them. He wouldn't, at the day's end, see that same sun going down behind the jagged lines of the Macgills or lie, his head pillowed on his hands and the smoke from his glowing camp-fire in his nostrils, watching the stars come out, one after the other, in the purple backcloth of the Queensland sky. He would be here, twelve thousand miles away, a stranger, still in a strange land, alone . . .

But . . . was he a stranger now? He remembered Logan: the great Castle, with its towering battlements that had looked down on eight centuries of history, saw again, in memory, the mountains which hemmed it in, the fertile arable land below them, the well-tended farms and crofts. These were his, his trust and his heritage to love and serve and cherish, to preserve for his son. The son he might never have, for . . . there was Fiona.

Johnny's lips tightened. He would have to face the ordeal of seeing Fiona again, of seeing her in David's arms, of watching David take her away from him.

The message he had received had given him no clue to what was happening nor had it told him why he was needed or what he might expect on his return. He could only conclude—since the message had come from David—that someone was ill. His cousin Catherine, probably. He hoped, his throat tight, that she was not seriously ill, for she had borne so much and accepted her tragic bereavement so bravely. But he knew, in spite of her courage and the brave show she made, that her health was far from robust. She suffered from headaches and broken nights and, of course, from loneliness. He wished, rather desperately, that the train would increase its speed and put an end to his anxious speculation, wished, too, that he had had time to telephone David for more precise news before he left.

But there simply hadn't been time. He had rung up the station and had only just got back there in time to catch this train which, it being Sunday, was the only one until late afternoon. And it was a comparatively slow train, stopping at countless stations he had never heard of, as the long, wearisome journey progressed.

But at last, at ten minutes to eight, it reached Ardloch and Johnny flung himself impatiently out of it. He hadn't wired for a car to meet him and it had slipped his mind to ask Pip to do this for him. There were usually taxis in the station yard, but, before going in search of one, he saw Jock, in his postman's uniform, helping to unload mail from the train, and strode over to him. Jock, he thought, would know if Cousin Catherine was ill.

"Jock," he said, "Jock, can you spare a minute? I want to talk to you."

Startled, Jock turned to face him. "Why, it's you! Guidsakes, man, I thought you were in London. They told me you were."

"I've come back. Dr. Cameron sent for me."

"Sent for you? Is there something wrong, then?"

Johnny shook his head helplessly. "I don't know. I hoped you might have heard." He explained the haste with which he had travelled and the terse message he had received and added, frowning: "I'd better get back to Logan and find out. I'm very much afraid my cousin Catherine must be ill."

"Her ladyship?" Jock's blue eyes widened. "I've heard nae word of that, but she could be, of course, poor lady. How are you going, Snow? Is there a car meeting you?"

"No. I'll get a taxi."

"There'll not be one in the station yard—'tis Sunday. You'll need tae phone or—" He hesitated, glancing at the man with him. "Wait on, I'll hae a wee crack wi' Alec here. Maybe we can arrange something that will not interfere too greatly wi' Her Majesty's mails."

"But look here, Jock, you're not supposed to carry unauthorized passengers in your van, are you?"

"Och," returned Jock cheerfully, "I'm not thinking of ony such thing, your lordship—I'm in enough trouble as it is, delaying the mails for the sake o' yon dam at Logan." He grinned. "I've ma motorbike at the Post Office. It'll not take ma twa minutes to fetch it, if Alec will take the van back. We'll be in Logan in half the time a taxi would take—and it having tae get here frae Campbell's Garage intae the bargain. Hold on. I'll not keep you."

He was as good as his word. Five minutes later, with Johnny riding pillion behind him, he crouched low over the handlebars of his powerful motor-cycle and they raced through the deserted streets of Ardloch and started to climb into the hills, the single headlamp cutting a bright swathe out of the darkness in front of them.

Conversation was almost impossible but Jock attempted it.

"I'll drop your suitcase in the morn," he promised.

"Thanks," said Johnny breathlessly, "there's no hurry for it." He felt suddenly no longer a stranger. Jock's welcome, his friendship and his spontaneous kindness were oddly heartwarming. They had been friends in Korea, but that had been because they had been thrown together by chance, sharing the same bunker and firing the same gun, partners of necessity. Now, so much had changed for both of them and yet, in a changing world, Jock was the same and their friendship hadn't altered. It had stood the test and was as staunch and strong as it had been before.

Johnny smiled in the darkness.

"You're a good bloke, Jock," he shouted, but the wind of their passing drowned his words.

"Oh, aye," Jock acknowledged, "'tis a cold night."

"I said . . . you were . . . a good bloke."

"I canna hear ye. But we'll no' be long getting you home—the bike runs sweetly, does she not? . . . I hope her ladyship's not seriously ill."

"I hope not too." He hoped it with all his heart, Johnny thought, but he was afraid. And he wondered about Fiona. She would be anxious and upset and it would take all the self-control, all the resolution he possessed if he were not to yield to the temptation to take her in his arms and comfort her . . .

"By the bye, Snow . . ." Jock's voice broke into his thoughts, carried back to him on the wind. "They're wanting you tae take the chair at the Legion Dinner next month."

"Me?" echoed Johnny, surprised. "Why me?" He had to repeat the question before Jock understood it.

"Och, man—you're the Earl of Logan, are ye not? His late lordship always took the chair—'twill be expected of you. And you've a fine wee string of gongs tae pin across your chest. I'll take a bet, though" —Jock's laugh was derisive—"you'll be the first Earl of Logan tae appear wi' the DCM!"

Johnny scarcely heard him. A long way away, across the glen, he could see the white ribbon of the Logan road, standing out very clearly in the moonlight, and, in imagination, saw the Castle at its end and Fiona, waiting. He was coming home, home to Logan, where they needed him, but—how would she receive him, what would she say? Would she be glad that he had come or would she, as she had done at first, continue to resent him and hold herself aloof?

Jock was still talking of his British Legion Dinner and Johnny made an effort to concentrate on what he was saying.

"The lads will be affy disappointed if you refuse, Snow. 'Tis you they want in the chair. They're all for you, you understand."

"I didn't think they knew who I was," Johnny said. "You promised you wouldn't tell them when I went there before."

"Och, man—do ye suppose they didna guess and you the split image o' Lord Alastair? Of course they knew. But I warned them tae keep quiet about it, just treat you like one o' themselves. They're my friends, ye ken, so they did as I asked. But they're wanting tae be your friends too."

"Are they?"

"Aye, they are. You've a place here

among us, Snow lad, whenever you care tae take it. As the Earl of Logan and as Snow Chisholm too. You're welcome and you're needed. I just thought"—Jock hesitated and then plunged in—"och, I just thought I'd better mention it, in case ye werena sure. There's whiles I think you're looking lost and no' verra certain o' yourself and—guidsakes, Snow, there's nae earthly reason why ye should be. Is this no' your home now?"

"Yes," Johnny admitted, "it is now. That is—it's going to be, from now on."

"That's fine," Jock told him and opened the throttle. They roared on towards Logan, the wind cold in their faces as the racing motor-cycle increased its speed.

A quarter of an hour later, Jock slowed down to enter the drive. The Castle came into sight, gaunt and strangely beautiful with the moon riding high above its central keep. So it had stood through the centuries, Johnny thought, looking up at it, aware, then, of how strong a hold it had taken of his imagination. His imagination and . . . his heart. For he loved it, he realized, with a surge of possessive pride. It was his and he was coming home. He was the last of the Logans. He had been born thousands of miles away, but—he had come home at last to Logan, and he was going to stay here, he wasn't going to run away.

They skidded to a halt outside the front door and Jock, with a brief: "I'll awa', Snow, you'll no' want me now," brushed aside his thanks and left him, his tail-light and the sound of his engine swiftly receding. Johnny went into the hall. It was deserted but the lights had been left burning, evidently for him, although Jamieson—his ears no doubt listening for the arrival of a car—did not appear as he crossed it and climbed the staircase, making for Cousin Catherine's rooms on the first floor. He wanted, before he did anything else, to reassure himself on his cousin's account.

He waited for a moment or two in the corridor, straining his ears for the sound of voices, but could hear none. He tapped very softly on the door of the sitting-room. To his surprise, it was opened by Catherine, who stood, fully dressed, regarding him with an astonishment that matched his own.

"John—John, my dear, what brings you back?" She held out her arms to him and, speechless with relief at finding her safe and well, he went into them, holding her close.

"I . . . thought you were ill. I came back because I thought you were ill."

"Dearest John, that was sweet of you" —her eyes were tender as they looked at him—"but, as you see, I'm not. What made you think I was?" She drew him after her into the warm, firelit room. "You're cold. Toast yourself by the fire and I'll pour you a cup of tea. It's just been made and there's a spare cup—I thought Fiona might want one." Lady Logan smiled and motioned him to a chair.

Johnny sat down and gratefully accepted the tea.

"David sent for me, Cousin Catherine —David Cameron. I got the message as soon as I arrived in London, but it wasn't very clear. I jumped to the conclusion that you must be ill. I didn't think he'd have sent for me otherwise."

"Didn't you? Well, perhaps it's understandable. What exactly was the message, John? Can you remember it?"

"Oh, yes." He repeated it and saw that she was smiling at him with deep, compassionate kindness.

"Didn't it occur to you, John, that you have more than one cousin who might . . . need you?"

Johnny reddened. "Fiona? But—Fiona doesn't need me, she never did. And she's going to marry David. She told me so."

"Does the thought of her marrying David distress you?" his cousin asked.

"Yes, I—I'm afraid it does. I like David, of course, he's a very decent chap, but—"

"But *you* are in love with Fiona, is that it?"

Shamefacedly, he nodded. "Yes, Cousin Catherine, I am. I don't know how you guessed, but it's true. Not that I'll let it make any difference, of course. I—I mean, there's David and—"

"Fiona isn't going to marry David," Lady Logan told him gently. "David's message—about which I knew nothing—was evidently meant to tell you so. I imagine it must have become a trifle distorted in transit, that's why you thought what you did. Wait, John dear"—as Johnny made to rise—"drink your tea. And calm yourself. Have a cigarette, won't you, before you go to Fiona? She hasn't come up yet, so you've plenty of time."

"Have I?" His heart was pounding but he waited obediently, feeling in his pockets for a packet of cigarettes.

Lady Logan watched him light one. "I thought you always rolled your own cigarettes?"

He shook his head. "Not now. I'm trying to do in Rome as the Romans do . . . no one rolls their own cigarettes here, do they?"

"No, I don't think they do. But"—she spoke with a hint of reproval—"you mustn't try too hard to change yourself, John. We love you as you are, you know, and . . . we respect you, too. You will bring new life to Logan, a fresh atmosphere. Perhaps, in the past, we have been a trifle remote, too much—how can I put it? Too much on our dignity. You will alter that and people will love you for it, as already many of them do. Your friend the young postman—what is his name?"

"Jock," Johnny supplied. He inhaled smoke and felt his taut nerves relax a little. "Jock MacPhail. We served together in Korea and—he brought me back this evening, on his motor-bike."

Lady Logan's lips curved into a delighted smile.

"It didn't enter your head to send for a car? No, of course it wouldn't. Dear John, that is one of the things I like about you, there is a complete absence of false pride in your make up. You mustn't ever change! But you must deal gently with Fiona's pride. She is not like you in this respect, but I think that each of you has something to give the other. You will make a good pair, you and she."

"Do you mean that you"—Johnny swallowed hard—"you don't mind? That I love Fiona, I mean?"

"How could I mind, John, when Fiona loves you?"

He looked into her sweet, gentle face and put out both hands to her, flinging his half-smoked cigarette into the fire.

"I'm going to her now, Cousin Catherine," he said huskily. "Will you give me your blessing before I go?"

"Oh, my dear boy—of course I will! With all my heart." She kissed him, holding him to her, her cheeks against his and he felt it damp with tears. "Now go," she whispered, turning her face away. "Go to Fiona. She doesn't know you're here but . . . she will be waiting for you."

Johnny rose and went to the door. "Goodnight, Cousin Catherine. Sleep well."

"I shall," she called after him. "Goodnight, John dear."

The hall was still deserted when he returned to it, the great house very silent. He found Fiona in the drawing-room, and as he entered the room she looked round, recognizing him with a little cry. In that instant, caught completely unprepared, her heart was in her eyes, her love there for him to see, as plainly as if she had spoken it aloud.

She said, her voice a small whisper of sound in the big, silent room: "Oh, John —Johnny, you came back . . ."

"Yes," he said, "I couldn't stay away. I had to come, Fiona. I had to tell you I love you, you see. I was afraid you didn't know."

"I didn't," she admitted shakily. "At least I—wasn't sure."

Johnny captured her hand, drew her to her feet and into his arms. As his mouth found hers he knew again the fierce, compelling upsurge of emotion her touch always engendered in him, but with it, as her lips yielded to his, came tenderness. He held her gently, though his blood was on fire and his pulses racing, and said humbly: "Fiona, will you be my wife? I need you so and I love you, more than I ever imagined it possible to love anyone . . . more than Logan, more than Wahrangi . . . more than life itself. But I am—what I am, and—"

"You're Johnny," Fiona told him.

"Yes, but—"

"It's Johnny I love," Fiona said simply. "Johnny I want to marry." She raised her face to his and then his arms closed hungrily about her and he kissed her with pride and passion and a new, masterful eagerness to which, with a tiny sigh of breathless ecstasy, Fiona surrendered.

For a timeless moment, for what seemed an eternity, they clung together, both bemused with the wonder of the love they had found, both shaken to the depths of their being by the intensity of their emotions, both reluctant to break the magic spell this kiss had cast over them.

But, at last Fiona drew back, trembling, letting her head droop, hiding her face against his chest. Johnny felt her shiver, knew that she was weeping. Lips in her hair, he reproached her tenderly:

"Tears, Fiona? Don't cry, my darling—don't."

She lifted her head then. "They're tears of happiness, Johnny. Such happiness, I don't know what to say."

"Just say you love me," Johnny begged.

A smile lit her eyes. "Oh, Johnny, as if you didn't know! I love you, love you, love you . . . for the rest of time, darling."

"That will do, to be going on with," he said exultantly, and kissed her tear-bright eyes. "Will you let me show you Australia —and Wahrangi—one day, Fiona? One day, after we're married and when Logan can spare us?"

Fiona inclined her dark, beautiful head. "Whither thou goest, I will go," she told him, very softly.

Johnny's arms tightened about her.

"Amen to that," he said and looked up, for a moment, at the portraits of his ancestors which lined the walls.

The last of the Logans met the painted eyes of one of the first of them and he smiled. He had come home and this was his destiny.

THE END

GUIDE
TO THE COLOUR CODING
OF
ULVERSCROFT BOOKS

Many of our readers have written to us expressing their appreciation for the way in which our colour coding has assisted them in selecting the Ulverscroft books of their choice.

To remind everyone of our colour coding— this is as follows:

BLACK COVERS
Mysteries

★

BLUE COVERS
Romances

★

RED COVERS
Adventure Suspense and General Fiction

★

ORANGE COVERS
Westerns

★

GREEN COVERS
Non-Fiction

ROMANCE TITLES
in the
Ulverscroft Large Print Series

DOM

Library at Home Service
Community Services
Hounslow Library, CentreSpace
24 Treaty Centre, High Street
Hounslow TW3 1ES

YOUR COMMUNITY
YOUR SERVICES

0	1	2	3	4	5	6	7	8	9
871			943	16+	883	346	658		929
	161		324	993	246	369	818	2568	
	861					086		308	
						6306		3209	
						36507	1588		
						706	34567	479	
						9567			
						9578			

P10-L-2061